Richard Marsh

Confessions of a Young Lady

Richard Marsh

Confessions of a Young Lady

1st Edition | ISBN: 978-3-75241-661-9

Place of Publication: Frankfurt am Main, Germany

Year of Publication: 2020

Outlook Verlag GmbH, Germany.

Confessions of a Young Lady
Her Doings and Misdoings
By

Richard Marsh

I

A WONDERFUL GIRL

As a small girl I must have been a curiosity. At least I hope so. Because if I was only an average child what a time parents, and guardians, and schoolmistresses, and those sort of persons, must have of it. To this hour I am a creature of impulse. But then—! I did a thing; started to regret it when it was about half done; and if I ever thought at all about the advisability of doing it, it was certainly only when everything was over.

Take the case of my very fleeting association with Bradford's Royal Theatre.

So far as I can fix it, at the time I must have been about twelve. A small, elf-like creature, with eyes which were ever so much too big for my face, and a mass of unruly, very dark brown, hair. Some people have told me that then it was black. But I doubt it. For there are those who tell me that it is black now, which I have the very best of reasons for knowing it is not. At that school they called me The Witch; in allusion, I believe, not only to my personal appearance but also to my uncanny goings-on.

The school was in a Sussex village. To that village there used to come each year a travelling theatre. It took the form of a good-sized oblong tent, which was erected in a field which was attached to the Half Moon Hotel. I imagine that the whole countryside must have patronised Bradford's Royal Theatre, because sometimes it would stay there for two months at a time. It put in its first appearance, so far as I was concerned, during my second term at Miss Pritchard's school. We girls were not supposed to know anything about it. But well do I remember the awe with which I used to gaze at the exceedingly dingy canvas structure as we passed it in our walks. And once when Nelly Haynes, with whom I was walking, pointing to an individual who was lounging in his shirt sleeves at the entrance to the field, observed that that was one of the principal actors—though what she knew about it I have not the faintest notion—I could not have stared at him with greater curiosity had he been the Slave of Aladdin's Wonderful Lamp.

Even yet, when I am in the mood, I read everything in the way of print that I can lay my hand on. In that respect, also, I fear that the girl was mother to the woman. I had recently come across an article in a magazine treating of infant phenomena; I am not quite sure if the plural ought to be written with an *a* or an *s* when using the word in that particular sense; but, any way, I will leave it. How I had lighted on the magazine I cannot remember. But I rather

2

fancy that it must have been the property of one of the governesses, who had left it lying about, and that I borrowed it without going through the form of asking leave. I know that I took it to a corner of the orchard of which we had the freedom when there was no fruit upon the trees, and that I devoured that article. It was all about precocious children. Recording how Mozart had composed masses—whatever they were!—at the age of two, or less, and how some little girl had won fame as a dancer at the age of three, or perhaps a trifle more. But in particular it told of the Infant Roscius. The story of that Wonderful Boy—he was throughout alluded to as The Wonderful Boy—set my brain in a whirl. I do not think that I have read much—if anything—about William Henry West Betty since; but I do believe that I recollect nearly all that I read then. He took London by storm when he was twelve years old; my age! the tale of my own years nearly to a tick! As Selim in *Barbarossa*— when one thinks of it, it must have been a wonderful part in a truly wonderful play for that Wonderful Boy!—the whole world of wit, and wealth, and fashion was at his feet. In the course of a single season he gained over seventeen thousand pounds.

Those are facts and figures for you. Especially were they facts and figures for me then. By the time I had reached the end of that article my mind was firmly resolved upon one point—that I would be an Infant Phenomenon. There should be a Wonderful Girl as well as a Wonderful Boy. It seemed clear to me that girls, of the proper type, might be made quite as attractive as boys. The mystery was that there should not have been a Wonderful Girl already. But the want should be immediately supplied.

Of course, one or two difficulties were in the way. I had never acted myself, or seen anybody else act, and knew as much about plays as about Mars. And then Betty was encouraged; while I had an inward conviction that that would not be the case with me. Under these circumstances I did not quite see, at the moment, how I was to play the principal part at Covent Garden, nor even begin to charm the world—as young Betty had done—at a theatre in Ireland. But not for one moment did I allow myself to be daunted by considerations of that kind.

I think it was the very next day—my enthusiasm lasted all through the night, which was not always the case, for I have gone to sleep intending to marry a missionary and woke up bent on being a queen of the cannibals—that Fate threw in my way the very opportunity I wanted—at Bradford's Royal Theatre.

I imagine that it must have been pretty bad weather about that time. When it was not raining it was blowing; and when, as the Irishman said, it was doing neither, it was doing both. Climatic conditions unfavourably affected the attendance at Bradford's Royal Theatre. I know such was the case because I heard the governesses saying so. It all comes back to me. It was after morning lessons; I was in the schoolroom writing to someone at home—in those days I was a tremendous correspondent—and some of the governesses were talking together close to where I sat. They paid no attention to the pair of large ears attached to the small person close at hand. The theme of their conversation was Bradford's Royal Theatre, and they were expressing their fears that things had lately gone very badly with the company thereof. Two remarks stick in my memory:—that on one occasion there had only been one and ninepence taken at the door; and that at the close of a recent week there had been less than two pounds to divide among seven people. What warrant they had for their statements I cannot say. But I know that they made a vivid impression on me at the time. And when they spoke of certain individuals being in actual want, it was all I could do to refrain from showing more interest in the topic under discussion than, under the circumstances, would have been discreet.

Because, as I listened, it burst in upon me in one of those sudden flashes of illumination to which I was singularly liable that here was the very opening I wanted. Here was a chance to figure, in a double sense, as a Wonderful Girl.

On the one hand I would dower these unfortunate people with the wealth of which they stood so much in need; on the other, I would take the world by storm. At Bradford's Royal Theatre, in the guise of a benevolent fairy, I would commence that career compared to which that of the Infant Roscius would be as nothing.

I did not stop to consider—it was not my custom. Stealing from the schoolroom, taking my hat from its peg, crossing the playground, paying no attention to the girls who spoke to me, through the gate out into the road, I marched right straight away to Bradford's Royal Theatre.

When I think of it I hardly know whether to laugh or cry. The eager little creature that I was, with my heart swelling in my bosom, my head full of unutterable things, striding along the country road, now breaking into a run, now compelled to relax my speed for want of breath. It must have been nearly one o'clock, our dinner-time at school. I remember that I had twopence in my pocket. I fancy that at Miss Pritchard's—my first boarding-school—my allowance was threepence a week; and as that was paid on Saturday, and I still had twopence left, it is probable that I adventured in the regions of infant phenomena upon a Monday. My way lay past a solitary shop. I got hungry as I walked—in those days I did get hungry—the presence of that shop brought the fact vividly home to me. I paused to see what might be bought. My instinct pointed to sweets. Just as I was about to follow my instinct I

4

perceived, on a dish in the corner of the window, a German sausage—or rather, a portion of one. I thought of the hungry folk at Bradford's Royal Theatre. My mind was made up on the instant. Into the shop I went and asked for two pennyworths of German sausage. Whoever it was that served me must have stared, for I can hardly have looked like an individual who might be expected to make a purchase of the kind. But, anyhow, I got what I desired, and with it in my hand, wrapped in a piece of newspaper, I pursued my way.

I would not only present these unfortunates with the first-fruits of my great gifts, I would furnish them with food as well.

Whether, while I was being served with that German sausage, I had time to begin to reflect, I cannot say, but I have a clear recollection that, after quitting that emporium of commerce, my steps were not marked by that enthusiasm which had originally sent me speeding like an arrow from a bow. Probably the whole distance was not more than three-quarters of a mile, and of that less than two hundred yards remained. But that two hundred yards took me longer than all the rest had done.

I was beginning—positively—to be afraid. When I reached a point at which the histrionic temple was only on the other side of the road I stood still. I was conscious of considerable reluctance to cross from the side on which I was to the side on which it was. For one thing, I was appalled by the peculiar dreariness of its appearance. I could not fancy the Infant Roscius commencing his career in that. The tent itself did look so shabby; the living waggons, which stood disconsolately together in the mud, were so much in want of painting; about the whole there was such an atmosphere of meanness, such a wealth of mire, that my heart began to sink. A small girl ran from the tent to a waggon, and from the waggon back to the tent. She struck me as being the dirtiest and most disreputable-looking creature I had ever seen. I called to her, meaning to give her that twopennyworth of German sausage and then retire, postponing the opening of my career until a future time. But either I did not call loud enough or she was in too much haste to heed. She disappeared without a glance in my direction.

The moment she was gone sudden consciousness of the shameful thing that I would do swept over me. I had come to help those poor people, and just because they evidently were so much in want of help I proposed to leave them to their fate. Was I attempting to quiet my conscience by pretending that it would be enough to present them with two pennyworths of German sausage? What—my thoughts flying back to what the governess had said—was two pennyworths of German sausage among seven? Why, I could eat it all myself —and more! Over the road I tore, clattered along the boards which formed a causeway through the thick, upstanding filth; in a flash was through the entrance and in the theatre.

Then I paused. Without, the day was dull. Inside, to my unaccustomed eyes, all at first was darkness. I have not forgotten the anguish with which I began to realise some of the details of my surroundings. It was all so dreadful —so different to anything I had expected. To begin with, there was the smell. As the merest dot I never could stand odours of any kind. Even now, whoever presents me with a bottle of scent makes of me an enemy. That smelt as if all the bad air was kept in and all the good kept out. Then it was so small; to me it perhaps appeared smaller than it actually was, because I thought that Miss Pritchard's pupils would have filled it. And dirty, untidy, comfortless, beyond my powers of description. There was nothing on the ground to protect one's feet from the oozing damp. If the audience sat at all I could not think. I saw nothing in the way of seats, unless they were represented by some boards which were piled upon each other at one side. At one end, raised a little from the ground, was a platform of rough planks, so small that there could hardly have been room on it for half a dozen persons standing abreast. It never occurred to me till afterwards that that was the stage. I kept wondering where the stage was. I knew that theatres had stages.

While, as they became used to the light, my keen young eyes were taking these things in, I perceived that the place had occupants. There were four men and three women. I should have put them down as the seven I had heard alluded to, had there not also been a litter of children. It was only the children who seemed to take any interest in me. They clustered round, a ragamuffin crowd, regarding me as if I were some strange beast. At last one of them exclaimed,—

"Mother, here's a little girl!"

The woman whom, I supposed, the child addressed, looked up from some potatoes which she was washing in a pail of water.

"Well, little girl, what is it you're wanting?"

The place, the people, their surroundings, everything was so altogether different to the vague something I had anticipated, that, like the creature of moods I was, I seemed, all at once, to have passed from a world of fact into a world of dream. It was like one in a dream I answered,—

"I have come to be the Infant Roscius."

Not unnaturally the lady who was washing the potatoes failed to understand.

"What's that?" she demanded.

I repeated my assertion.

"I have come to be the Infant Roscius."

Other of the grown-ups roused themselves to stare at me.

"What's she talking about?" inquired a second woman, who had a baby at her breast.

An elderly man, who was perched on the edge of the platform smoking a pipe, hazarded an explanation.

"She's after tickets; that's what it is she wants."

The potato washer seemed to be brightened by the hint.

"Has your mother sent you to buy some tickets?"

I shook my head solemnly.

"I have come to act."

"To—what?"

That my appearance, words and manner together were creating some sort of a sensation I understood. That these were ignorant people I had already— with my wonted promptitude—concluded. It seemed to me that it would be necessary to treat them as children—and dull of comprehension at that—to whom I, as a grown-up person, had to explain, in the clearest possible manner, exactly what it was that had brought me there. This I at once proceeded to do, with what I have no doubt whatever was an air of ineffable superiority.

"I am going to be a Wonderful Girl. I am nearly twelve, and Young Betty was only twelve, and he earned over seventeen thousand pounds in one season, and if I earn as much as that I will give it all to you." I paused—to reflect. "At least I would give you a great deal of it. Of course, I should like to keep some, because a Wonderful Girl mayn't go on long, and when I stop of course I should want to have a fortune to live upon, like Young Betty had. But still that wouldn't matter, because there'd be plenty for seven."

Amid my confused imaginings I had pictured the announcement of my purpose being received with wild applause. Those who heard would cast themselves at my feet, throw their arms about me, and rain tears upon my head. Not that that sort of thing would be altogether agreeable. But something of the kind would have to be put up with. When people were beside themselves with gratitude at seeing themselves snatched from the gaping jaws of feelings had to be allowed them. If, however, the persons to whom my explanation was actually addressed were beside themselves with gratitude they managed to conceal the fact with astonishing success. It struck me that they did not understand me even yet, which showed that they must be excessively dull. More stupid even than the teeny weeny tots in the first class who could not be got to see things.

The seven looked from me to each other, then back again to me. The woman with the baby repeated her former question, as if she had no sense of comprehension. I wondered if she was deaf.

"What's she talking about?"

The man who had dropped the hint about the tickets, descending from his perch upon the platform, came sauntering in my direction. As he moved he placed his hand against his forehead.

"Barmy on the crumpet," he observed.

What he meant I had not a notion. It moved a third woman, whose girth precluded any notion of her being on the verge of famine, to exclaim,—

"Poor dear!"

The potato washer began to put me through an examination.

"What's your name?"

"Molly Boyes."

"Where d'ye live?"

"West Marden."

"You ain't come all the way from West Marden here?"

"I've come from Miss Pritchard's school."

The statement seemed to fill the man with illuminating light.

"Ah, that's just what I thought! D'rectly I see her that's just what I thought. Miss Pritchard's—that's the girls' school on the Brighton road, house is inside a wall. I went there to try to get them for *Uncle Tom's Cabin*. First the lady said there wasn't to be no flogging, then that she couldn't possibly bring her pupils if there wasn't any chairs for them to sit up. I told Mr Biffin what she said. And he said, well there wasn't any chairs, and there was an end of it."

The woman with the baby interposed an observation.

"We should do better if there was chairs. It isn't likely that the front seat people will want to sit on boards."

The big woman proffered a reminder.

"On the front seats there's baize."

Which the woman with the baby spurned.

"What's baize?"

The man addressed himself to me. He was a thin man, with iron-grey hair, and there was something about his face which made me think that though he was untidy, and I wished he would not wear such a very greasy cap, I might induce myself in time to like him. Never once did he remove his pipe from his mouth, nor his hands from his trouser pockets.

"Well, Miss Boyes, it's a pity you should have come to act, seeing that there's a good many of us here that does that sort of thing already. The difficulty is to get people to come and see us do it. Do you think that many of your friends would come and see you act?"

"Well, not many of my friends."

"That, again, is unfortunate."

"But strangers would."

"It's that way with you, is it? With us it's different. We look to friends for our support. Strangers are sometimes disagreeable. What plays were you thinking of acting?"

"I don't know any plays as yet. But I soon could."

"Of course. That's easy enough. *Hamlet*, I suppose, and that kind of thing. And what sort of part were you thinking of playing?"

"I really haven't thought."

"No, you wouldn't, such a trifle being of no consequence. You weren't thinking of playing old women?"

"Well, I don't think I could act old women. But I might try. Young Betty acted an old man."

"Young Betty did. Is that so? And who might young Betty be? A friend of yours? That young lady over there, her name's Betty."

He jerked his elbow towards the woman with the baby. I was shocked, although, having already taken their ignorance for granted, I was able to conceal my feelings with comparative ease.

"He was a boy."

"A boy? With a name like Betty? What was his father and mother up to then?"

"His name was William Henry West Betty. He was the Infant Roscius."

"Was he?"

"He was The Wonderful Boy. I am going to be a Wonderful Girl."

"You're that already. Seeing that you are a Wonderful Girl, what might have put it into your head to come here?"

"You are very poor, aren't you?"

"Poor? That's what you might call a leading question. We're not rich. Who told you we were poor?"

"Didn't you only take one and ninepence at the door one night?"

By this time general interest was being roused in our conversation. As soon as the words were out of my mouth I was aware that they had been heard with more attention than anything I yet had said. Though why that should be the case was beyond my capacity of perception.

"Only took one and ninepence at the door one night, did we? Oh! Looks as if someone had been talking. From whom might you have heard that piece of news?"

"And one week weren't there less than two pounds to divide among seven? You could not live on that. No one could. It's not to be done. It simply means starvation."

I merely repeated, with all the earnestness of which I was capable, what I had heard the governesses saying. My remarks were followed by what even I felt was a significant silence. My interlocutor, bringing forward with his foot what looked like an empty egg-box, placed himself upon a corner. It creaked under his weight.

"It would seem as if somebody knows almost as much about this temple of the drama as it knows about itself. And it certainly is true that, regarded as a week's earnings, two pounds isn't much between seven. So you thought—?"

"I thought I'd come and help you."

"Come and help us? By acting?"

"If I'm going to be a Wonderful Girl—and I am going to be—it's quite time I was beginning. Young Betty was at the height of his fame when he was twelve. So I thought I would commence by making a lot of money for you here, which would keep you all from starving; and then, of course, I shall go on to London and make the rest of my fortune there."

"I see. Well, this bangs Banagher. Banagher it bangs."

What he meant I could not say. But he should have been a capital actor, because not a muscle of his face moved. A man behind him laughed—stinging me as with the lash of a whip.

The big woman delivered herself of her former ejaculation.

"Poor dear!"

The potato washer remarked,—

"Strikes me, my girl, that you've a good opinion of yourself."

The grey-headed man had his eyes upon what I had in my hand.

"What might you happen to have there?"

"It's some food which I have brought for you."

"For me in particular, or for all the lot of us?"

"It's for the seven."

"The seven? I see. The seven who divided those two sovereigns."

"Yes. It's some German sausage. I hope you like German sausage."

"It's my favourite joint."

I endeavoured to correct what I imagined to be a still further display of his ignorance.

"I don't think that German sausage is a joint. It's not generally looked upon as such. It's a long, round, cold thing, off which, you know, they cut it in slices."

I passed him the parcel, he removing—for the first time—one of his hands from his pockets for the purpose of taking it, balancing it on his open palm as if on a scale. It was a pretty grimy piece of newspaper, and was not of a size to suggest extensive contents. I became more and more conscious of its wretched smallness as, with every outward appearance of care and gravity, he slowly unwrapped it. The others gathered closer round, as if agog with curiosity. Finally there were revealed three or four attenuated slices. He held them out at arm's length in front of them.

"For seven!"

"There isn't much," I managed to murmur, oppressed, all at once, by the discovery of what a dreadful little there really was. "But I had only twopence."

"You had only twopence, so you purchased two pennyworths of German sausage—for seven."

"Of course I'll earn a deal of money for you besides."

A girl came rushing into the tent behind me. The interruption was welcome, for I instinctively felt that matters had reached a point at which a diversion of any sort was to be desired. But I was far from being prepared for the proclamation which she instantly made.

"Here's the lady come!—I've been and fetched her!"

To my blank astonishment there appeared—Miss Pritchard. That intelligent young woman, having a shrewd eye for a possible reward, had availed herself of the information which had been extracted from me to rush off to the school to proclaim my whereabouts, receiving, as I afterwards learnt, a shilling for her pains. Never before had I seen Miss Pritchard in such a state of agitation; and no wonder, considering the pace at which she must have torn along the road.

"Molly!—Molly Boyes, what is the meaning of this?"

The sight of her had driven me speechless. I could not have told her for everything the world contained. My interlocutory friend explained instead— in a fashion of his own.

"It's all right, madam—everything's quite right! Having heard that things were in a bad way with us in this temple of the drama this young lady has brought us two pennyworths of German sausage to save us from actual starvation, and has expressed her intention—I don't quite follow that part, but so far as I can make out she's proposing to make our fortunes by beginning to be a Wonderful Girl; which it isn't necessary for her to begin to be, seeing as how I should say that she's been a Wonderful Girl ever since the moment she was born."

Of what immediately followed I have but a dim appreciation. I know that, on the instant, I was turned into a common butt—or I felt as if I was. The children pointed their fingers at me and jeered. The grown-ups were all talking at once. There was general confusion. The whole rickety tent was filled with a tumult of scorn and laughter.

Presently I was being escorted by Miss Pritchard back to school, the children standing in the middle of the road to point after me as I went. I was in an agony of shame. With that keenness of vision with which I have been dowered I perceived, as I was wont to do, too late, what an idiot I had been! What a simpleton! What a conceited, presumptuous, ignorant little wretch! How I had made of myself a mock and a show for the amusement of the company of Bradford's Royal Theatre! I felt as if the hideous fact was written on my face—on every line of me. All I wanted was to hide, to bury myself somewhere where none might witness my distress. Although my worthy schoolmistress was walking faster than I ever saw her walk before or afterwards, I kept tugging at her hand—she was not going fast enough for me.

So soon as we reached the school she took me into her little private sitting-room, and, without removing her hat, or giving me time to take off mine, required from me an immediate explanation of my conduct. Amid my blinding sobs I gave her as full and complete an explanation as she could possibly have desired. The bump of frankness was—and is—marked on my phrenological chart as developed to an even ridiculous extent. When I have been indulging in one of my usual escapades nothing contents me but an unrestrained declaration of all the motives which impelled me to do the thing or things which I ought to have left undone.

I told her about the article in the magazine, and about what I had heard of the pitiful state of things at Bradford's Royal Theatre, and my determination to assist them while starting on my meteoric career. And before I had gone very far, instead of scolding, she had her arm about me, and was endeavouring to soothe my sobs. She must have been a very sensitive person for a schoolmistress—though I do not know why I should say that, because I have not the least idea why schoolmistresses should not be as sensitive as anybody else, since they are human—for when I began to tell her of how I had expended my capital on the purchase of what that grey-headed man had called his "favourite joint," she drew me quite close to her, and in the midst of my own anguish I actually felt the tears upon her cheeks. She took me on her knee, and instead of sending me to bed, or into the corner, or punishing me in any way whatever, she kissed and comforted me as if I had not been the most ridiculous child in the world. It might not have been the sort of treatment I deserved, but I loved her for it ever afterwards.

What was more, she promised not to betray me to the governesses, or to my schoolfellows, or to anyone. Though I think that she wrote and told my mother, though mother never breathed a hint of her having done anything of the sort to me. But I always thought so. It was weeks and weeks before I could bear the slightest allusion to anything "wonderful" without becoming conscious of an internal quiver. I fancy Miss Pritchard must have given instructions as to the direction our walks were to take. It was some little time before the governess led us past the site of Bradford's Royal Theatre. When next we went that way every vestige of the "temple of the drama" had disappeared. The dingy—and odious—tent had gone.

It was with a positive gasp of satisfaction that I recognised the fact. A weight seemed lifted off my bosom, and my heart grew lighter there and then. When, the walk being over, we returned, before anyone could stop me, or had an inkling of my intention, I dashed headlong into Miss Pritchard's private room. She was seated at the table writing.

"It's gone!" I cried.

She must have been very quick of understanding. She did not ask me what had gone. She just put her arm about me, as she had done before, and pushed my hair from off my brow, and, I think, she laughed.

II

CUPID'S MESSENGER

I do protest that it was not altogether my fault. At least—; but if I tell you exactly how it was you will understand what I mean.

I was fifteen. It was after I had left Miss Pritchard's. Not that I was much wiser than I was when I was at Miss Pritchard's. Though that was not my opinion at the time. In what I then called my judgment I was the wisest person the world had ever seen—perhaps it would be more correct to write that that was my estimate of myself as a rule. There were between-whiles when I knew better. I was at Mrs Sawyer's—Lingfield House School—at Brighton to be finished. And a nice finish they made of me.

It was the summer term and I was romantic, I had my phases. One term I was cynical; another philosophical; a third filled with a wild despair. That one I was all for sentiment. I had been reading all manner of stuff, prose and poetry; I had even written some poems myself. As I burned them years and years ago I do not mind owning it. I was convinced that there was nothing in the world worth living for except love. Given Love—it ought to have a capital L; in my poems it always had—you had everything a reasonable being could desire. Lacking it, wealth, fame, clothes, and even chocolate creams, were as dust and ashes.

There was, that term, a governess who must have been almost as great a goose I was. I am not sure that she was quite so right in the head as she might have been. She only stayed that term. Why Mrs Sawyer ever had her is more than I can say. Her name was Frazer—Mamie Frazer. Her autograph—suggestive of a fly slipping over the paper after a visit to the inkstand—stares at me out of my birthday book at this moment. She was the most speechless person I ever encountered. So to speak, you might carry on a conversation with her for hours and she would never say a word. As a listener she was immense. By degrees her attitude so got upon your nerves that I, for one, would feel like murder.

"Say something!" I would beseech of her. "Do please say something! Don't you know that I have been talking myself hoarse and you haven't uttered a single word."

She would only sigh. To a person who was fond of conversational give-and-take it was trying.

And the name of the girl who shared my bedroom was Travers—Hester—generally known as Hetty—Travers. She was, well, she is one of my dearest friends at this hour, and she may see this, so I don't want to say anything to hurt her feelings, but she certainly was a mischievous imp. Mischief brimmed out of her finger-tips. And the point was that she had such an excessively demure air that you never had the faintest notion that she was that kind of person till the truth was forced upon you. Even then you gave her the benefit of the doubt; or you tried to—at least I did—until it was obviously absurd to attempt to do so any longer since there was no doubt. Reverence! she did not know what it was. She had not a mite of respect for me, though I was a good three months her senior. She used to make fun of all the varying things I held most sacred—that is, while the mood was on me.

That inveterate habit of hers ought to have made me suspect her. But I was ever a Una for innocence. She was always taking me in. She had an insidious way about her which would take in anybody.

One night we were going to bed. I had one stocking off, and was wondering how the holes did get into the toes; I used to bribe other girls to do my darning. It cost me frightful sums. We were talking about other people's peculiarities, as was our agreeable custom.

"You know Miss Frazer told me to walk with her when she took us out to-night. I kept talking to her all the time, and yet the whole way there and back she never spoke a word. I believe she's going mad."

"I shouldn't wonder."

Hetty was doing her hair. I was wishing she would make haste, because she was using the only glass we had, and it seemed to me that she never would have done with it. What discussions we had about that looking-glass! We took it in turns to use it first, and whoever had first turn used to hang on to it as if it was the Koh-i-noor. Something struck me in her tone.

"Why shouldn't you wonder?"

"I shouldn't." This was cryptic. But I was aware that it was advisable to give her a little rope. So I held my peace and found another hole. And presently she added, "When a woman's heart is breaking she sometimes does go mad."

"Hetty!"

I had been giving utterance to my sentiments on the subject of the importance which love plays in human lives; I think I got them from Byron. Hetty had been scoffing. I suspected her of paraphrasing my words with mischievous intention. But it seemed that she was actually in earnest.

"You talk about love wrecking people's lives, as if you know anything at all about it; I saw that paper-covered Byron in your workbox—and you can't see what's taking place underneath your very eyes."

"Hetty, what do you mean?"

"Poor Miss Frazer!"

She sighed, actually. Or she emitted a sound which appeared to me to be a sigh. A light dawned on me.

"You don't mean—you don't mean that you think that she's in love?"

Miss Frazer was short, square, and squat. Sandy-haired, with not much of that. Short-sighted, her spectacles would not keep straight owing to the absence of a bridge on her abbreviated nose. Freckled, you might have been able to stick a pin between some of the freckles, but I doubt it. To me, then, she seemed ancient; but I suppose she was about forty. And, considering her general appearance and style of figure, she had a most unfortunate fondness for Scotch plaids. Up to that moment my sentimentalism had been all theory. I had not associated the tender passion with Miss Frazer. It was left for Hetty to direct my theoretical sympathy into a practical channel.

"Do I think? No, I do not think."

"Do you know that she's in love?"

"I know nothing. I want to know nothing. I will know nothing. But with you, who are always talking, it is different."

"Hetty, if you don't tell me what you mean, I—I—I'll throw my shoe at you."

"Throw away. You never hit anything you aimed at yet." She went on calmly brushing her hair, as if she had not made me all over pins and needles. Presently she gave utterance to an observation which was Sphinx-like in its mystery: "A Frenchman thinks no more of breaking an Englishwoman's heart than—than of eating his breakfast."

"Hetty! what do you mean?"

"Ask Monsieur Doumer."

Monsieur Doumer! Ask Monsieur Doumer! Why, M. Doumer was our French master, as unromantic-looking an example of the one sex as Miss Frazer was of the other. He was immensely stout, perfectly bald-headed, with cheeks and skin which looked as if they were covered with iron-mould, because he never shaved them. That anything feminine could regard with equanimity the prospect of being brought within measurable distance of that scrubby countenance did seem incredible. And yet here was Hetty hinting.

"Do you mean to say that Miss Frazer's in love with M. Doumer?"

"You say yourself that she seems to be going mad."

"Yes; but I don't quite see what that has to do with it."

"Not when a woman's being trampled on?"

"Trampled on? Really, Hetty, I do wish you would say straight out what it is you're driving at. You can't be suggesting that M. Doumer has been literally trampling on Miss Frazer, because, since he weighs about two tons, she'd have been killed upon the spot."

"There are more ways of killing a pig than one."

"You are mysterious. I daresay you think it's clever, but I think it's stupid."

"Are there not more ways of killing a pig than one?"

"I daresay there may be; but I don't see what that has to do with Miss Frazer."

"I don't say that it has anything to do with Miss Frazer. But, as I began by observing, when you consider how every Frenchman considers himself entitled to treat an Englishwoman exactly as he pleases, and perceive where Miss Frazer is plainly drifting, I should have thought you would have been able to see something for yourself." She seemed to me to be more mysterious than ever. "Perhaps," she added, as if by an afterthought, "if someone were to take him to task, and give him to understand that an Englishwoman is not a football for anyone to kick about, matters might be brought to wear a different aspect. But no doubt, as she is alone and unprotected, he knows that there is nothing of that kind to be feared. Because, of course, no one is going to play Don Quixote for a freckled Scotchwoman."

"I don't see why not. I should have thought that the fact of her being alone and—and not good-looking—would have made anyone with a grain of chivalry in them stand up for her all the more on that account."

"It looks like it! When you yourself just said that she is going mad because of the way she has been treated."

I had not said that or anything of the kind. I was trying to think of what I had said when the door opened and Miss Frazer herself came in. She had her watch in her hand, at which she was pointing an accusatory finger. I do not know what time it was—she did not give us a chance to see—but I expect it was later than we had supposed, because, taking the candle off the dressing-table, she marched straight out of the room with it without a word, and left us in total darkness.

"Well," I exclaimed, "this is pleasant. I'm not undressed, you've had the looking-glass all the time, and I haven't done a single thing to my hair, and I never can do anything to it in the dark."

"When a woman is in the state of mind in which she is, those who have to do with her have to put up with her. Don't blame her. Don't even think hard things of her. Try sometimes to practise, what you preach."

What Hetty Travers meant I again had not the faintest notion. She certainly had no right to hint such things of me. It seemed impossible that the mere contemplation of Miss Frazer's doleful plight could have moved her to tears; but while I fumbled with my hair in my indignant efforts to do it up in one decent plait in the darkness she did make some extraordinary noises, which might have been stifled sobs.

The following morning, during recreation, when I went into the schoolroom to get a book which I had left, I found Miss Frazer crouching over her desk, not only what I should call crying, but positively bellowing into her pocket-handkerchief. I stared at her in astonishment.

"Miss Frazer! What is the matter?" She bellowed on. A thought occurred to me. "Has—has anyone been treating you badly?"

Since she was so taciturn when calm, I expected her to be dumb when torn by her emotions. But I was mistaken. Taking her handkerchief from before her streaming eyes—her spectacles lay on the top of the desk, and I noticed how comical she looked without them—she spluttered out,—

"I'm the worst treated woman in the whole world!"

"Someone has been making you unhappy?"

"Cruelly, wickedly unhappy!"

"But have you no one to whom you can go for advice and assistance?"

"Not a single creature! Not a living soul! I am helpless! It is because I am helpless that I am trampled on."

Trampled on? I recalled Hetty's words. So she had been trampled on. Was being trampled on at that very moment. My blood, as usual, began to boil. Here was still another forlorn woman who had fallen a helpless victim to what Lord Byron called the "divine fever." And so a Frenchman did think that he could kick an Englishwoman about as if she were a football! I jumped at my conclusions with an ease and a rapidity which set all my pulses glowing.

"Do you think that it would make any difference if anyone spoke for you?"

"It must make a difference; it must! It is impossible that it should not make a difference! But who is there who would speak for me? Not one being on the earth!"

Was there not? There she was mistaken, as she should see. But I did not tell her so. Indeed, she must have thought me also lacking in that rare human sympathy, the absence of which she mourned in others, because I hurried out of the schoolroom without another word. To be entirely frank, I was more than half afraid. Unattractive enough in her normal condition, she was absolutely repulsive in her woe. Had I dared I would have advised her, strongly, never under any circumstances to cry. But had I done so I might have wounded her sensitive nature still more deeply. She might have started boohooing with still greater vehemence. Then what would she have looked like? And what would have happened to me?

Mrs Sawyer had instructed me to go into town to get a particular kind of drawing block for the drawing class which was to take place that afternoon. I knew where M. Doumer lived. When a newcomer appeared in his class it was his custom to present her—with an original article in bows which we irreverently described as the "Doumer twiddle"—with his card, in the corner of which was printed his address, so that the place of his habitation was known to all of us. It was close to the shop where they sold the drawing blocks. In returning one needed to go scarcely out of one's way at all to pass his house. I made it my business to pass his house. And when I reached it I marched straight up to the door, and I knocked.

The door was opened by a nondescript-looking person whom I took for the landlady. There was a card in the window—"Apartments To Let"—so I immediately concluded that M. Doumer lived in lodgings and that this was the person who kept them. She was a small, thin, hungry, acidulated female, who struck me as being an old maid of the most pronounced type. I have a fatal facility for drawing instant definite deductions from altogether insufficient premises which will one of these days land me goodness alone knows where.

"I wish to see M. Doumer."

She led me into the room on the left, in the window of which appeared the legend about apartments.

"M. Doumer is out. Is it anything which I can say to him?"

It struck me, even in the midst of the boiling-over state of mind in which I was, that she might have informed me that the man was out before taking me into the house. But I was in much too explosive a condition to allow a trifle of that sort to deter me from letting off some of my steam.

"Will you please ask him what he means by the way in which he has behaved to Miss Frazer?"

To judge from the way in which she looked at me I might have said something extraordinary. She had rather nut-cracker jaws, and all at once her mouth went in such a way that one felt sure there must have been a click. And she did look at me.

"I don't understand," she said.

"I don't understand either. That's why I want M. Doumer to explain. He has been trampling on Miss Frazer, and broken her heart, so that she's crying her eyes out."

The landlady person had not quite closed the door when showing me into the room, but had remained standing with her back to it, holding the handle in her hand. Now she turned right round, carefully shut it fast, and moved two or three steps towards me. There was something in her behaviour which, in a person in her position, I thought odd.

"Who are you?"

She asked the question in an exceedingly inquisitorial sort of way. I held up my chin as high as I could in the air.

"I am Molly Boyes."

"Molly Boyes?" She seemed to be searching in her mind for something with which to associate the name. "I don't remember to have heard of you."

"Perhaps not. I shouldn't think it likely that you had. I don't suppose that M. Doumer talks to everyone about all of his pupils."

"Are you one of his pupils?

"I am. I am at Lingfield House School, and I have been in his French class for now going on for four terms."

"And who's Miss— What's-her-name? Is she another of the pupils?"

"Miss Frazer is one of our governesses; and if he thinks that because she is an Englishwoman he can use her as if she were a football he's mistaken."

"Use her as if she were a football? What do you mean? What's he been doing to her?"

"He's broken her heart, that's what he's been doing to her. And when I came away just now she was crying so that if someone doesn't stop her soon I know she'll do herself an injury."

The landlady person made a noise with her nose which I should describe as a sniff. She straightened herself up as if she were trying to add another three or four inches to her stature, which would not have made her very tall even if she had succeeded.

"I thought as much. I have suspected it for months. But I am not one to speak unless I know. The man's a regular Bluebeard."

"A regular Bluebeard!—M. Doumer!"

"A complete Don Juan. I have long been convinced of it. He fascinates every woman he comes across. But he doesn't care."

The idea of calling that barrel-shaped monster, with his shining yellow head and scrubbing-brush physiognomy, a "complete Don Juan" so filled me with astonishment that for a second or two I could only look my feelings.

"M. Doumer is not like my idea of Don Juan in the very least."

"Indeed! And pray what do you know about Don Juan? A chit of your age! At my time of life I suppose I may be allowed to know something of what I'm talking about, and I tell you that I'm persuaded that he breaks hearts like walnuts."

"But—he's so ugly!"

"Ugly! Maximilian Doumer ugly! Misguided girl! But it's not becoming that I should discuss such subjects with a mere child like you. I know what I know. But it is none the less my duty on that account to see that he trifles with no woman's affections. And as his wife my duty shall be done."

When she said that I do believe the blood nearly froze in my veins. I am sure it turned cold, because I know I shivered from head to foot. His wife? She said his wife. And all the time I had been taking her for his landlady and an old maid, and had been calling M. Doumer ugly, and accusing him to her face of breaking Miss Frazer's heart. I do not know why, but I had never imagined for a single moment that he could be anything but a bachelor. We girls at Mrs Sawyer's had always taken it for granted that he was. At least, the general impression on my mind was that we had. The horror of the situation deprived me of the use of the tiny scrap of sense which I possessed. My own impulse was to run for it. But it was far from being Madame Doumer's intention that I should do anything of the kind. And though I think that she was in every respect smaller than I was, I am convinced that I never encountered a person of whom I all at once felt so much afraid. I stammered out something.

"I—I'm afraid I must go."

I made a faltering movement towards the door. She simply placed herself in my way and crushed me.

"You must what?"

"I—I shall be late for dinner."

"Then you will be late for dinner. You will not quit this apartment until M. Doumer returns. Not that that will necessitate your being detained long, because here he is."

I had been desirous of seeing M. Doumer, even anxious. In order to do so I had gone a good deal out of my way, and behaved in a characteristically considerate manner. But so far as I could judge, amid the rush of very curious sensations with which I was struggling, on a sudden, the entire situation had changed. It was far from being my wish to have an interview with him at that particular moment. Quite the contrary. I really do not know what I would not have given—certainly all the remainder of that term's pocket-money!—to have escaped such an encounter. Picture, therefore, my sensations when I heard the garden gate slam, the front door open, a heavy footstep enter the hall, and, on Madame Doumer opening the sitting-room door, perceived her husband standing without.

"Here is someone who wants to see you."

The lady's tone was sour as sour could be, and what she said was perfectly untrue. I could have wanted nothing less. I should have been only too glad to have been able to disappear up the chimney on a broomstick, or on nothing at all, if I could only have got out of that room. In came M. Doumer, all smiles and smirks, looking to me more shiny-headed and scrubbing-brush faced than ever.

"Ah!—it is Miss Boyes!—Sarah"—he addressed his wife as Sarah, and she looked it—"this is one of my charming pupils at Lingfield House School."

"So she's not an impostor. That's something." The insinuation made my cheeks flame. "You appear to have a number of charming pupils, M. Doumer. Is Miss Frazer one of them?"

"Miss Frazer? Who is Miss Frazer?" He turned to me. "Is that the young lady who joined the class a week or two ago? I have forgotten her name."

I was tongue-tied. A conviction was stealing over me that the whole thing was a hideous mistake, that I had been making a spectacle of myself on an unusually handsome scale. The tone in which he put his question was sincerity itself. It was impossible to suspect him of an intention to deceive. At least I should have thought so, though it pleased his wife, apparently, to think otherwise.

"It is odd that you should have forgotten the name of the woman whose heart you have broken."

"Whose heart I have broken?"

"Though perhaps that is because it has become such a frequent custom of yours to trample your victims under foot that one more or less is hardly worth your noticing."

"My dear, I do not understand."

He evidently did not. He looked from one to the other of us as if struck by a sudden foreboding that there was trouble in the air. Such a comical-looking distress came over his peculiar physiognomy that I positively began to feel sorry for him.

"Still, considering that a short time ago she was crying to such a degree that it was feared that she might do herself an injury—all because of you!—it does seem strange that you cannot even remember her name."

He held out his hands in front of him in the funny way we knew so well.

"My dear, of what are you talking? I wish that you would explain."

"It seems that that is what she wants you to do. She has sent this insignificant child to demand an explanation."

He turned to me.

"She has sent you? Who has sent you? Miss Frazer?—who is Miss Frazer?"

"She's one of the governesses."

"One of the governesses?—which of the governesses?"

"So there are several. It is to be hoped that you haven't broken the hearts of the entire staff. It is plain that you know them all."

"My dear, I have to meet these ladies in the performance of my duties."

I thrust in my oar.

"M. Doumer, I've made a mistake, I know I've made a mistake—I'm sure of it. I've been very silly. Madame Doumer, I'm quite sure I've made a mistake; please do let me go."

"So that's the tone you take on now. It was a different one at first. I can see as far through a brick wall as most people, and I rather fancy that there may be a brick wall here. Perhaps you expected to see M. Doumer alone."

"I did; I thought he was a bachelor."

"Oh-h!—now I begin to see. You thought he was a bachelor. I suppose, M. Doumer, that that is because you have always behaved as a bachelor. In your profession it is so easy. And with your natural advantages, so much more agreeable."

"I tell you, Madame Doumer, it's a mistake. It's all my fault. I have been silly. I am so sorry, I beg your pardon and M. Doumer's too. Please forgive me!—and let me go!"

"Oh, you shall go. And I'm as sure as you are that there's a mistake— somewhere. Exactly where I intend to ascertain. So M. Doumer and I will go with you. I will request to be introduced to this Miss Frazer, and M. Doumer shall make the explanation you require before her face. Then we shall know precisely where the mistake has lain."

The prospect of such a climax to my adventure as her words suggested appalled me into something approaching a fury. I made a little rush at her.

"You sha'n't keep me!—I will go!"

She looked me straight in the face. Then she moved towards me. As she advanced I retreated. I found the little woman very terrible. M. Doumer tried his hand at expostulation.

"My dear, you do not know what you talk about. If you do not take care you will do mischief—great mischief I do not know what silly tale Miss Boyes has been telling you, but there is not a word of truth in it, whatever it is." He seemed to have a way of taking certain things for granted which was nice for me! "You must not listen to the talk of silly girls—never! never!"

He waved his hand as if he were dismissing the matter finally as being unworthy anyone's consideration. His wife, however, regarded neither his words nor his gestures. She spoke to him as if it were hers to command and his to obey.

"Go upstairs and get my hat, my coat, my gloves and my umbrella; and be quick about it. I have no intention of quitting this apartment until this young person quits it with me. Nor do I propose to leave you two together to arrange an explanation of the mistake between you and to hatch plots behind my back. Did you hear what I told you to get me?"

He did hear; and he obeyed. Some faint attempt at remonstrance he ventured on. But he might as well have spoken to a wooden image. Though it certainly is true that a figure of that description would not have been quite so dictatorial. She opened the door, she pointed through it with her fingers.

Shrugging his shoulders, with an air of piteous resignation he went in the direction in which the finger pointed. During his absence not a word was spoken, his wife contenting herself with looking me up and down in a way I never was looked at either before or since. I felt as if I were momentarily dwindling in size. She called out to him.

"How long are you going to be up there?"

"Coming, my dear, coming!"

And he came.

A delightful walk we had, three abreast. The lady was in the centre, her husband on the left, I on the right. She treated us as if we were prisoners. I am sure I felt like one. Every now and then M. Doumer endeavoured to induce his wife to listen to a word or two of what he considered reason. She snapped him into silence. In vain he tried to make her realise the indignity of the situation into which she was thrusting both of us. Not a syllable would she have of it. Forced into speechlessness, he hinted at what was taking place within him by a variety of odd little gestures which, had I not been so conscious of my own ignominy, would have made me laugh outright in the street.

We reached Lingfield House. Madame made Monsieur knock at the door. But when it was opened it was she who inquired if Mrs Sawyer was in. It is my impression that he would have turned tail even at the last moment had she not insisted on his entering first, with me next, while she herself brought up the rear. We were shown into a sitting-room, where presently Mrs Sawyer appeared. M. Doumer, who had been fidgeting about like a cat on hot bricks, at once burst into speech.

"Mrs Sawyer, will you permit me to explain to you that I do not know—"

His wife cut short his flow of eloquence.

"M. Doumer, I will say all that is necessary. I am Madame Doumer, the wife of M. Doumer." Mrs Sawyer bowed. "Have you a person here of the name of Frazer?"

"Miss Frazer? Certainly, she is one of my governesses." Mrs Sawyer turned to me. "Molly, we have begun dinner without you. Where have you been?"

I essayed to explain, though I do not know what sort of explanation I should have offered. But Madame Doumer was acting as explainer-in-chief.

"She has been to visit M. Doumer. It is on that account that I am here; very much on that account. May I ask you to request Miss Frazer to favour us with her company? It is indispensable that what has to be said should be said in Miss Frazer's presence."

"I don't understand," began Mrs Sawyer.

She did look puzzled. And no wonder. M. Doumer interrupted.

"My dear, once more I beg of you to permit me to say—"

But his wife would not.

"Silence, sir! If you will be so good as to request Miss Frazer to come into this room I will endeavour to make myself as plain as the extremely peculiar circumstances will permit."

The end of it was that Miss Frazer was requested to come, and she came. She evidently had not a notion why she had been sent for. She gazed at us like a startled sheep. Mrs Sawyer introduced her.

"This is Miss Frazer. Miss Frazer, this is Madame Doumer. It appears that she has something which she wishes to say to you."

Miss Frazer looked more sheep-like than before; Madame Doumer could not have regarded her as a dangerous rival. But her manner could not have been more acid if Miss Frazer had been a queen of beauty.

"It is not my intention to give offence, therefore I trust that no offence will be taken. But it is my duty, as a woman, to invite you to state, publicly, what grounds you have for the assertion that M. Doumer has broken your heart."

"Broken my heart!"

Instantly Miss Frazer was all of a fluster, which was not surprising.

"And, also, why you charge him with trampling on you."

"Trampling on me? Why, I have never spoken to M. Doumer!"

M. Doumer was promptly in the breach.

"There, my dear—you hear! What did I say to you? What did I say? I have never spoken to this lady in my life—nor she to me! So far as I recollect I have not had the pleasure of seeing her before."

"Then what do you mean?" This question was addressed to me. I was beginning to ask myself what I could have meant. Oh, my feelings! "What do you mean by coming and telling me that this person was crying as if she would do herself an injury because of the way in which she had been treated by M. Doumer? And by saying that she had sent you to demand from him an explanation?"

"I did not say that she had sent me, I did not say it! And you were crying, Miss Frazer, you know you were!"

"Crying?"

"You know that I came and found you crying in the schoolroom."

She began to cry again then and there. As for me, I was swimming in tears already.

"I know that I was crying, but it wasn't because of that."

Mrs Sawyer interposed.

"Gently, Miss Frazer. Perhaps, if we keep cool, by degrees we shall begin to understand what this is all about. Can you tell us what you were crying about when this impulsive young lady intruded on your grief?"

"I was crying because of what you said to me."

"Because of what I said to you?"

It was Mrs Sawyer's turn to look bewildered.

"You said that you didn't wish me to wear plaids, not even my own plaid, and—I'm—a—Frazer!"

Exactly what happened afterwards I do not know. Mrs Sawyer bundled me out of the room and up to my bedroom. And well I deserved it. And more besides.

I threw myself on to the bed in a passion of sobs, though I could not pretend to emulate the boo-hooing I had left Miss Frazer indulging in downstairs. What an imbecile I was to suppose that she was bellowing like a bull calf because of the injury M. Doumer had wrought her virgin heart, when all the time it was because Mrs Sawyer had ventured to suggest that she did not think plaids were altogether suited to her style of figure, and that, in particular, the one to which she was partial was a trifle obvious. What a Frazer she must have been! And how devoted to the Frazer plaid!

I could have beaten myself. I was wild with everyone—with Madame Doumer, with Miss Frazer, and, last but not least, with Hetty Travers, that I should have allowed her to delude me into believing that unrequited love was driving Miss Frazer mad, and that it would be playing a chivalrous part to take that deceitful Frenchman to task. When, as soon as she had swallowed her dinner, Hetty stole up to learn what had become of me, I stormed at her like some wild thing. When she understood what I had been doing, instead of exhibiting penitence, or the least scrap of sympathy, she burst into peal after peal of laughter. I could have shaken her. But she had such a way about her, and could be so lovely when she chose, that, by degrees, I forgave her, though I never meant to. That tale was told. Everybody in the place had it off by heart within four-and-twenty hours. I believe that Miss Frazer blurted it out to one or two of them; it seemed that she could talk when she was not wanted to. And, of course, they told everybody else. I never heard the last of it while I was at Lingfield House. Mrs Sawyer merely remarked, with that dry smile which was peculiar to her, that she had always found young ladies difficult creatures to manage, but that I certainly did seem to be a curiosity even among girls.

And when I look back, and go hot all over—as I do when I recall that adventure to this hour—I really am disposed to think I must have been.

III

THE OGRE

Mother died while sitting in her chair writing to me. It was tea-time, and she did not come, so Con went to see what she was doing. She was leaning over her writing-table, and as she did not seem to have noticed his coming in —though I am sure that he made noise enough, because he always did—he called out to her.

"Mother! tea's on the table!"

Then, as she neither moved nor answered, he ran forward and put his hand upon her shoulder.

"Mother!"

When he found how still she was, and how unresponsive to his touch, he rushed off, frightened half out of his wits.

Then they all trooped into the room and found that she was dead. She had a pen in her hand, and a sheet of paper in front of her, and had begun the first line of a letter to me—"My dear Molly." Death must have come upon her as she was writing my name, for there is a blot at the end of it, as if her pen had jabbed into the paper. No one knew what she was going to say to me, or ever will. It was just her weekly letter—she wrote to me each Monday. And I expect she was just going to tell me the home news: what Nora had been doing, and what mischief the boys had been in, and beg me to be a good girl and think before I did things sometimes, and keep my stockings darned; those stockings were almost as great a trouble to her as they were to me. Not a creature had a notion that she was ailing. Indeed she was not. She was in good spirits—mother always was in good spirits!—and in perfect health half-an-hour before. It seemed that something extraordinary must have happened to her heart, which no one could have expected. Death must have come upon her in an instant. She must have gone before she had the least idea of what was going to happen. When she got to heaven how grieved she must have been to think that she had been compelled to leave us all without a word.

Never shall I forget receiving the telegram at Mrs Sawyer's. We were just going to bed, and the last train was nearly due to start. But I rushed off to catch it; and Mrs Sawyer went with me. She bought my ticket and sent a telegram to let them know that I was coming. At the other end I had a drive of nearly six miles. It seemed the middle of the night when I got home.

The state the house was in! And the children! They were in much more need of help than mother was. She was calm enough. When I first saw her I could not believe that she was dead. I thought that she was sleeping, and dreaming one of those happy dreams which, she used to tell us, she liked to dream. On her face was the smile with which she always greeted me. She always did look happy, mother did; but I never saw her look happier than when she was lying dead.

But the children! They were half beside themselves. It was dreadful; the boys especially. We could not get Con away from the bed on which mother lay. And Dick, great fellow though he was, was almost as bad. The whole house was topsy-turvy. Nobody knew what to do; everybody seemed to have lost their wits.

That is how it was the Ogre came on the scene. Of course his name was not the Ogre. It was Miller—Stephen Miller. But it was not very long before we only knew him as the Ogre among ourselves. He was not very tall, but he was big; at least, he seemed big to us. He had a loud voice, and a loud way about him generally. We liked neither his looks nor his manners—nor had mother liked them either. But at the beginning I do not know what we should have done without him. That is, I did not know then what we should have done. Though I am inclined to think now that if we had been left to ourselves, and been forced to act, we should have done as well, if not better. Yet one must confess that at the very beginning he was a help, though a comfort one never could have called him.

He was our nearest neighbour. His house was about half a mile down the lane. It was only a cottage. He inhabited it with a dreadful drunken old woman as his only servant. It was said that he could get no one else to stop in the house. He himself was not a teetotaller, and his general character was pretty bad. He seemed to have enough money to live on, because he did nothing except go about with a lot of dogs at his heels. In the charitable way which children have of talking we used to say that he was hiding from the law, and would speculate as to the nature of the crime of which he had been guilty. When he first came he tried to cultivate mamma's acquaintance, but she would have nothing to do with him, and would scarcely recognise him when she met him in the lane. I once heard Dick speak of him as an "unmannerly ruffian"; but I never knew why. And as Dick, like his sister Molly, sometimes said stronger things than the occasion warranted, I did not pay much heed.

The morning after mother's death he came marching into the house to ask if he could be of any assistance. No one, so far as I could ever gather, said either yes or no, which shows the condition we were in. He seems to have taken our consent for granted—to such an extent that he at once took into his hands the entire management of everything. He managed the inquest—for that I was grateful. Oh, that dreadful inquest! He also managed the funeral; for his services in that direction my gratitude assumed a mitigated form. Although the world was still upside down, and everything seemed happening in a land of topsy-turvydom, I yet was conscious that a good deal took place at mother's funeral which I would rather had not have taken place. For one thing I felt sure that a great quantity of money was being spent on it, much more than need have been. A number of people were invited who had not the slightest right to be present, so that we children were almost lost amid a crowd of strangers. In spite of the dreadful trouble I was in it made me burn when I saw them. Many of them were people whom mother would never have allowed to enter the house. Then there was an excessive amount of eating and drinking, especially drinking. Some time after we had returned from the grave I went into the hall and there were rows of bottles stacked against the wall. A lot of people seemed to be in the drawing and dining-rooms, who were talking at the top of their voices. I could not go in to see what it meant then—but I could guess.

But the trouble really began after the funeral was over.

We children were in such a strange position. So far as we knew, except mother we had not a relation in the world. There certainly were none with whom we were in communication. I had always fancied, from what mother said, that she and father were married without the approval of their relatives. I did not know if it was father's or mother's side which objected, but I felt sure it was one or the other. And I thought it was just possible that it was both. I believe that, when father died, mother was not nicely treated. This hurt her pride, because, though she was such a darling, and so sweet, and beautiful, and clever, and true, and tender, she was proud, as she had every right to be. And I think, because they were so unkind, she took us straight off to that Sussex village, miles and miles away from everyone, and bought The Chase. Con was a baby when father died, and now he was nearly eleven, so we must have been there quite nine years. And during all that time I do not think we ever had a visitor. This may sound incredible, but I do not remember one. Not that people were unfriendly. But then there were so few people thereabouts. And those who were there mother did not seem to care for. They were either country folk, villagers, farmers, and that sort of thing, or else they were very rich people, who were scattered here and there. I know they called; but I also know that mother did not encourage their advances. She used to tell us, laughingly, that she had six children, and that they were society enough for her.

But the consequence was that when she was gone we knew nothing about anything. We did not know who or where she got her money from, or what money she had. In two months I should be sixteen. That was to be my last term at school. And it is my belief that it was her intention, when I left school for good, to tell me everything, or at least as much as it was desirable that I should know. But if such was her intention she had gone before she had a chance of putting it into execution, or of dropping a hint, or even saying a word. And there we were, as ignorant and as helpless a family as ever was seen upon this earth.

It was under these circumstances that the Ogre showed a disposition to take entire control as if everything about the place—we included—belonged to him. Already there had not been wanting signs that the entire establishment more than sufficiently appreciated the change which had taken place. One of the chief difficulties with which mother had had to contend had been servants. In that remote part of the world it was almost impossible to get them. And sometimes when they were got they were hardly worth house-room. At the time mother died there were five—cook and two housemaids, a coachman, who was also gardener because his duties as coachman did not occupy anything like the whole of his time, and an odd lad, who was supposed to do whatever he was asked to do. The cook was a new one—she had come since my last holidays. On the day of mother's funeral she was intoxicated; she had indulged too freely in the refreshments which Mr Miller had so liberally ordered. So it may be imagined what sort of character she must have been. The next morning the housemaid, who had been with us longest, came and told me that she could not continue in a house in which there was no mistress. When I mildly suggested that I was the mistress now she remarked, quite frankly, that she could not think of taking her orders from me. Mr Miller, who had been standing at the morning-room door, listening, called her in to him. The details of what took place between them I never learned. But that afternoon she took herself off without another word to me. When, after she had gone, I went into mother's room, I found that all sorts of things were missing. I feared that Mary Sharp had taken them, and that that was the real explanation of her anxiety to depart. It made me conscious of such an added sense of misery, the feeling that henceforward we were going to be taken advantage of by everyone.

But the Ogre was the thorn in our sides. The day after Mary left we held a council of war in Dick's bedroom.

"I'm not going to stand this sort of thing," Dick announced. "And the sooner that beggar downstairs is brought to understand as much the better. Why, he's messing about with mother's papers at this very moment."

"A punch on the nose would do him good," declared Jack. He is one of the twins.

"A sound licking wouldn't do him any harm," added Jim. He is the other twin.

"He'll get both if he doesn't take care."

Dick drew himself up as straight as a dart. Although he was only fifteen he was five feet eight inches high, and as strong as anything—and so good-looking.

"But surely mother must have left a will. There must be something to tell us what is going to happen."

That was what I said. Dick took up my words at once.

"That point shall soon be settled. We'll go down and tackle the beggar right away."

Off we trooped to interview the Ogre in a body. He was in the morning-room—mother's own particular apartment. Outside the door we might have hesitated, but it was only for a moment. In strode Dick, and in we all went after him. The Ogre seemed surprised and not too pleased to see us. A bottle and a glass were on the table; both of those articles seemed to be his inseparable companions. One of his horrid dogs, which had been lying on the hearth-rug, came and sniffed at us as if we were the intruders. The whole room was in confusion. It looked as if it had not been tidied for days, and I daresay it had not been. When I thought of how different it used to be when it was mother's very own room, a pang went right through my heart. I could not keep the tears out of my eyes; and it was only because I was so angry that I managed to choke them back again. Papers and things were everywhere. At the moment of our entrance he had both his hands full of what I was convinced were mother's private letters.

It did seem like sacrilege, that that disreputable-looking man, with his pipe stuck in the corner of his mouth, who was nothing and no one to us, should be handling mother's treasures as if they were so much rubbish. I am almost certain that if I had been a big strong giant I should have been tempted to knock him down. It was not surprising that Dick spoke to him in the fiery way he did. When I looked at him I saw that he had gone red all over, and that his eyes were gleaming. He was not very polite in his manner, but more polite than the Ogre deserved.

"What are you doing with those things? What do you want here at all?"

The Ogre glanced up, then down again. I do not believe he could meet Dick's eyes. He smiled—a nasty smile, for which I could have pinched him.

And he continued to turn over the things which he was holding.

"My dear boy, I'm putting these papers into something like order. I never saw anything like the state of confusion which everything is in."

"Don't call me your dear boy! And what business of yours is it what state they're in? Who asked you to put them in order? What right have you to touch them?"

The Ogre calmly went on with what he was doing as if Dick was a person of not the slightest consequence. And he continued to indulge in that extremely objectionable smile.

"You haven't a very nice way of asking questions. And some people might think that the questions themselves were a little suggestive of ingratitude."

"What have I to be grateful for? I never asked you to come here. You are not a friend of ours."

"That you most emphatically are not!"

It was I who came blazing out with that. He looked at me out of the corner of his bloodshot eyes, his smile more pronounced than ever.

"Now, Miss Molly, that's unkind of you."

I was in a rage.

"You appear to be oblivious of the fact that you were not even an acquaintance of my mother's; and as those persons she did not wish to know we do not care to know either, we shall be obliged by your leaving the house at your earliest possible convenience."

"Inside two seconds," added Dick.

"Perhaps you'd like a little assistance."

"It's always to be got."

These two remarks came from the twins. The Ogre laid down on the table what he had been holding. A very ugly look came on his face.

"This is an extraordinary world. I don't want to say anything offensive—"

"You can say what you like," cried Dick.

"I intend to, my lad."

"Don't call me your lad!"

The Ogre looked at Dick. And this time he gave him glance for glance. And I knew, from the expression which was on both their faces, that if we were not careful there was going to be trouble. I am not sure that my heart did not quail. The Ogre spoke as if my brother was unworthy even his contempt.

"Mr Dick Boyes, you appear to be under the impression that you are still at school, and can play the bully here, and treat me as I have no doubt you are in the habit of treating the smaller chaps there. You never made a greater mistake in the course of your short life. I am not the kind of man who will allow himself to be bullied by a hobbledehoy. I give you fair warning that if you treat me to any of your insolence the consequences will be on your own head—and other parts of you as well. Don't you flatter yourself that the presence of your little sisters will shield you from them."

"Throw   something   at   him!"

"Down him with a pail of water!"

These suggestions proceeded from the twins. The Ogre turned his attention to them.

"If you two youngsters want a row you shall have it. And it will take the shape of the best licking you've ever had yet. You'll not be the first pair of unmannerly cubs I've had to take in hand."

I spoke; I wanted peace.

"There's not the slightest necessity for you to talk like that, Mr Miller. We're quite willing to believe that you're more than a match for any number of helpless children. But this is our house—"

"Indeed! Are you sure of that?"

"Of course I am sure. Do you mean to say that it is not?"

"At present I am saying nothing. I only advise you not to be too confident on a point on which some very disagreeable surprise may be in store for you."

"At anyrate, it is not your house. And all we ask—with all possible politeness—is that you should leave it."

"So that is all you ask. It seems to me to be a good deal."

"I don't know why it should. If you were a gentleman it would not be necessary to ask you twice."

"If I were a gentleman? I suppose if I came up to a school-girl's notion of what a gentleman ought to be—a sort of glorified schoolboy. I'm a good deal older than you, Miss Boyes—"

"You certainly are!"

"I certainly am, thank goodness!"

"I am glad you are thankful for something."

"I am glad that you are glad. As I was observing, when you interrupted me, I am older than you—for which I have every cause to be thankful—and my experience of the world has taught me not to pay much heed to a girl's display of temper. I undertook the management of affairs at your own request—"

"At my request? It's not true!"

A voice came from behind me. Looking round, there, in the doorway, was cook; and, on her heels, Betsy, the remaining housemaid. While—actually!—at the open window was Harris, the coachman, staring into the room as if what was taking place was the slightest concern of his. It was cook's voice which I heard, raised in accents of surprise, as if my point-blank denial of the Ogre's wicked falsehood had amazed her.

"Oh, Miss Molly, however can you say such a thing! When I heard you thanking Mr Miller with my own ears! And after all he has done for you. Well, I never did!"

"What did you hear?"

"I heard Mr Miller ask you in the hall if there was anything he could do for you, and you said you'd be very much obliged. Then he went on to say, I'm sure as kind as kind could be, that if you liked he'd take the whole trouble off your hands and manage everything; and you said,' Thank you.' And now for you to stand there and declare you didn't, and to behave to him like this after all he's done for you, in one so young I shouldn't have believed that it was possible."

In the first frenzy of my grief and bewilderment I had scarcely understood what I was saying to anybody. I remembered Mr Miller coming, as cook said, but that anything which had been said on either side had been intended to bear the construction which was being put upon it was untrue.

"I was not in a state of mind to understand much of what Mr Miller was saying, but I supposed that he was offering to assist in the arrangements for mother's funeral, and that offer I accepted."

"You did so. And what you'd have done without him I can't think. He arranged everything—and beautifully too. He's made the family more thought of in this neighbourhood than it ever was before. If ever helpless orphans had a friend in need you've had one in him—you have that."

Betsy had her say.

"He got us our black. There wouldn't have been a word said about it by anyone if it hadn't been for him."

"And he bought me two suits of clothes—blacks."

That was Harris, at the window.

"Bought you two suits of clothes!"

"Yes, miss," said cook, "we've all of us had full mourning, as was only decent. And I happen to know that Mr Miller paid for it. Indeed, he paid for everything. And considering the handsome way in which it has all been done, nothing stinted, nothing mean, a pretty penny it must have cost."

I exchanged glances with Dick and perceived that we were both of opinion that we had had enough of cook. I told her so.

"I have heard what you have had to say. And now, please, will you leave the room?"

"Excuse me, miss, but that's exactly what I don't intend to do—not till I know how I stand."

"How you stand?"

"I'll soon tell you how you stand," declared Dick. "You'll be paid a month's wages and you'll take yourself off."

"Oh, shall I, sir? That's just the sort of thing I thought you would say after the way you've been trying to behave to Mr Miller. And in any case I shouldn't think of stopping in the house with a pack of rude, ungrateful children. But I should like more than one month's wages, if it's the same to you. There's three months nearly due. I've not had one penny since I've been inside this house."

"Not since you've been inside this house?"

"Not one penny; and it's getting on for three months now."

"But I thought mother always paid you every month regularly."

"Did she, miss? Then perhaps you'll prove it. She never paid me; nor more she didn't Betsy. There's three months owing to you, isn't there, Betsy?"

"That there is."

"And so there is to you, isn't there, Harris?"

"Well—I don't know that it's quite three months."

"Why, you told me yourself as how it was."

Harris tilted his hat on one side and scratched his head as if to jog his memory.

"Well—it might be."

At this Dick fired up.

"It's all a pack of lies! I'm sure that my mother paid you your wages as they fell due, and that you're trying to cheat us."

Then it was cook's turn.

"Don't you talk to me like that, not if you do call yourself a young gentleman. And I'll learn you to know that a woman of my age is not going to be called a cheat by a young lad like you. You ought to be ashamed of yourself, that's what you ought to be, standing there disgracing of yourself."

The Ogre held up his hand, as if to play the part of peacemaker.

"Gently, cook, gently. You leave it to me and I will see that you have what is due to you. We must remember how ignorant these young people are of their position, and try to make allowances. Though I grant that under the circumstances it's a little difficult." He put his hands into his trouser pockets, tilted back the chair on which he was seated, and considered the ceiling. "What I intend to do is this. At Miss Molly's request I have, reluctantly, incurred certain liabilities and assumed certain responsibilities. To know exactly what those responsibilities are it is necessary that I should examine thoroughly the condition of affairs. When I have done so—it cannot, I am sorry to say, be done in a moment—I will lay the results before the more responsible members of the family—if there are any such—and without waiting for the thanks which I possibly shall not receive I will at once withdraw."

Such a prospect did not commend itself to me at all. That we were already being cheated all round I was sure. That we ran a great risk of being cheated to a much more serious extent if the Ogre was allowed to do as he suggested I felt equally convinced. And in any case I did not want his interference in our private affairs. It was dreadful to think of him peering and prying into mother's secrets, into the things which she held sacred. The way he was behaving now showed how much we could trust him and what use he would make of any knowledge he might acquire. Instead of being our friend he would be our bitterest enemy. And yet I did not see how we were going to get rid of him without a desperate struggle—of which, after all, we might get the worst.

But I was not going to let him see that I was afraid of him.

"Where is the money which was in mother's desk?"

"Money? What money?"

"Mother always kept a large sum of money in her desk. You have had access to her desk, though you'd no right to touch it. How much was there? and where is it now?"

"I've seen no money."

"Why, it is with mother's money that you have been paying for everything."

"I wish it had been. I've been paying for every blessed thing out of my own pocket."

"That's a lie!" shouted Dick. "I know there was money in her desk."

"Look here, my lad—if you'll excuse my calling you my lad—the next time you speak to me like that I'll make you smart for it. Now, don't you expect another warning."

"That's right," cried cook. "You give him a good sound thrashing, Mr Miller. He wants it. Accusing everyone of robbing him, when it's him who's trying to rob everybody!"

The Ogre brought down his clenched fist heavily on the table.

"Listen to me, you children. For all you know, and for all I know, you're nothing but a lot of paupers; and if you don't want to find yourself inside a workhouse you'll leave it to me to make the best of things. So now you've got it."

We had got it. I saw Dick's cheeks blanch. I was conscious that my own went pale. If the awful thing at which he hinted was true, then things were miles worse than I had ever supposed. But was it true? And how, with him sitting there, were we going to look for proof of either its truth or falsehood?

Just as I was beginning to fear that I should make a goose of myself and cry, I heard someone come up the front doorsteps and ask,—

"Is Miss Boyes at home? Miss Molly Boyes?"

I rushed out into the hall. There, standing at the hall door, which was wide open, was the handsomest man I had ever seen. He was very tall and sunburned. He had his cap in his hand, so that you could see that he had short curly hair. And his moustache was just beginning to come. I wondered if he was a harbinger of more trouble. He did not look as if he was; but he might be.

"I am Molly Boyes."

"My name is Sanford. I am afraid I ought to apologise for my intrusion, but I am a cousin of Hetty Travers, who tells me you are a friend of hers. I am

40

staying a few miles from here, and she has written to say that she is afraid you are in trouble, and to ask me to run over and see if I can be of assistance."

Hetty's cousin! That did not sound like trouble. How sweet of her to think of me, and to send that great strong man! She might have guessed what was happening to us—the dear!

"I am in trouble. I have lost my mother. And now, there is Mr Miller."

"Mr Miller? Who is he?"

The children had already trooped into the hall. Then Dick appeared. I introduced him.

"This is my brother Dick. Dick, this is Mr Sanford, a cousin of Hetty Travers. You have heard me speak of Hetty. Mr Sanford has come to know if he can be of any assistance to us."

"If you really would like to do something to help us—"

There Dick stopped, as if in doubt.

"I should," said Mr Sanford.

I rather fancied from the way he smiled that he had taken a liking to Dick upon the spot. I did so hope he had.

"Then perhaps you'll lend me a hand in chucking this man Miller through the window. He's almost a size too large for me. Come inside here."

We all trooped back into the morning-room, Mr Sanford and Dick in front. Dick pointed to the Ogre.

"You see that individual. His name's Miller. He's taken possession of the place as though it belongs to him; he's made free with my mother's property and papers; and when I ask him to leave the house he talks about treating me to a good sound thrashing."

"He does, does he? Is he a relation of yours?"

"Relation! He's not even an acquaintance. He came here uninvited when my mother lay dead, took advantage of the state of mind we were in to gain a footing in the house, and now we can't get rid of him."

Mr Sanford turned to me.

"Is it your wish, Miss Boyes, that this person should leave the house?"

"It is very much my wish. He knows it is."

"You hear, sir. I hope it is not necessary to emphasise the wish which Miss Boyes has expressed so clearly."

Cook struck in.

"A pretty way of talking, upon my word. Perhaps, my fine gentleman, while you are putting your nose into other people's business you'll see that our wages are paid. Mr Miller's only trying to save us from being robbed, that's all he's doing. Three months' wages there is due to each of us servants, and over."

Mr Sanford paid no heed at all to cook. He continued to eye the Ogre.

"Well, sir?"

"Well, sir, to you."

"You heard what I said?"

"I did. And if you are wise you'll hear what I say, and not interfere in what is absolutely no concern of yours."

"Nothing in this house is any concern of yours," burst out Dick. "And well you know it!"

"Who's dog is this?" asked Mr Sanford.

The Ogre's dog—a horrid, savage-looking creature—was sniffing at Mr Sanford's ankles, showing his teeth and growling in a way that was anything but friendly. Its owner grinned, as if the animal's behaviour met with his approval.

"That's my dog. It objects to strangers—of a certain class."

Suddenly Mr Sanford stooped down, gripped the brute by the scruff of its neck and the root of its tail, swung it through the air and out of the window. Harris happened to be staring in at the time. The dog struck him as it passed. Over he went, and off tore the dog down the drive, yelping and howling as if it had had more than enough of our establishment. The Ogre sprang from his chair, and he used a very bad word.

"What do you mean by doing that?"

Harris, as he regained his feet, gave utterance to his woes.

"That's a nice thing to do, to throw a great dog like that right into a man's face! What next, I wonder?"

Mr Sanford was most civil.

"Hope it hasn't hurt you, but I'm afraid that your face must have been in the way." Then to the Ogre: "Well, sir, we are still waiting. By which route do you propose to follow your dog?"

There was something in Mr Sanford's looks and manner which, in view of the little adventure his dog had had, apparently caused the Ogre to suspect that the moment had arrived when discretion might be the better part of valour.

"Before we go any further, perhaps you'll let me know who's going to repay what I've advanced? Nearly two hundred pounds I'm out of pocket."

"You're nearly two hundred pounds out of pocket!" cried Dick. "What for?"

"Why, for seeing that your mother was buried like a respectable woman. It begins to strike me that you'd have liked to have had her buried by the parish."

The Ogre thrust his red face so very close to Dick's that I suppose the provocation and temptation together were more than Dick could stand. Anyhow, Dick gave him a tremendous slap on the cheek. In a moment Mr Sanford was between them.

"It serves you right," he declared. "It shows what sort of person you must be that you should permit yourself to use such language in this house of mourning."

"Harris," shouted the Ogre, "run round to Charlie Radford and Bill Perkins and tell 'em I want 'em, quick! And loose the dogs and bring 'em back with you!"

"Begging of your pardon, Mr Miller," replied Harris, possibly perceiving in which direction the wind was about to blow, "but if you want any more of your dirty work done you'll do it yourself."

Cook was horrified.

"Well, the likes of that! After all Mr Miller has done for you!"

"Done for me! He has made me do what I'm ashamed of, that's what he's done for me! I've had enough of him, and of you too, Mrs Boyes was as good a mistress as anyone need have. I know it if no one else does. And, Miss Molly, your mother always paid my wages regular to the moment; you don't owe me nothing. And you don't owe cook and Betsy nothing either."

"What do you know about what is and is not owing me?" screamed cook.

"I know you were paid each month; and, what's more, I know you gave a receipt for it. Why, you told me yourself that you took the wages' receipt book from the little cupboard in the corner."

Cook's virtuous indignation was beautiful to behold.

"It only shows how sensible Mary Sharp was to pack her box and take herself outside of such a place. And I'll do the same within the hour."

"So will I," said Betsy.

"Mr Sanford," I said, "all sorts of mother's things are missing, and I shouldn't be at all surprised if cook and Betsy have taken some of them."

"Me taken your mother's things!" screamed cook. I believe that if it had not been for Mr Sanford she would have scratched me.

"I think it not at all improbable," he agreed. "Is there a constable hereabouts?"

"There's one in the village." This was Harris, who seemed to have arrived at a sudden resolution to attack his late allies at every possible point, "Name of Parker."

"If you will be so good as to request Mr Parker's immediate attendance you shall have no reason to regret it, Mr Harris. Neither of you women will leave this house until the contents of your boxes have been examined in the presence of a policeman."

Cook looked uncomfortable as she met Mr Sanford's stern glance. And it was stern! Betsy began to cry.

"And what's more," added Harris, pointing at the Ogre, "I happen to know that there was money in Mrs Boyes's desk, and he knows it too."

With that parting shot Harris hurried off down the avenue.

"Things are beginning to wear rather an ugly aspect, Mr Miller."

"Ugly aspect! What do you mean? You needn't think I want to stop in this hugger-muggering hole! I am just as anxious to get out of it as anyone can be to get me out."

"I should hardly think that possible."

"I only regret that I ever set foot in it."

"Then the regret is general."

"As for these ungrateful little wretches, and especially you, my lad!"—this was Dick—"they shall hear of me very soon in quite another fashion, when they haven't got a bully to back them up."

Mr Sanford laughed.

"He's cramming mother's things into his pocket at this very moment!" cried Jim.

"Aren't you making a mistake, Mr Miller?"

Mr Sanford's politeness seemed to make the Ogre feel dreadful. He looked as if he would have liked to have killed him.

"I don't want the miserable rubbish!"

He banged the letters and things down on the table. Dick went on,—

"I believe that what Harris says about there having been money in mother's desk is true, and this man hasn't accounted for a penny. And it's my belief too that he's been taking what he likes out of the house. He lives just up the lane—I shouldn't be surprised to find plenty of mother's property at his own place."

The Ogre moved towards the door, but it was too late, Mr Sanford interposed.

"Excuse me, Mr Miller, but I think that now I would rather you waited till Mr Parker arrives. We will accompany you to your own establishment. There —together—we will make certain inquiries."

He blustered a little, but he was a coward at heart, and he had to give in. As it chanced, Harris met Parker in the lane, so that he came back with him almost at once.

All sorts of things which did not belong to them were found in cook's and Betsy's boxes; and actually the book of which Harris had spoken, in which they themselves had signed receipts for their wages. There was a tremendous scene. Parker badly wanted to lock them up, but we had had trouble enough already, so we let them go.

While we were examining the servants' boxes upstairs the Ogre was offering Mr Sanford what he called an explanation. When they went round with him to his own house he handed over quite a collection of miscellaneous articles which belonged to mother. Her cheque-book, all sorts of papers, some of them representing stocks and shares, even some of her jewellery. He said he had taken them home to examine. Which seemed a very curious thing to do. The next morning he had vanished. He had left no address, and nothing was seen or heard of him in that neighbourhood again. So we concluded that he had escaped with something much more valuable than anything which he had given up. But it was a long time before we suspected what it was.

What we should have done without Mr Sanford—if he had not come in the very nick of time—I do not dare to think. We might have been plundered of every single thing we had. It was very nice of Hetty Travers to have a big strong cousin, and it was perfectly lovely of her to send him to us.

IV

THE HANDWRITING

It was some time after mother's death before we knew if we were or were not penniless. And as, of course, it was our duty to be prepared for the very worst, we used to discuss among ourselves how, if we were left without a farthing, we should earn one. Though I am perfectly well aware that a single farthing would not have been of much service to us. But then I suppose everybody knows what I mean.

When there are six children, and the eldest is a girl, and she is only sixteen, and they have no relatives, and not one grown-up person to advise them, it does seem strange what a very few ways there are of making a fortune. That is, within a reasonable space of time. So far as I could make out, from what the others said, for every one of them you wanted money to start with. And if you had no money, it was not the slightest use your doing anything. Then the boys had such impracticable notions. Dick was full of South Africa. He declared that nothing was easier than to go to South Africa; find what he called a "claim," on which there were tons of gold, or so many pounds to the ton, I do not quite know which; turn it into a company, and there you were, a millionaire, in what he termed "a brace of shakes." But it appeared to me that that "brace of shakes" would be some time in coming. First, he would have to get to South Africa, then he would have to find his "claim,"—and there was no proof that they were found by everyone; then he would have to get his company up, which might take weeks; and, in the meantime, were we supposed to starve? I seemed to have read somewhere that a human being could not be kept alive without food for more than seven days. I doubted if there would be much left of me after four-and-twenty hours. Jack wanted to be an engine-driver on the railway line, a profession which I feel sure is not too highly paid; while Jim actually yearned to be a fireman in the fire brigade, though how he imagined that he was going to earn a fortune that way was beyond my comprehension.

Nora and I were reluctantly compelled to admit that if our means of sustenance were to depend on the efforts of the masculine portion of the family we should apparently have to go very short indeed. And the field for girls did seem to be so circumscribed. As I said to her—

"There do seem to be such a few ways in which girls can get money."

"There aren't any."

We were in the kitchen, she and I alone together. We were supposed to be getting the tea ready. There was not a servant about the place. And the condition the house was getting into in consequence was beyond anything. She was sitting on the edge of the table, with a coal scoop in one hand and a toasting-fork in the other. Nora always was of a pessimistic description. She invariably looked on the blackest side of everything. So one got into the habit of allowing for the peculiarity of her outlook. Besides, I had in my head at that moment the glimmering of an idea of how to earn an immense amount.

"There are some ways. For instance, there's writing. There are girls who write for papers, and all kinds of things."

"Only those who can't write get paid anything."

I wondered if she had been trying her own hand. The statement did sound so sweeping.

"There's teaching. Look at the lots of governesses that must be wanted."

"Let 'em be wanted. I prefer prussic acid."

"There's drawing for the magazines."

"You might as well talk about drawing for the moon—unless you're a perfect idiot, then you might have a chance."

I felt sure that she had had experiences of her own. Her tone was so extremely bitter.

"And then there are prize competitions. There do seem to be a tremendous number of them about. And some of them for really large prizes."

"Prize competitions!" Nora seemed all at once to have wakened to life and vigour. "Promise you won't split if I tell you something?" I promised. "I believe that all prize competitions are frauds run by robbers. Do you know"— she brought the toasting-fork and coal scoop together with a bang—"that I've gone in for seventy-two of all sorts and kinds, and never won a single prize, not even a consolation. And some of them were hard enough to kill you. I've guessed how much money there was at the Bank of England; how many babies were born on a Tuesday; picked out twelve successful football teams; named three winners at a horse race—"

"Nora!"

"I have—or, at least, I've tried to. Much the largest prizes are offered for that. I've drawn things, written things, calculated things, prophesied things, made things, collected things, solved things, sold things,—once I tried to sell a lot of papers in the village for the sake of the coupons, but no one would buy a single copy. It was a frightful loss. I do believe I've tried my hand at

47

every sort and kind of thing you can think of—and heaps you can't—and, as I say, I've never even won a consolation prize. No more prize competitions for me!"

That was not encouraging, especially as it was a prize competition which I had got in my mind's eye. After her disclosures I did not breathe a word of it to Nora, but when I got up to my bedroom I took out the paper in which I had seen all about it, and considered. The part which told you about the competition was headed "Delineation of Character by Handwriting." You had to write, on a sheet of paper, a sentence not exceeding twelve words in length. This you had to put into an envelope, which you had to seal and endorse with a pseudonym. This envelope you had to put into another envelope, together with your real name and address, and a postal order for a shilling, or twelve stamps, and send to the paper. The person whose caligraphy was considered to show that the writer was the possessor of the finest character was to receive one hundred pounds.

One hundred pounds!—for a shilling! Of course, I was perfectly well aware that hosts of people would go in, and that, as the chances of success were presumably equal, one's own individual chance was but a small one. But, on the other hand, what was a shilling? And, also, some people's writing was better than others. As a matter of fact, I rather fancied my own. It had been admired by several persons. It was large, bold, and, I was persuaded, distinctly characteristic. I perceived that the sentences had to be despatched to the office of the paper on the following day.

Why should not one of mine go with them? There really seemed no reason. I had twelve stamps. There were pens, ink, and paper. My non-success would merely add to the list of failures with which the family was already credited— making seventy-three. What was that? The question was, what sentence should I send. You were left to choose your own. But the presumption was that your chances of success would not be lessened if the one selected was a good one. I had it on the instant. My desk chanced to be open. There, staring at me on the top, was the very thing.

At Mrs Sawyer's school there had once been a governess named Winston —Sophia Winston. We all of us liked her. I adored her. She was one of the best and sweetest creatures that ever lived. But her health was not very good and she had to leave. Before she left I asked her to write a motto in my book of mottoes. Although she said she would, when I came to look for the book I could not find it anywhere. Somehow, in those days, my things always were playing games of hide-and-seek with me. So, instead, she wrote a motto on a sheet of paper. There lay the identical sheet of paper in front of me at that moment. I took it up; opened it; read it:—

"Who goes slowly goes safely and goes far."

The very thing! I more than fancied that it was with *malice prepense* that Miss Winston had referred me to that rendering of what I knew was an Italian proverb. It was not my custom to go slowly, or safely, or—in the sense in which the word was there used—far. But, for the purpose of the present competition, that was not a matter of the slightest consequence. I made six copies of Miss Winston's sentence; picked out the one which I judged was the best; and, after destroying the other five, packed it up with the requisite twelve stamps, and sent it off to the office of the paper.

Of course I told no one of what I had done. I was not quite so silly as that. The boys would have laughed—especially Dick, who was once rude enough to ask me if I wrote with the end of a broom-stick. While Nora—after her revelations of the hollowness and deceitfulness of such things—would have concluded I was mad. I simply held my tongue. And I waited.

The paper to which I had sent was a weekly one—it came out every Wednesday. It appeared that the competition was a weekly one also. The sentences had to reach the office on the one Wednesday morning, and in the paper which came out on the following Wednesday the results were announced. Either not many sentences were sent in, or there must have been someone in the office who was uncommonly quick at reading character. There used to be a girl at Lingfield House who pretended to read character from handwriting. She wanted pages of it before she would attempt to say what kind of character you had. Then she would take days to form an opinion. And then it would be all wrong. I daresay that in the office of the paper they had had a deal of practice.

On the Thursday morning of the week following I was down first as, I am sorry to say, I generally had to be; sometimes I actually had to drag the others out of bed; and Nora was every bit as bad as the boys—and as I came into the hall I saw a letter lying on the floor. Smith the postman had pushed it through the slit in the door. I picked it up. It was addressed to "Miss Molly Boyes, The Chase, West Marden, Sussex." On the top of the envelope was printed "*Trifles*. The Paper For The Whole World." When I saw it something seemed to give a jump inside me, so that I trembled all over. I could hardly tear it open. There were three things inside. One—could I believe my eyes? at first I felt that they must be playing me a trick—but one really was a cheque—"Pay Molly Boyes or Order One Hundred Pounds." I believe that at the sight of it I very nearly fainted. I never have done quite; but I think that I very nearly did do then. It was a most odd sensation. I was positively glad to feel the wall at my back, and I went hot and cold all over. Of the other two enclosures the first was a letter—from the editor himself! though, as it had been done by a typewriter, it was not in his own writing—perhaps that was because he was afraid of having his character told—saying that he was glad to inform me that I had been adjudged the winner of that week's competition; that he had pleasure in handing me a cheque for one hundred pounds herewith; and that he would be obliged by my signing and returning the accompanying form of receipt. The second inclosure was the receipt.

As soon as I recovered my senses I tore up the stairs about three at a time. I rushed in to Nora.

"Nora," I cried, "I've won a hundred pounds!"

She was lying reading in bed, and was so engrossed in her book that she did not catch what I said. She grumbled.

"I wish you wouldn't come interrupting me like that; especially as I've just got to where the hero is killing his second wife."

"Bother his second wife! and bother the hero too! Look at that!" I held out before her the editor's letter and the cheque. "Seventy-two times you've tried, at least, you said you had; and I've only tried once. And the very first time I've won!"

"What are you talking about?"

"If you'll come to Dick's room I'll tell you all about it."

Off I raced to Dick's room, calling out to Con and Jack and Jim as I passed. Presently the whole family were gathered about Dick's bed. Nora had put on a dressing-gown, but the three younger boys were just as they had got out of the sheets.

"Well," said Dick, when he had turned the cheque over and over and over, and held it up to the light to see if it was a forgery, "some rum things do happen, and those who deserve least get most."

"I always have thought," observed Nora, "that those prize competitions were frauds, and now I know it."

Jack was more sympathetic—or he meant to be.

"Never mind what they say; it's only their beastly jealousy. I'm jolly glad you have won, because now we can have new bicycles."

"About time too," declared Jim. "I've had mine tinkered so many times that there's none of the original machine left."

"I punctured my tyre again yesterday," groaned Con. "That's about the twentieth time this week. It's hardly anything but holes."

I had not contemplated providing the whole family with new bicycles. But they did seem a necessity. I knew that I wanted a new machine, and so did Nora. And in a little matter of that kind the boys were pretty sure not to be very far behind. Fortunately nowadays bicycles are so cheap; and then we could always give our old ones in exchange; so, supposing the worst came to the worst, and we were all penniless, even after buying six new bicycles, I ought to have a good deal of money left, to keep us in food and things. Because, of course, I had to remember that I could not expect to win a hundred pounds every time I tried.

The nearest place to us where they sold papers was the bookstall at the station, and that was six miles away. So after breakfast we all mounted the machines we had, and dashed off to get a copy of *Trifles*. On the road Con had another puncture. It would not be stopped. As he said, his tyres did seem to have all they wanted in the way of ventilation. So as Jim's handle-bar had come off, and could not be induced to remain where it ought to be, we left them to console each other. Of course Dick, who rides tremendously fast, got to the station first, and Jack next. Nora and I never got there at all. They came flying back to us when we were about two hundred yards away, each waving a paper above his head, and laughing like anything. I was half afraid that there was something wrong, and that although I had got the prize, I had not won it. But it was something else which was amusing them.

"If ever anyone ought to be sent to a lunatic asylum it's the man who runs this paper," shouted Dick. "Let's get to the stile, and I'll prove my words to your entire satisfaction."

At the stile we all four of us dismounted. Unfolding his paper Dick read aloud from it, Jack following him in his own particular copy.

"'We have much pleasure in announcing that, this week, the possessor of the finest character, as revealed by her handwriting, is Molly Boyes, The Chase, West Marden, Sussex, to whom a cheque for one hundred pounds has accordingly been sent. Her character, as declared by her caligraphy, is as follows.'—Now then, all you chappies, listen! attention, please, and mind you, the character 'declared' is supposed to be Molly's—'This writing shows a character of unusual nobility—'"

"Hear, hear!" from Jack.

"'The motto chosen is singularly appropriate'—By the way, the motto chosen was 'Who goes slowly, goes safely and goes far,' so everyone who knows her will perceive its peculiar fitness. Now do just listen to this Johnny, and I ask the lady herself if he doesn't credit her with exactly those qualities which she hasn't got—'Patience and thoughtfulness, a high standard of honour, clear-sightedness, resolution combined with a sweet and tranquil temper,'—what ho!—'are all clearly shown. The writer is strong on both the moral and the intellectual side. A large and beautiful faith is obvious. To a serene tranquillity of temperament is united a keen insight and a calm persistence in following to a successful issue well-considered purposes, instinct with a lofty rectitude.'—As an example of how not to delineate character from handwriting, I should say that takes the record."

I felt myself that here and there that expert was a trifle out. I certainly should not have called the sentence selected "singularly appropriate" to me. Nor should I have laid much stress upon my patience or my thoughtfulness. I had not been hitherto aware that I was the owner of "a sweet and tranquil temper," or of "a serene tranquillity of temperament," or of "calm persistence." Indeed, there were one or two little matters in which I more than suspected that that character reader was a trifle at fault. But, after all, these were questions of opinion, and had nothing to do with the real point, which was, that I had won the hundred pounds.

When we returned home I went upstairs, fetched my desk, carried it down to the morning-room, and prepared to write and tell everyone of my good fortune. In the frame of mind in which I was, it was not a piece of news which I was disposed to keep to myself. I opened the desk, got out the note-paper, found the pen, and just as I had got as far as—"My darling Hetty,—I've won a fortune! You never will guess how!"—I thought of Miss Winston's sentence. It was that which had brought me luck. I was convinced of it. If it had not been for the motto which that curiosity in character readers had found so singularly appropriate, I seriously doubted if I should have won. The least I could do was to kiss it, in memory of the writer.

I had placed it—after making those six copies—in an envelope which I had endorsed "Miss Winston's Motto." I laid down my pen, raked out the envelope, took out the sheet of paper. On it was the sentence, not in Miss Winston's small, exquisite penmanship, but in my own great sprawling hand. For a moment or two I stared at it in bewildered surprise. Then, in the twinkling of an eye, I understood what had happened.

In my characteristic blundering fashion I had confused my copy with her original. My writing I had packed into the envelope I was holding, and hers I had put into the one which I had sent to the paper. It was her caligraphy which had been adjudicated on, her character which had been deduced therefrom. The thing was as plain as plain could be—the whole business had had nothing whatever to do with me. I re-perused the winning character as it appeared in the paper. The man was not such an idiot as we had all supposed. It was not a bit like me; but it exactly described Miss Winston. She was all the lovely things he said she was, while I—I was none of them—I was just an addle-headed donkey.

Talk about sensations! My feelings when I found the cheque in the letter were nothing compared to what they were when I realised precisely what the situation was. The world seemed to have all at once stood still; as if something had happened to the works. It was perfectly awful. Here was my name printed in great big letters in the paper; with my character underneath. I had flaunted the cheque in the face of all the family. In imagination the money was already spent. I had practically promised to buy each one of them a bicycle. And now, after all—

Whose was the money after all?

Never, till that dreadful time, did I thoroughly appreciate what it means about not leading us into temptation. It would be quite easy to say nothing. They were my twelve stamps which I had sent; and the sentence on the piece of paper was my property. Really, if you looked at it from one point of view, the hundred pounds belonged to me as much as to anybody else. I had only to keep my own counsel and it was impossible that anyone should even guess that there was anything the least bit odd about the matter. Of course, I knew what I knew; and the misfortune was that I did know. If I had only never looked inside that horrid envelope, and never found out what had happened, how much happier I should have been.

I laid my head straight down upon the table, and I did cry.

While I was in the very middle of enjoying myself—like a great overgrown baby!—someone came into the room, and a voice said, a voice which I knew well—

"Miss Boyes!—I beg your pardon, but I knocked at the door, and when no one answered I thought I would come in to see if there was anyone about."

It was Mr Sanford! It only wanted him to find me going on like that to finish everything. As usual, all the luck was on my side. I was perfectly aware that the slightest scrap of crying makes me look an object; and here I had been howling myself inside out for goodness alone knew how long. I dabbed at my eyes with my pocket-handkerchief—though I knew I made a fresh smear every time I touched myself, because I had the best of reasons for knowing that tears made me positively grimy—and I tried to pretend that I was not yearning to sink into the ground. He seemed concerned.

"I hope there's nothing wrong?—that the Ogre has been giving you no further trouble?"

I did manage to gasp out something.

"No—thank you—he's—been—giving—us—no—trouble."

He apparently concluded that it might be advisable to seem not to notice that there was anything strange in my demeanour.

"I am the bearer of good news."—We wanted some, badly. I know I did. —"You have been good enough to allow me to examine somewhat closely into the condition of your affairs."—We had been good enough to allow him! As if it had not been perfectly splendid of him to do it; he being, not only Betty's cousin, but a barrister.—"Your mother appears to have managed everything herself—and very well she seems to have done it too; but the fact makes it somewhat difficult for a stranger to probe quickly to the bottom of everything; and the Ogre's proceedings have not made it easier. But so far as I have gone, I have ascertained beyond all doubt that instead of being in fear of the workhouse—as someone suggested—you are very comfortably off. As time goes on I shall not be surprised if you find yourselves—financially—in a still better position."—It was a consolation to know so much. That hundred pounds would not be wanted—"By-the-bye, I saw my cousin Hetty yesterday, and she entrusted me with what she called a note to you. I fancy you will find that it extends to about six sheets of paper."

It is not necessary to tell me it was ill-manners; I knew it was; but I felt that I must do something to avoid meeting his eyes; so I opened the envelope, and started reading Hetty's letter then and there. The opening words seemed to leap up off the paper and strike me in the face.

"My very own dearest little Molly!"—she always would call me little, though I was every bit as big as she was—"What do you think? You remember Miss Winston? She's starving! And she's not only starving, but she's dying of consumption. I've only just found it out by the merest accident. It seems that she's living in a little cottage at a place called Angmering, somewhere near Worthing. She's been ill ever so long, and able to do no work, or earn a penny. So that she has absolutely no money to buy herself food, or even to pay her rent. If someone doesn't come to her help soon they'll have to take her to the workhouse—to die! Poor Miss Winston! And she such a darling! Isn't it dreadful to think of?"

It was. So dreadful, that I could not bear to think. I hope it was not wicked, but I almost felt as if that letter must have dropped out of heaven. It did seem a miracle that it should have come to me at that very moment. Penniless! Starving! And there was that hundred pounds—her hundred pounds—lying on the table. Was it possible that I had even remotely contemplated the possibility of—of doing what? My conscience so rose up at me that, whether Mr Sanford was or was not there, I had to hide my face with my hands and start crying all over again. My behaviour seemed to positively frighten him.

"I hope that Hetty has not said anything disagreeable—nothing to cause you pain. I assure you that nothing was further from her intention, and that the letter was accompanied by all sorts of loving messages."

Then I felt that I must tell him everything. So I did—every morsel, right from the beginning. He was so patient, so full of understanding and of sympathy; indeed, he was much more sympathetic than I deserved. Still, even if you are not deserving of sympathy, it is a comfort to receive it, particularly if it is nicely offered.

I do not wish to breathe a word against my own family. I am perfectly certain that no one could be fonder of Nora and the boys than I am. Yet I am inclined to think that there are times, when if one must confess, it is just as well to do it to someone who is not exactly a relation. One's relatives are apt to take such a narrow view. I am convinced that no one could have taken a broader view than Mr Sanford did; and he never laughed once. That, in itself, was an immense relief. I have noticed in Nora, even when I have been confiding to her the most serious things, a tendency to treat me as if I was not quite in earnest. There was nothing of that sort about Mr Sanford, not a trace; or, at least, if he did show some faint sign of my having afforded him amusement, he did not do it in a brutal way.

"Poor little soul!" he said, when I had finished. "Poor little soul!"—I was not certain that I liked him to address me in quite that form of words. But there was something so extremely soothing in his manner that I let it pass.
—"And so this has been the cause of the trouble." He picked up the copy of the sentence which I had meant to send to the paper. "I see no reason why this should not have succeeded in winning the prize. If you will forgive me for posing as an expert, this handwriting is eminently characteristic."

"Don't be horrid!"

"Such is not my intention. I am not suggesting that the character given in the paper is particularly applicable to this."

"I know it isn't!"

"But it does not follow that this does not hint at something equally fine, though in a different way."

"Mr Sanford!"

"I must ask you to forgive me if I annoy you by the expression of my opinion. In any case, you are to be congratulated on what you have done."

55

"How do you make that out? When I have been winning other people's money with somebody else's writing?"

"Precisely. Though I should not phrase it quite like that. Hetty informs me that this lady is in sore straits. Well, you have gained for her what, in her position, she will regard as a fortune—which she never could have done for herself."

"I never meant to."

"Which actually makes it more delightful. Because, while you have been trying to do a good deed, you have really done a better." He had a very nice way of putting things. "I would suggest that you yourself take the money to this lady at once. Her pleasure at seeing it will only be eclipsed by her delight at seeing you. And I shall be only too proud and happy if you will allow me to accompany you on your errand of mercy."

That was what did happen. Scarcely had he stopped speaking than Harris appeared at the window.

"If you please, Miss Molly, Miss Nora and the young gentlemen asked me to tell you that they've gone off for the day, and won't be back till the evening."

"We also," observed Mr Sanford, "will go off for the day. You see, the stars in their courses are on the side of Miss Winston. I came over on my machine; if you'll jump on yours we'll be off!"

He seemed to imagine that I could rush off to the other side of the county just as I was. Masculine persons do have such curious notions—even when they are grown up. I had to scrub my face to make it clean. The condition of my hair was frightful. I seemed to have cried it into a tangled mass. Just as I was struggling with it his voice came up the stairs.

"I don't know, Miss Boyes, if you are aware that you have been five-and-thirty minutes. If you can get down inside the next five we may catch the train; but if you can't, I'm afraid we sha'n't."

Of course after that I simply flew. I left my hair nearly as it was; jammed my hat on anyhow; and bounded down the stairs.

"I hope I haven't kept you waiting," I remarked.

"I'm used to it," he said. "I have two sisters."

I do not know what he meant. It sounded very rude. Almost like one of my own relations.

We caught the train; and, after changing at Chichester, reached Angmering at last. By that time I had come to the conclusion that Mr Sanford was one of the most delightful persons I had ever encountered. And so intellectual. A trifle dogmatic perhaps, and a little inclined to regard me as younger than I was. We had a long and most interesting discussion about women in politics. A subject of which I knew absolutely nothing. But it was not necessary, on that account, that he should hint as much. Which he very nearly did. Yet, on the whole, I could not but regard him as the kind of cousin to do one credit. And, at the risk of making her conceited, almost made up my mind to tell Hetty so next time I wrote to her.

Dear Miss Winston! We found her, looking like the shadow of her former self, lying on such a hard old couch, in such a poor little room. Had I been an angel she could not have seemed more glad to see me. As I told her all about it she was so sweet. And when I gave her the twenty five-pound notes for which Mr Sanford had changed the cheque at Chichester, the way in which she thanked me did make me feel so strange. As if I had done anything to deserve her thanks. I never knew how happy it made one to be the bearer of good news until that day. As I came away I almost felt as if I had been in the presence of something sacred.

On our way home Mr Sanford and I had a warm argument about old-age pensions, which nearly ended in a tiff. After we had been talking about them for more than half an hour he as good as said that he did not believe that I knew what an old age-pension was. Even if that was true—and it was, perfectly—I did not propose to allow him—almost a stranger—to accuse me of downright ignorance; as if I were an untutored savage. He might know something about everything; and anyone could see that he was awfully clever, while I might know nothing about anything,—which possibly was the case. Still, it was not civil for him to remark on it. The fact was, that he would persist in regarding me—I could see quite plainly what was in his mind—as if I were a mere child. Which, at sixteen, one emphatically is not. I do not hesitate to admit that I snubbed him in order to let him see that I resented his quite intolerable airs of superior wisdom.

Which made it the more singular that he should have told me, as we were entering the drive, that he had to thank me for one of the pleasantest days he had spent in his life. Considering that I had been metaphorically sitting upon him for ever so long, I did not at all understand what he had to thank me for.

When I got out my desk, to commence a letter to Hetty, my copy of Miss Winston's sentence was nowhere to be found. I could not think what had become of it. I distinctly remembered Mr Sanford taking it off the table, and making some uninvited comments on the writing—he seemed fond of criticising other people. But I did not recall what had happened to it afterwards. He could not have put it into his pocket by mistake. It seemed such a very odd thing for him to have done. And so excessively careless.

V

THE PEOPLE'S STOCK EXCHANGE

Although we were not paupers, for ever so long after mother's death we lived pretty much as if we were. We hated the idea of living in a town; especially London, and we could not get a servant to stop at The Chase. Considering that the family consisted of Dick and me, and the four children, who all of them insisted on doing exactly as they pleased, it really was no wonder. The consequence was, that we generally had to do everything for ourselves, and the way in which things were done was beyond description. A stranger dropping in suddenly would have supposed himself to have wandered into something between a lunatic asylum and a workhouse.

Of course, as the head of the family, this state of things occasioned me much concern. I knew that it was not what mother would have wished. But when I spoke to the others about it, they all started laying the blame upon each other, and even upon me. The fact is, when we were servantless, the boys expected Nora and me to do everything. We did not see it. Especially as it was almost invariably their fault that we were without a creature to do a thing. Their habits were so erratic. You could not expect a properly trained servant—or indeed anyone—to take them up their breakfasts in bed at intervals of half an hour or so. Or—if they had made up their minds to fly off to the other side of the county—to have a regular meal ready at perhaps five o'clock in the morning. As for lunch, they expected that to be on all day. And always something hot and really nice. As for tea, as a rule, Nora and I had ours together; but no one ever knew when the boys would insist on having theirs. It was the same with dinner. We always had had a proper dinner, and I felt, strongly, that because mother was dead we ought not all at once to behave as if we were barbarians, and leave off everything she had accustomed us to. And Dick said that he agreed with me. So I fixed it first for seven; then half-past; then eight; then for all sorts of times. But it was no use. Either one of the boys would come in half an hour before the proper time, starving, because—through his own fault—he had had nothing to eat all day, and, before anyone could stop him, would seize whatever was cooking, and make a meal off it there and then. Or else some of them would be ever so late, and make a tremendous fuss because we had not waited—even to the extent of expecting another dinner to be served there and then. In that respect Dick was as bad as anyone. No cook would stand that sort of thing—and no cook did.

If we could only have found mother's will it might all have been so different. Because it was not at all unlikely that she had appointed someone as guardian, and to take proper control of everything until the children had grown up. As it was, so far as we knew, no one had a right to even send the boys to school. And as they refused, point-blank, to go of their own accord, educationally they bade fair to shine. At Mr Sanford's suggestion we tried a tutor. The tricks they played him were beyond conception. Nothing would induce him to stop. He actually threatened us with an action for damages. I do not quite know what for, but Mr Sanford had to pay him something extra before he would be satisfied.

I do not wish it to be supposed that the boys were bad boys. They were not. They had loved mother dearly, and I do not believe they had ever given her any trouble. But I fancy they had never been very fond of school. And the sudden chance of liberty had turned their heads. Besides, they had all made up their minds to be things for which much book-learning was not required. And if Jack was going to be an engine-driver, and Jim either a fireman or an aeronaut, and Con a naturalist, it did seem a pity to spend a lot of money on unnecessary schooling.

Unfortunately we could not find a will. The presumption was that mother had made one, but that it had been stolen, because one day I came upon a box of papers which was locked up in one of the drawers in her wardrobe.

Oh dear, how strange I felt as I looked through them. Almost as if I were prying into mother's secrets. Although I know perfectly well that there was nothing which now she would have wished to have kept hidden from me. There were all father's letters—even the love-letters which he had written to her before they were married. If I had only known that they were there, I would have had them placed with her in the coffin, so that they might have been hers only, even in the grave. I think she would have liked it. By the beautiful way in which they had been kept bound about with ribbons tied in true lovers' knots, you could see how sacred she had held them. There were all sorts of things besides. In particular, quantities of ball programmes. She must have seen a great deal of Society at one time. What a strange change must have taken place in her life, because I did not remember her once going anywhere. Some of the things were beyond my comprehension. I wondered what history was attached to a tiny Maltese cross wrapped in silver paper. There were lots of things which suggested us children. Actually, there were the first letters we had each of us written to mother! Such scrawls! Locks of hair, tiny shoes, a baby's cap, a beautiful christening gown, and I do not know what else besides. Fancy her keeping them all those years! I wondered if, when Nora and I were grown-up, and were married, and had children of our own, we should have a treasure-box like mother's, containing mementoes of our dear ones. I think if I ever do, I should like to have it with me in my grave. If I had known of its existence mother should have had hers.

All except one thing which was in it. And it is that to which I have been coming all this time. It was a sheet of foolscap paper, folded in three. On one side was written, in mother's writing: "Contents of Brown Despatch-Box." When I opened it I perceived that it was a sort of inventory. It began,—

"In the brown despatch-box are—

"My husband's will, My own will, My husband's jewels,"

—and then it went on to give quite a long list. Now I knew the brown despatch-box. We all did. It had been father's. There were his initials—R. B. —in gold letters on the lid. It was unlocked by a tiny little key. I had always understood from mother that she had kept all sorts of wonderful things inside of it. Yet, after she had been buried, and we had got rid of the Ogre, and had found her keys, it was empty. It contained not a vestige of anything. I thought it curious at the time. We all had done. But I thought it still more curious by the time I had reached the bottom of that list.

Next time Mr Sanford came to see us—which was a day or two afterwards —I handed it to him. He made inquiries at Somerset House, where, it appears, they keep such things, and there, sure enough, was a copy of father's will. It was simplicity itself, just two lines—

"I give and bequeath everything of which I die possessed to my dear wife, for her sole and absolute use."

So that, so far as we were concerned, everything depended upon what was in mother's will. Mr Sanford explained to us that at Somerset House they only keep a copy when the original will has been what they call "proved." And the whereabouts of the original will was just the question. Was it in existence? and, if so, where?

Dick expressed all our sentiments in language of his own.

"The Ogre collared it; that's what's come to the thing. What asses we were, not to have suspected him of it at the time!"

"If," observed Mr Sanford, "he collared that, then the probability is that he collared a good deal else besides. For instance, your father's jewels. Do any of you know anything about them?"

"It's a most extraordinary thing," I explained, "that I should ever have forgotten them. Mother's death was so sudden, and everything was in such confusion, that, except the one fact that she was dead, all the rest passed clean out of my mind. But I remember them perfectly. Why, it was only during the last holidays before she died that she showed some of them to me. I went into the morning-room one day, and she had the brown despatch-box on the table, and it was full of things. She had a leather case open in her hand. In it were a number of rings. 'See, Molly,' she said, 'there are some of your father's rings. Your father had some beautiful jewels. I am keeping it for Dick and the boys!"

"You are sure she said that she was keeping it?"

"Perfectly certain. Another small case was lying on the table. She took it up. 'Look,' she said, 'this was a present to your father. It is one of the most beautiful diamonds I have ever seen. It can be worn either in a ring, or as a pin, or as a stud.' She attached it to three pieces of gold which were with it in the case, to let me see how that was managed. 'Did he often wear it?' I asked. 'No,' she said; 'he didn't.' And she laughed. 'Your father scarcely ever wore ornaments of any kind. And this is much too fine a stone for a gentleman to wear. But it is worth a great deal of money all the same.'"

"Of course I knew about father's jewels," chorused Dick. "Once, when I was quite a little chap, she showed me a magnificent gold repeater watch, and told me it was father's, and that perhaps one day it would be mine. She touched a spring and let me hear it chime the hours, and the quarters, and the minutes. There were a lot of other things besides, though I can't tell you quite what, and I fancy there were two or three more watches."

"Where did your mother keep this despatch-box?' asked Mr Sanford.

"Where we found it, and where she kept all her private papers—locked up in her bureau."

"But neither the bureau nor the box showed any signs of having been tampered with."

"Of course not. Mr Miller borrowed mother's keys, without asking leave, and had the free run of everything. We knew nothing about what was going on. All he had to do was to unlock things, and walk off with what he wanted. Pretty idiots we were to let him get clean away with them. Goodness only knows what he has taken."

Mr Sanford, who had been serious enough all through, looked graver than ever when Dick said that.

"That is exactly the point. Under the circumstances it is difficult for us to determine what may not be missing. I am afraid that Mr Miller is an unprincipled person."

"There's no fear about that—it's a dead sure thing. He's a confounded highway robber, as well as a miserable area sneak."

Dick's language is so strong. But Mr Sanford did not seem to notice it.

"If all the items mentioned were in the despatch-box at the time of your mother's decease, and the correctness of her list is to be implicitly relied upon—"

"If mother says a thing was there, it was there; you can bet on that."

"Then, in that case, it seems only too probable that Mr Miller has robbed you of a very large amount of valuable property—"

"I'd like to have the flogging of him!"

"Besides the will, which is itself of cardinal importance; and your father's jewels, which evidently were worth a considerable sum—"

"I should think so!"

"There is here a list of no less than thirteen securities, all of the highest class, which are stated to have represented—apparently at par value—over £50,000. At present prices they would be worth more. The presumption is that scrip, or bonds, or other legal documents representing ownership, were in that box. If such was the case, the question is—where are they now?"

"£50,000!" I cried.

I have no doubt that we all of us looked amazed at the magnitude of the sum.

"That scoundrel," declared Dick, "is living on them—on the fat of the land."

"Since they were all easily negotiable, and could be turned into cash at a moment's notice, if our suspicions are well founded—"

"Which they are!"

"It is practically certain that Mr Miller is in the enjoyment of a comfortable little fortune. Not the least extraordinary part of the matter is, that had not your sister come upon this list, almost, as it seems, by accident, we might never have known that such securities were in existence. As it is, I fear we shall have some trouble in tracing their possession to Mr Miller; and still more trouble in tracing him."

It was ever so long—months and months—after I had found out what ought to have been in the despatch-box, that I went on a tremendous expedition—to London, all by myself. I was to meet Hetty Travers and her mother at St James's Hall—and perhaps Mr Sanford might be there, but he could not be sure—and then we were all going to a concert together. That was a Saturday. Hetty lived at Beckenham. And after the concert I was going to stay with her until the Monday.

That was the programme.

At home it was a lovely morning. So I thought I would go up by a pretty early train and do some shopping. I had quite a lot of money, and I wanted ever so many things, and you can buy things much better in London than at West Marden. It was true that I did not know much about London; for instance, I could not have found my way from St Paul's Churchyard to Regent Street. But I had heard Dick say that when you did not know your way to a place, all you had to do was to jump into a hansom and trust to the driver. He maintained that while there was a hansom to be found no one need be lost in town. So that was just what I did do. I took one from London Bridge to Oxford Street; then, when I had got what I wanted there, another to Regent Street, which, driving, seemed really no distance at all; and then a third to St Paul's Churchyard. Then, just as I was getting as hungry as anything, and was wondering where I could get something to eat, I found that all the shops were actually closing, and that I had scarcely any time left in which to get to St James's Hall. I get into a cab, and told the man to drive as fast as he could; it was then past two, and I was supposed to be there at half-past.

He went off at a pretty good pace. But he had scarcely gone any distance when I saw on the pavement, a little way in front—the Ogre! Mr Stephen Miller! The sight of him drove everything else clean out of my head. I jumped up in the cab, exclaiming,—

"Stop! stop!"

I daresay the cabman though I was going to jump out while he was going; and I believe I should have done so if he had gone on. But he pulled his horse back on to its haunches, and out I jumped. The Ogre, sublimely unconscious of who was behind him, had moved aside as if he were about to enter a great stone building which he had just reached. However, I was in front of him before he could get to the door; and I lost no time in coming to the point.

"Mr Miller," I cried, "where's mother's will, and father's jewels, and all our money?"

He stared at me as if I were the last person he expected—or desired—to see; and I daresay I was. I thought at first that he was going to turn on his heel and run. But that was only for a moment. After he had recovered from the sudden shock—and the sight of me must have been a shock to him—he glared with his horrid bloodshot eyes as if he would have liked to devour me, bones and all.

"I fancy there must be some mistake. I have not the pleasure of knowing who you are."

His wicked untruthfulness took me aback.

"You don't know who I am?—You do!—I'm Molly Boyes!"

"Unfortunately I have not the honour of knowing who Molly Boyes may be. And as I have a pressing appointment, I am afraid you must excuse me."

He put out his arm and, thrusting me on one side, dashed through the swing door into the building in front of which we were standing. He gave me such a push that it was a wonder I did not fall right over. By the time I had recovered myself sufficiently to rush after him there was nothing of him to be seen. He had either vanished into air, or into one of the innumerable offices which apparently the place contained. In front of me was a staircase; beyond it was a passage; on my right was a second passage; on my left a third. In which direction he had gone there was nothing to show. While I was standing there, feeling rather silly, a gentleman came out of one of the doors towards me. He was not bad looking; but he wore a green tie with pink spots which I did not like at all.

"Can you tell me," I asked, "where Mr Miller has gone?"

"Mr Miller? I'm afraid I don't know the name. Has he offices here?"

"He just came in!"

I described him as well as I could. The stranger seemed interested. He even smiled.

"Your description sounds like Mr Kenrick, of The People's Stock Exchange. The offices are on the fourth floor. You will see the name on a tablet against the wall."

It did not seem very promising. Kenrick did not sound like Miller. And I could not conceive of his having any connection with such an institution as The People's Stock Exchange. I was sorry for it if he had. Still up the stairs I went—it was a long way up to the fourth floor; and there, in black letters on a white tablet, amidst lots of other names, was "No. 169. The People's Stock Exchange. Mr George Kenrick." I went first round one corner, then round another—there was not a soul to be seen from whom to ask the way—and I was commencing to wonder if I should have to keep on chasing myself round corners for the rest of the afternoon when all of a sudden I heard someone shouting at the top of his voice. A door opened at the end of the passage in which I was and someone came out, addressing to someone within remarks which were uttered in such stentorian tones that it was quite impossible to avoid hearing what he said—

"I'll tell you what you are, Mr Kenrick—you're a scoundrel and a thief! And clever though you are, you'll find yourself at the Old Bailey yet before you've done—you dirty rascal!"

He shut the door with a bang which thundered through the place. He was very tall, with a long grey beard, and his hat crammed over his eyes; and as he strode past me he did look so very angry that I did not dare ask who he had been speaking to. But the language he had used was so extremely applicable to the Ogre, that I felt convinced it must be he. So I went to the room out of which he had come. Sure enough, on the glass door was "The People's Stock Exchange." I entered, and there, on the other side of a polished counter, was Mr Stephen Miller.

"I have found you again," I remarked.

He was talking to a young man—quite a boy, in fact—who was moving towards the door as I went in.

"You'll be here at the usual time on Monday?"

"Yes, sir."

The youth regarded me with what I almost felt was a twinkle in his eye; though I had not the remotest notion what he meant by such behaviour. And the Ogre and I were left alone. I repeated my previous observation.

"You perceive that I have found you again."

"It would seem so." He stood rubbing his chin and regarding me with a contemplative kind of air. He was ever so much better dressed than he ever was in our part of the world; but, in spite of it, he looked just the same disreputable, untrustworthy object. If anything, his face was fatter and redder than it used to be; and his eyes more bloodshot. "Come into my private office."

He led the way into a room beyond, and I followed. When we were in he stared at me again; and this time he grinned.

"You're quite a beauty—that's a pretty frock of yours. Perhaps it's the frock that does it—you never know." His manner made my cheeks burn. "Well, and how are they all at The Chase?"

Fancy his having the impudence to ask such a question!

"Thank you; they are all quite well. I want my mother's will—and father's jewels—and the securities which were in the brown despatch-box."

"You do, do you? Are they missing?"

"You know very well that they are missing—since you took them."

"Took them, did I? Odd what things one sometimes does by accident."

"It was no accident, as you are perfectly aware. Will you give them to me, please, as I am in a hurry?"

"Give them to you? Do you expect me to hand them over now—at once?"

"Most certainly. I don't intend to leave until I have them."

"Suppose I leave?"

"Then I shall follow you until we come to a policeman, to whom I shall give you in charge."

He laughed; though what there was to laugh at in the notion of being locked up was beyond my comprehension.

"So that's the idea. Well, I shouldn't like being sent to prison—it's not to be expected—"

"You will have brought it upon yourself."

"So I'll tell you what I'll do; you give me a kiss and I'll hand over."

I flamed up.

"How dare you say such a thing!"

"All right! all right!—you look spiteful; and it seems you are. Sorry I asked for what isn't to be had. I keep what you want outside; if you wait here I'll go and fetch it."

His insolent suggestion had made me so furious that, without stopping to think, supposing he meant what he said, I let him go. The door closed behind him as he went; but as there was a spring which made it close, I saw nothing strange in that. And I waited. His horrible proposal—and something, too, about his words, looks and manner made me conscious of a distinct sense of discomfort. I half wished that I had allowed him to escape, and made no attempt to follow. I glanced at my watch. It was past half-past two! What would the cabman think of me outside—and I had left three parcels in his cab!—and Hetty and her mother waiting for me at St James' Hall. I went to the door and turned the handle. It declined to yield. Imagining that there might be some trick in opening it, perhaps connected with the spring— because I knew that they had all sorts of queer inventions in the city—I rapped at the panel.

"Mr Miller!" I cried. "Mr Miller! Will you open this door, please, and be quick, because I'm late already!"

No answer. I rapped again—and called again. Then—at last!—I suspected.

I stooped down and saw that the door was locked. I banged at it with both my fists.

"Mr Miller! How dare you lock the door. Open it at once and let me out!"

But not a bit of it. That was not his intention at all. Whether he was or was not on the other side I could not tell. It was a great, strong, heavy door, and so long as he chose to keep it locked, it was impossible for me to find out.

Suppose he was not there? if it was all a trick? and if he had imposed on my simplicity and made a fool of me? The mere possibility of such a thing made me so mad that tears of rage came into my eyes. There must be a bell somewhere. There was; an electric bell, represented by an ivory button. I pressed it: kept on pressing it. No result seemed to follow. I could hear no sound. Was it ringing? If so, where?

As I listened, I was struck by the curious silence. I had no idea that in London it could be so still. Considering the hugeness of the buildings, and the clatter of the great thoroughfare through which I had come, it seemed so odd. Could I be alone in that great place? The prospect did not appear agreeable. I turned to the window. It was quite narrow, though tremendously high, and filled with frosted glass, or whatever they call it, so that I could not see through. I had to stand on a chair to reach the top of the sash. Then I could not see out.

I seemed to have got myself into a thoroughly delightful position. Time was getting on. Hetty and her mother would be wondering if anything had happened to me. Something certainly had. But they would never guess what. How long was I to stop in that room? This was Saturday. I seemed to remember having heard that people left business early on Saturdays. I myself had seen that the shops were being closed. Perhaps that was the explanation of the silence. Everybody might have gone. The whole place might be deserted. In that case not a creature might be back till Monday. I had heard the Ogre say to the departing youth,—

"You'll be here at the usual time on Monday?"

Monday! Was it conceivable that I might have to stay in that wretch's office till—Monday! Long before then I should be raving mad. I picked up a ruler off the table and hammered with it on the door and shouted. How I shouted! But no one took the slightest notice—I doubted very much if there was anyone to hear. The room through which I had come was much larger than the one in which I was. The passage was beyond. If, as was probable, the outer door was also closed, then my noise would hardly penetrate into the passage. Apart from the fact that the offices were at the end of the passage, and that no one would be likely to come that way, except on business. And if business was over until Monday?

But I was not disposed to simply hammer and shout. I proposed to do something. Monte Cristo escaped from the Chateau d'If. And if by any possible means I could win my way out I did not intend to remain the Ogre's prisoner a moment longer than I could help. So, by way of a commencement, I smashed the window. With the ruler I deliberately knocked out as much of the frosted glass as I could. Most of it went outside and, amid the prevailing stillness, it seemed to make quite a terrible noise. I found that the look-out was into a sort of well. The frame was so narrow, and the fringe of broken glass so obvious, that I could not lean right out; and from as far as I could get I could not see the bottom, nor the top either. There were walls and windows above, below, all around. And, so far as I could perceive, nothing else.

While I was wondering whatever I should do next, a window right opposite, on the other side of the well, was thrown up, and someone looked out, a masculine someone. I do not think I was ever so glad to see anyone in my life as I was to see that boy—he appeared to me to be a boy, though I daresay he supposed himself to be a man. The sight of me seemed to occasion him surprise—which was not to be wondered at.

"I beg your pardon, but—have you just broken that window?

"I have!"

"It made such an all-fired din that I thought something had happened."

"Something has happened! I'm shut up in here!"

"No? Are you? What a horrid shame. We're in the same box, because I'm shut up in here. Governor told me not to go till he came back from lunch, and as he's gone off with some other fellows to a regular spread, it looks as though he's never coming back again. And I ought to be down at Richmond for a cricket match. It looks like getting there! Though what they'll do without me I can't think. Because, apart from batting, with the leather I'm a marvel. My name's Clifford—perhaps you know my name? Last Saturday, playing for the Putney Pilgrims, I took eight wickets in nine overs. It was in the papers. Perhaps you saw it there. I don't know if you're interested in that sort of thing."

He rattled on at such a rate that he did not give me a chance to speak.

"I'm afraid you don't understand: I'm locked in here."

"Locked in? No? Not really?"

"Yes, really!" He was dense. "And I want you to come and break down the door and let me out."

"Break down the door? Me? What ho! Pray, are you trying to take a rise out of yours truly? I'm more than seven, you know."

"You don't look it; and you don't sound it either."

I tried to explain.

"If you will listen, I will endeavour to make you understand. This place belongs to a robber and a thief. I came to get back some of the things he has stolen. He's gone away and locked the door, and left me here, and I want you to come and let me out!"

"I say! Isn't that rather a rummy story?"

"I don't know if it's rummy or not—it's true! And if you don't want to see me throw myself out of the window you'll come, at once!"

"For goodness' sake, don't talk about throwing yourself out of the window. You'd make an awful mess if you did. It's a bit of a drop—Hollo! here's the governor!"

I heard a voice speaking behind him.

"Yes, here is the governor. And pray, Master Clifford, what are you doing there?" Master Clifford vanished. In his place appeared a short dark man, with an eyeglass and a moustache turned up at the ends. He smiled in my direction as if he had known me all his life. "Delighted to see you. Lovely afternoon, isn't it? You make a charming picture in that frame."

"I'm a prisoner!" I cried.

"You're what?"

"A prisoner!"

"You look as if it were more your custom to make captives of others. Are you in earnest?"

"Don't I sound as if I were in earnest? Of course I am in earnest!"

I tried to explain all over again. The stupidity of some people is extraordinary. Even when I had finished he did not seem to comprehend.

"Do you know that you're proposing that I should break into another man's premises?"

"Do you want me to stop locked in here till you do! Because I shall go mad and kill myself long before then."

"May I ask your name?"

"My name is Molly Boyes, and I live at The Chase, West Marden, and I ought to have met Hetty Travers at St James's Hall at half-past two, and now I don't know what time it is!"

"But I do. It's time I was off."

He spoke as if he did not care a button about me. I was seized with a perfect paroxysm of fear.

"Oh please—please—please—don't go and leave me!—please let me out! —please—please!"

I could not see his face through my blinding tears; but I fancy I startled him.

"My dear Miss Boyes! Don't distress yourself like that! You'll spoil those pretty eyes of yours! You mustn't think me a brute; but yours is such an extraordinary statement. But, as you do seem serious, I'll come round and see what I can do. By the way, where are you?"

"I'm at 169; it's called The People's Stock Exchange, and belongs to a man who calls himself Kenrick, but—his—real—name's—Stephen—Miller!"

"So that's The People's Stock Exchange! I wasn't aware we were such close neighbours. I begin to see daylight. So you're one of the sheep, and you've been fleeced! I fancy it won't be the first shindy they've had at that establishment. Here, Clifford, just go and find a policeman and bring him here! If you'll wait, Miss Boyes, I'll come round to you as soon as I possibly can."

He vanished—and I waited. As if there was anything else I could do! My heart sank directly he vanished from the window. He did not seem a bit in earnest. I felt convinced that he would not care a scrap if I was locked in there until the crack of given another glance at his watch, he would come to the conclusion that it was more than time for him to go off home to tea, and that it really was not worth while bothering about the girl over the way. He seemed that kind of man. Supposing he did? My last straw would be gone!

As the hours—which, I suppose, according to the clock, were only minutes —dragged past, and still nothing happened, I concluded that that was what he had done. What a state of mind I was in! I hammered with the ruler, and yelled and shouted, so that I might attract attention if anyone was about. And at last—such a long at last—I heard the outside door being opened; footsteps approached my door; there was a little fumbling with the keyhole; and—I was unlocked! There stood a porter-looking sort of person, a policeman, and the eye-glassed man from over the way. He had had more sense—and more heart —than I had imagined. He had hunted up a caretaker, who actually possessed a key—I think it was one key, though I own I do not see how it could have been—which opened every door in the place, and with it he had opened the one behind which I was imprisoned.

Oh, with what rapture I greeted those three extremely plain-looking men! No wonder they seemed pleased with themselves when I almost jumped into their arms!

That night I slept at Beckenham. Hetty and her mother were nearly out of their minds. Mr Sanford had gone to the concert. When I did not appear he telegraphed home to know what had become of me. On their replying that I had gone to London with the intention of going to the concert, he tore about in every direction. By the time I did turn up they appeared to have concluded that I must be dead. Their countenances when I told them my adventures!

When the Ogre left me locked in his private office he left The People's Stock Exchange for good. He never showed his face in that neighbourhood again. It seemed that he had used the money of which he had robbed us to help him to rob others. The People's Stock Exchange was a gigantic swindle. I did not quite understand how; but Mr Sanford said that he deserved penal servitude for life. Next time I see him he will probably get it.

I do not know what became of that cab of mine. Nor of the parcels which I left inside. And in them were some lovely things. It's a dreadful shame!

VI

<u>BREAKING THE ICE</u>

Shortly after my seventeenth birthday Mr Sanford and I had a serious difference of opinion which almost amounted to a quarrel. I do not say that the fault was entirely his. But that is not the point. The point is whether, every time you happen to be not quite exactly right, you are to be treated as if you were a mere worm, and have your age thrown in your face.

It was not my fault that I was only seventeen. As Mr Pitt said—I remember reading about it at Mrs Sawyer's—being young is a crime one grows out of. Rome was not built in a day. You cannot do everything at once. It is quite certain that you cannot be ninety in five minutes. I was perfectly aware that Mr Sanford was twenty-five. It is not a time of life against which I have a word to say. I feel sure that it is a delightful age. But I cannot understand why persons who are twenty-five should consider themselves so immensely superior to persons who are only seventeen. Or, if they are superior, and are known to be, that is no reason why they should show it.

On my birthday Mr Sanford gave me a box of gloves. Now I am five feet five and a half inches high. I know I am, because when Dick made me stand up against the wall with my hair down and a book on my head, he said he never should have thought it from the look of me. Which was not a nice thing to say. But then brothers have manners of their own. I want to know what size of hand a person who is nearly five feet six high ought to have. Because, directly I opened the box, I saw that they were lovely gloves, but that they were all six and a half.

"Oh, what a pity!" I cried. "They'll be like boats on me! I take six and a quarter!"

Of course, I am conscious that it was not precisely a civil remark to make; and, had I reflected, I might not have made it. But it was out before I even guessed it was coming. As it was out, it was. And, anyhow, it was simply the truth. At the time, Mr Sanford was as nice as possible. He expressed his regret for the mistake which had occurred, and volunteered to change them.

He did change them. Four or five days afterwards he came with another box. It was the sixteenth of November, a Thursday. As it turned out to be a memorable day to me, I have the best of reasons for keeping the exact date in my mind. I shall never forget it—never—not if I live long enough to lose my memory. It was very cold. All the week it had been freezing. That is, off and on. Because I admit that it might occasionally have risen above freezing point. But it certainly had been freezing all the day before, and all that morning—hard. Ice was everywhere. I had made up my mind to try it, and had just finished cleaning my skates when Mr Sanford came in.

"Why," he exclaimed, when he saw them, "what are you going to do with those?"

"I'm going to skate with them. What is one generally supposed to do with skates?"

"But, my dear Miss Boyes, it's impossible. After two or three days' more frost, perhaps, but at present the ice won't bear."

Now there was just that something about his tone which nettled me. It was the way he had of taking it for granted that, because he said a thing, the matter was necessarily at an end, since it was impossible to imagine that anyone would venture on remonstrance.

"I daresay it will be strong enough to bear me."

"I very much doubt it."

"Do you? Do you skate?"

"A little."

"Then, since that sister and those brothers of mine have gone off, they alone know where, may I venture to suggest that you should come with me?"

"I shall be delighted—as far as the ice. I'm sure you'll find that it won't bear. And, anyhow, I've no skates."

"There are a pair of Dick's. They're not very rusty. And I don't suppose you'll find them very much too small."

He took them up—and smiled.

"As you say, they're not very rusty, and I daresay my feet are not very much more gigantic than Dick's, but—"

"But what?"

"I shall be very glad to come with you to examine the ice. But when you get to it you'll find that skating is out of the question."

"If I get to the ice I promise you that I'll go on it. I am passionately fond of skating, and as we so seldom get any, I like to take advantage of every chance I get. Besides, I am not afraid of a little cold water, even if it does happen to be a degree or two under the usual temperature."

He laughed. He had a way of laughing when I said things which were not meant to be comical which puzzled me and annoyed me too. Fortunately for himself he changed the subject, handing me the box he had been carrying.

"I've brought the gloves. This time I hope you will find that they are not like boats. I am credibly informed that they are six and a quarter."

"Thank you so much. I really am ashamed of myself for giving you so much trouble—it's so sweet of you. Oh, what lovely gloves. Just the shades I like. As I have brought none down with me I think I'll put a pair on now."

I ought to have known better. I had, as I have said, just finished cleaning my skates, and had been washing my hands, and, in consequence, they were cold. It is not, at any time, the work of only a moment to put on a brand new pair of properly-fitting gloves. Everybody knows that, who knows anything at all. They require coaxing. Especially is this the case when your hands are cold. And certainly the task is not rendered easier by the knowledge that you are being observed by critical, supercilious eyes, towards whose owner you entertain a touch of resentment. Those gloves would not go on. The consciousness that Mr Sanford was staring at me with obvious amusement made me, perhaps, more awkward than I should have been. But, whatever the cause, I do not think I ever had so much trouble with a pair of gloves either before or since.

Presently he spoke.

"Rather tight, aren't they?"

"Tight? What do you mean? I suppose they're six and a quarter?"

"Oh, yes, they're six and a quarter. But don't you think it might have been better to have kept the original six and a half for the sake of the additional ease?"

"Ease? You don't want ease in a glove."

"No? That's rather a novel point of view. Do you want it to be uneasy, then?"

"A properly fitting glove never is uneasy. You are possibly not aware that a new glove always is a little difficult to get on the first time."

"Yes—so it seems."

Something in his tone annoyed me, particularly the impertinent suggestion which I felt sure it was intended to convey. I gave an angry try at the glove, and, behold! it split. I know I went crimson all over. Mr Sanford laughed outright.

"When you try to cram a quart into a pint pot something is bound to go."

A ruder remark I had never had addressed to me. My own brothers could not have been more vulgar. Even they had never compared my hand with either a quart or a pint pot. An observation of that kind it was impossible that I should condescend to notice. Removing the glove, with all the dignity at my command, I replaced it in the box.

"I think that I had better wear a pair of gloves which have become adapted to the unfortunate conformation of my hands."

"But, Molly—"

"I don't know who has given you permission to use my Christian name, Mr Sanford. I have noticed that you have done so two or three times recently. I am not a relative of yours."

His eyes twinkled. Although I did not look at him I knew they did, because of the peculiar way in which he spoke. When they twinkled there was always something in his voice which, to the trained ear, was unmistakable. Not that I wish it to be inferred that I had paid any attention to Mr Sanford's oddities. It was the mere result of my tendency to notice trifles.

"But, Miss Boyes, I never could understand why a woman of reasonable and proper and delightful proportions should show a desire to be the possessor of a hand which, as regards dimensions, would be only suited to a dwarf."

"Is it I you are calling a monster, or only my hand?"

"Neither. I should not presume to call you anything. But I would take leave to observe that you have as dainty, as well-shaped, as capable, and, I may add, as characteristic a pair of hands as I have ever seen."

"Personal remarks are not in the best of taste, are they? I believe I have had occasion to point that out to you before."

I took that box of gloves upstairs and I banged them on the dressing-table. When I looked into the glass I saw that my cheeks were glowing, and my eyes too. It was plain that I was in a perfect passion. The most exasperating part of it was that I knew what a fright bad temper made of me. It always does of your black sort of people.

Never did I meet anyone with a greater capacity for rubbing you the wrong way than Mr Sanford. And so autocratic! I suppose that if he is of opinion that I ought to wear six and three-quarters I shall have to. But I will give him clearly to understand that, whatever size my hands may be, I shall wear sixes if I like. I do not propose to allow him to lay down the law to me, even on the question of gloves.

I kept him waiting as long as ever I could, though up in my bedroom, where there was no fire, it was positively freezing, and every moment I grew colder and colder, till I felt I must be congealing. But I knew that he hated waiting, so, while I dawdled, I wondered if everybody was crushed by everybody else as some people crushed me, or, at least, as they tried to. When I got down he was standing at the window, staring out into the grounds.

"Are you still there? I thought you would have gone. I trust that you have not remained on my account. I didn't hurry. Even an old pair of gloves cannot be put on in half a second."

"So it would appear."

"As you are not going to skate, and I am, I won't keep you."

"You were good enough to ask me to come with you to see if the ice would bear."

"I'm sure it will bear enough for me, though probably not enough for you. And as you're nervous, it's hardly worth while to put you to any further trouble. You would hardly find it amusing to stand on the bank and watch me skating."

"Well, I can fancy more objectionable occupations."

"Can you? There is no accounting for people's fancies."

"There certainly isn't."

"So, as I am already later than I intended, I will wish you good-day. And thank you so much for the gloves."

"Good-day, and pray don't mention the gloves—ever again. But I'm going with you all the same. I'll borrow Dick's skates on the off-chance, and ask his permission afterwards."

"Oh, I've no doubt that Dick will have no objection to your taking them; but as you're not going to skate, really, Mr Sanford, it's not the slightest use your coming."

"No use, but a great deal of pleasure for me. Let me carry your skates."

"Thank you, but I prefer to carry them myself."

He planted himself in front of me, looked me in the face, stretched out his arm, and took the skates from my hand. The astonishing part of it being that I did not offer the slightest resistance.

"I do declare, Mr Sanford, that you're the most dictatorial person I ever met. You appear to be under the impression that people are not entitled to have opinions of their own on any subject whatever. I suppose I may carry my own skates if I want to."

"Quite so. Suppose we start."

We did start; though I was more than half inclined—since he was evidently bent on accompanying me—not to go at all. From the way we were beginning I foresaw what would be the end; or, at least, I imagined I did. Because, of course, what actually did happen never entered my head even as a remote possibility.

I was in a vitriolic temper, which was not improved by the knowledge that I was behaving badly, and should, in all probability before long, behave much worse. There is nothing more galling than the consciousness that the person with whom you are angry is in the right, and knows it, and is therefore indisposed to take any notice of your tantrums, being resolved, do what you will, not to take you seriously. That was what used to make me so mad with Mr Sanford; he would not regard me as if I were a serious character. He would persist in treating me as if I were a child. Even if I did sometimes behave like one, it ought to have made no difference, since at seventeen you are not a child, and can behave exactly as you please, because you are grown up. Especially after the experience of the world which I had had.

The lake was more than a mile away from the house; amid the pine-trees in Mr Glennon's wood. A lovely walk. Particularly in that sort of weather. But, as the poet does not say, no prospect pleases when your temper is vile. The mere fact that I yearned to beg Mr Sanford's pardon for being so disagreeable made me nastier than ever. It may sound incredible; it is true. Such conversation as there was suggested that horrid game called "Snap"—played ill-naturedly.

"Are you an expert skater, Miss Boyes?"

"I can keep myself from falling, though, of course, I cannot compare with you."

"I assure you that I have no pretensions in that direction. Like you, I can keep myself from falling and that's all."

"Meaning, I presume, that I cannot even do that. Thank you."

Silence. I knew the man was smiling, although I did not look at him. After we had gone about another hundred yards he spoke again.

"I always think a woman looks so graceful on the ice."

"You won't think so any longer after you have seen me."

"I think I shall. I cannot conceive you as looking anything but graceful, anywhere, in any position."

"I don't think you need sneer."

"Miss Boyes."

"Mr Sanford?"

"I beg your pardon?"

"You beg my pardon? What for?"

"I don't quite know. But I feel you feel that it would be more becoming on my part. So I do so. Please will you forgive me?"

"If you have no objection I should prefer to turn back. I do not care to skate to-day."

"You need not skate. As I have already remarked, I am convinced that the ice will not bear. But we can at least continue our walk."

"I shall skate if we do go on. On that I am determined."

"You are not always so aggressive."

"Nor are you always so domineering. Though I admit that as a rule you are. At home they must find you unbearable."

"I hope not. I am sorry you find me domineering. Particularly as you are yourself so—plastic."

"I am not plastic. I don't know what you mean. But I am sure I am nothing of the kind."

"Molly."

We had reached the stile over which you have to climb to get into the wood. He had crossed first, and I was standing on the top step—he was holding my hand in his to help me over. I did not notice that he had called me Molly.

"Yes?"

"I wish you would be pleasant to me sometimes. You don't know what a difference it would make to me."

"What nonsense! I am perfectly convinced that, under any circumstances, nothing I could say or do could be of the slightest consequence to you."

"Couldn't it? You try!"

"I am much too young."

"Too young! Too young!"

There was all at once something in his voice and manner which gave me quite a start. I snatched my hand away and jumped down to the ground.

"We can't stop here all day if we mean to do any skating, and I for one certainly do."

I marched off at about five miles an hour. He wore an air of meekness which was so little in keeping with his general character that, at the bottom of my heart, it rather appalled me.

"I would sooner be snubbed by you than flattered by another woman."

"Snubbed by me! Considering how you're always snubbing me, that's amusing."

"I never mean to snub you."

"You never mean to? Then you must be singularly unfortunate in having to so constantly act in direct opposition to your intentions. To begin with, you hardly ever treat me as if I were a woman at all."

"Well, you are not a woman—are you—quite?"

"Mr Sanford! When you talk like that I feel—! Pray what sort of remark do you call that?"

"You are standing at the stepping stones."

"At the stepping-stones?"

"Happy is the man who is to lead you across them."

"I don't in the least understand you. And I would have you to know that I feel that it is high time that I should put childish things behind me; and I should like other people to recognise that I have done so."

"Childish things? What are childish things? Oh, Molly, I wish that you could always be a child. And the pity is that one of these days you'll be wishing it too."

"I'm sure I sha'n't. It's horrid to be a child."

"Is it?"

"You are always being snubbed."

"Are you?"

"No one treats you with the least respect; or imagines that you can possibly ever be in earnest. As for opinions of your own—it's considered an absurdity that you should ever have them. Look at you! You're laughing at me at this very moment."

"Don't you know why I am laughing at you, Molly?"

Again there was something in the way in which he asked the question which gave me the oddest feeling. As if I was half afraid. Ever since we had left the stile I had been conscious of the most ridiculous sense of nervousness. A thing with which, as a rule, I am never troubled. I was suddenly filled with a wild desire to divert the conversation from ourselves, no matter how. So I made a desperate plunge.

"Have you seen anything of Hetty lately?"

He was still for a moment, as if the sudden reference to his cousin occasioned him surprise; and that not altogether of a pleasant kind. Though I did not see why it should have done.

"I was not speaking of Hetty. Nor am I anxious to, just now."

"Aren't you? Have you quarrelled with her, as well?"

"As well? Why do you say as well?"

"Oh, I don't know. You're always quarrelling."

"That's not true."

"Thank you. Is that a snub? Or merely a compliment?"

"Molly, why will you treat me like this? It's you who treat me like a child, not I you."

"There's the lake at last, thank goodness!"

I did not care if it was rude or not. I was delighted to see it, so I said so plainly. What is more, I tore off towards it as hard as I could. My rush was so unexpected that I was clean away before he knew it. All the same he reached the lake as soon as I did. He could run, just as he could do everything else. The ice looked splendid, smooth as a sheet of glass. All about were the pines with their frosted branches. They seemed to stand in rows, so that they looked like the pillars in the aisles of some great cathedral. And then pine-trees always are so solemn and so still.

"Give me my skates, please. I want to get them on at once. Doesn't the ice look too lovely for anything?

"It's not a question of what it looks like, but of what it will bear." He stepped on to the edge. It gave an ominous crack. I daresay, if he had waited, long enough, it would have given way beneath him. But he did not. He hopped back on to the solid ground. "You see!"

"Excuse me, but that is exactly what I do not do. Here it is under the shadow of the trees. Besides, the water is so shallow that it is practically cat's ice. I'm sure it's all right a little further round and in the middle. It's often cracky near the edge."

"I am sure it is not safe anywhere."

"Will you please give me my skates, Mr Sanford?"

He looked at me. So as to let him see that I had no intention of being cowed, I looked back at him.

"I hope that, this once, you will be advised. I assure you it is unsafe."

"Please give me my skates."

He laughed, in that queer way he had of laughing at unexpected moments, when there certainly seemed nothing to laugh at.

"Good. Then it is decided. We will both go skating."

"Both? It is not necessary that we should do anything of the kind. I wish you would let me do as I like, without criticism. Who appointed you to have authority over me? Who suggested that because I choose to do a thing you should do it too? I prefer not to have you attached to my apron-strings. Give me my skates. You can go home. I would rather you did."

"If you skate, I skate also."

"As you please, if you can get over your timidity. There is room on the lake for two. If you will choose one end I will have the other."

"I shall skate where you do."

"Mr Sanford—you are intolerable!"

"Indeed, I am disposed to act on your courteous suggestion, and go home, and take your skates with me.

"If you do, I will never speak to you again."

"Don't pledge yourself too deeply. You spoke of having put childish things behind you. I did not suspect you of having been such a mistress of irony."

"Will you give me my skates?"

"Certainly. I will put them on for you. Where do you think the ice is—strongest?"

We were walking along the bank, I with my nose in the air, he white with rage. It wasn't easy to make him lose his temper, but when you did succeed, he was wicked.

"This will do. I won't trouble you for your assistance. I prefer to put on my own skates, thank you."

He dug his heel right through the ice.

"Do you call this strong?"

"I wish you would not do that. You forget that I am not quite so heavy as you." We went on a little further. Then I stood on the edge. "You perceive that it will bear me. Now—for about the dozenth time—will you give me my skates?"

"I will put them on for you."

"I have already told you that I will do that for myself."

"Don't be absurd. Sit down on the bank." He spoke to me as if I were a slave. As it was evidently useless to remonstrate, I obeyed, placing myself on the sloping bank. "There is a condition I must make. If I put your skates on first you must promise not to start till I am ready."

"I shall promise nothing of the kind."

"Then in that case I am afraid I shall have to keep you waiting till I am equipped."

He actually did too. And as Dick's skates were in rather a muddle, or he did not understand them, or something, it took him a tremendous time to get them properly attached to his boots, while I sat on the bank and froze. But I tried to keep myself as warm as I could by an occasional genial remark.

"You understand, Mr Sanford, that when we do get home I will never speak to you again. I never want to see you again either."

"The betting is that we never shall get home again, since it is probable that we shall both of us be drowned in the lake. That is, if there is a sufficient depth of water to drown us."

"Sufficient depth! Why, I'm told that in places there are twenty feet. I imagine that that is enough to drown even you, big though you seem to think yourself. Though I totally fail to see why we should both of us be drowned. Why can't I drown by myself?"

"If you drown I drown."

"That is really too ridiculous. Pray, who is talking like a child now? I quite fail to see how it can matter to you what becomes of me."

"You do know."

"I do not know. I have not the faintest shadow of a notion."

"Don't you know?"

He twisted himself round and glared at me in such a fashion that I was alarmed.

"Mr Sanford, don't look at me like that!"

"Then kindly remember that there are limits even to my patience."

"I should think that your patience was like the jam in the tart; the first bite you don't get to it, and the second you go clean over it."

"I am glad to be able to afford you so favourable an opportunity for the exercise of your extremely pretty wit. Please give me your foot."

He took it without waiting for any giving. Then immediately proceeded to comment on it, as if it had not belonged to me, or as if I had not been there.

"A dainty foot it is; and reasonably shod in decently fitting boots; not six and a quarter."

"You still seem not to understand that my size in gloves is six and a quarter."

"I'm so dull."

"You are. And something else besides."

He simply ignored my hint. I hate people not to notice when I intend to sting them. It makes you feel so helpless. He went on calmly discussing my foot.

"It's worth while allowing you to flesh the arrows of your malice in one's hide for the privilege of holding this between one's fingers."

"Do you think so?"

"I do."

It was strange how excessively odd an effect his touch had on me. It made me thrill from top to toe. I could scarcely speak. When I stood, to my amazement I found that I was trembling.

"Are your skates comfortable?"

"They seem all right."

"Molly, let us understand each other. Are you bent on skating?"

"I am. Though there is not the slightest reason why you should."

"The ice may be sufficiently thick in places, but it certainly is not all over, and, as you don't know where the weak points are, it will be at the risk of your life if you venture on it."

"It is strong enough to bear me, though it is very possible that it may not be strong enough to bear you also. So, if you do not desire to add to the risk on which you are so insistent, you will not force on me your company."

"If you go I go also."

"Then don't talk so much—and come!"

He had been holding my hand. I snatched it from him and was on the ice. In an instant he was at my side. I was filled with a curious excitement. Something had got into my blood, microbes perhaps, of a fever-generating kind. The various passages of arms which we had had together seemed, all at once, to have reached their climax. I was seized with a sudden frenzy of resolve to show him, once for all, that what it was my pleasure to do that I would do. I craved for motion; yearned for movement—if only as a means of relief for my pent-up feelings. Longed for a flight through the air, to rush through it, to race. Especially to race that man—or to escape from him. I did not care much which.

I struck out for all that I was worth. As I had surmised, the ice was in perfect condition as regards its surface. Sufficiently elastic to enable the blade of one's skates to bite on to it, smooth enough to offer no impediment to their onward glide. One skimmed over it almost without conscious effort. The ecstasy of doing something; the sense of freedom which it gave; the delight of tearing through the keen, clear atmosphere; of feeling it upon one's cheeks—ruffling one's hair—exhilarating one's whole being—breathing it in great gulps into one's lungs—these were the things I needed. And I had hardly been enjoying them half a dozen seconds when the bonds which had seemed to bind me parted, proving themselves to be but the phantasmal creations of a crooked mood. And I laughed, in my turn.

"Isn't it glorious?"

"While it lasts."

"Why the reservation? Isn't it glorious, now?"

We had gone right across the lake. We swung round at a right angle.

"I thought it wasn't safe!"

"What's that?"

Just my luck! Scarcely were the words out of my lips than there was an ominous sound.

"That's nothing. I thought everybody knew that virgin ice make eccentric noises; we're the first to test its quality. That shows how safe it is."

"Does it? I think there may be something in your theory about the middle being best. Suppose we cross to the other side again."

The sound did go on.

"It's because we're skirting the shore. If you'll admit that I am right for once in a way I'll concede that you may be."

"I'll concede anything if you'll come away from this."

"Then I'll race you to our starting-point!"

We had been keeping within perhaps a dozen feet of the land. Sharply turning I made for the centre. I had not taken half a dozen strides when the cracking noise increased to a distinctly uncomfortable degree. I felt the ice heaving beneath my feet. He was at my side; it was preposterous to talk about racing him level. He could have given me seventy-five yards out of a hundred.

"We have struck a bad place. Don't stop; go as fast as you can."

"I'm going as fast as I can. I shall be all right. You go in front."

"Give me your hand!"

"No!"

"Give me your hand!"

I did not give him my hand—he snatched it. As he did so, something went. We did not stop to see what. How he managed I did not, and do not, understand. But I know he gripped my hand as in an iron vice, started off at about seventy miles an hour, and made me keep up with him.

"Don't!" I cried; as well as I could while I gasped for breath.

"Come!" he said.

And I had to come. And before I knew it we were standing on the shore, and I was half beside myself with rage.

"How dare you? Do you suppose that I'm an idiot, and that you can haul me about as if you were my keeper? What did you do it for?"

"I fancy I saved your life."

"Saved my life! Saved your own, you mean. You are an elephant, not I; and if you would only relieve the ice of the weight of your huge bulk, everything would be all right. But you are so grossly selfish that you hate the idea of anyone engaging in a pleasure which you cannot share—and better still, go home; and let me amuse myself exactly as I choose."

"Molly! you are not going on again!"

"I am going on again!—I am! And you dare to try and stop me—you dare!

I imagine that the expression of my countenance startled him. He had planted himself directly in front of me. But when he saw me looking like black murder he moved aside. In an instant I had passed him, and was off towards the centre of the lake.

Whether the double burden which the ice had had to bear had been too severe a strain for its, as yet, still delicate constitution, I cannot say. I only know that, as soon as I was clear off the shore, in spite of my blind fury, I realised that I really was an idiot, and one, too, who was badly in need of a keeper. It groaned and creaked, and heaved in every direction; seeming to emit an increasingly loud crack with every forward stride I took. Mr Sanford shouted.

"Molly, for God's sake, come back!"

I recognised—too late—the reason that was on his side. But the very vigour of his appeal served as a climax. I lost my head. I did not know what to do, where to go; turning this way and that, only to find the threats of danger greater. The question was settled for me. For the second time something went; the ice disappeared from beneath my feet—and I went in.

I felt—when I felt anything—almost as much surprise as consternation. Fortunately, I did not appear to have hit on a spot where the depth was twenty feet—or anything like it. For, instead of being drowned, the water did not come up to my armpits.

"Can you feel the bottom?"

The agony of fear which was in Philip Sanford's voice as he asked the question calmed me as if by magic.

"I think so; I seem to be standing in what feels like mud."

"Can you get your arms on to the ice and raise yourself? If you do it carefully it will probably bear you."

"I am afraid not. I seem to be too deep in to get a proper purchase."

"Where can I get a rope?

"Jennings' farm is the nearest house; and that's the other side of the stile."

"Do you very much mind waiting there? I'll be back inside five minutes."

My heart sank at the prospect of being left alone, even for an instant.

"I'd rather—I'd rather you did something now. I'm afraid—I'm afraid I'm sinking deeper. And it's so cold. Can't you do anything at all?"

"I'll do my best."

He did his best; while I watched—how I watched! He selected a part where the ice had not as yet been subjected to any strain, and carefully advanced towards me. It bore him better than I—and perhaps he—had expected.

"It's all right," he cried. "I shall get to you! Cheer up! And keep as still as you can!"

Then it cracked. And I feared for him. If he should have chanced on a spot where the depth was twenty feet! And should be drowned before my eyes! The cracking noise grew more instead of less.

"I fancy I shall do better by lying down and taking to my hands and knees; it will be spreading my weight over a larger surface."

He lay flat on the ice; wriggling towards me somehow, like a snake. It was a pretty slow process; especially as the icy water was wrapping my draperies about me and freezing the blood in my veins; and I was either sinking lower and lower, or else imagining that I was, which was just as bad. At last he came within three feet of me—within two—within reach. When I got my hands in his I burst out crying.

"Will you ever forgive me?" I sobbed.

"My darling!"

"I'll always do as you wish me to in the future—always—if I'm not drowned."

"My sweet!"

I did not notice what he was saying to me; nor, for the matter of that, what I was saying to him. Though I should not have cared if I had. I was too far gone. He put his hands underneath my arms; but directly he began raising me the ice on which he was lying gave way, and, in another second he was standing beside me in the water. Just as I was thinking of starting screaming, for I made sure that it was all over with both of us, he lifted me as if I were a baby, and I found that the water scarcely came over his waist, and he kissed me.

And I never was so happy; although, for all I knew, at that very moment we might be drowning.

But we did not drown. We reached the shore, though it took us a tremendous time to do it. Because Philip had to break every bit of ice in front of us. And though none of it was strong enough to bear, it was not easy to break. Luckily the water grew shallower as we advanced. So it must have been somewhere else that it was twenty feet.

"Do you think you can run?" Philip asked, when we stood on the dry ground at the end.

"I can—and will—do anything you tell me to—anything on earth."

He laughed.

"It occurs to me that it was perhaps as well you had that little attack of eccentricity just now; otherwise it might have been ages before we arrived at an understanding."

I was entirely of his opinion. I knew he was right. But then he always is.

We ran all the way home; except when we stopped at intervals, to say things. Though it was frightfully difficult; because, of course, all my clothes were sopping. But I was never the least bit ill. Nor was Philip. I changed directly I got in; and Philip changed into a suit of Dick's. It did not fit him, but he looked awfully handsome. And so like a great overgrown boy. So it did not matter if I did behave like a child.

When Nora and the boys came home they opened their eyes when they heard of our adventures. And what amazed me was that they seemed to take it quite for granted that Philip and I should be on the terms we were. Dick offered his congratulations—if they could be called congratulations—in the most extraordinary form.

"Well, old man, you've escaped one funeral, but you're booked for another —that's a cert.!"

The opinions which brothers allow themselves to utter of their sisters are astonishing. Fancy Dick calling me a funeral!

VII

A GIRL WHO COULDN'T

I am almost perfectly happy; but an unfaltering regard for the strict truth compels me to state that I am not quite. I wish I could—conscientiously—say that I was. But I cannot. I am aware that when a girl is engaged—especially when she is just engaged—her happiness ought to be flawless. And mine was, until—

However, perhaps I had better come to the point.

It is not my fault if I cannot do everything. I can do some things. When I turn the matter over in my mind, systematically, I feel justified in asserting that I can do a good many things. It is a well-known scientific fact that a Jack-of-all-trades is master of none. Therefore it seems to me to follow as a matter of course that because I can do the things which I can do, I cannot do the things which I cannot do. Nothing could be simpler. Or more obvious. We cannot all of us be Admirable Crichtons. And it is just as well that we cannot. And yet, merely on that account, I have lately suffered—well, I have suffered a good deal.

Nothing could have given me greater pleasure than the knowledge that Philip had a mother and two sisters. When Mrs Sandford—that is his mother —wrote and said that Philip had told her about the understanding he and I had come to; that she would very much like to know her dear son's future wife; so would I spend a few days with her in her cottage on the Thames, I was delighted. There was a note from each of the sisters—Bertha and Margaret— echoing their mother's words, and that also was very nice. I sat down then and there, and replied to them all three, arranging to go to them on the Tuesday following.

As soon as I had despatched my letters I became conscious of feeling—I hardly know how to put it—of feeling just the slightest atom unsettled; as if I had the shadow of a shade of a suspicion that I had let myself in for something which might turn out to be, I didn't quite know what. Directly I got there—or very nearly directly—certainly within half an hour of my arrival, I realised that my premonitions had not been airy fictions of my imagination; but sound and solid forebodings, which might—and probably would—turn out to be only too well justified by events.

In the first place I had to go without Philip. He was to have gone with me. And, of course, I had looked forward to our journey together in the train. But, at the last moment, he telegraphed to say that business detained him in town; would I go down without him, and he would join us on the morrow. I went without him. And, on the whole, I think I bore up very well. Especially considering that, just as the train was starting from Paddington, a woman got into my carriage with two dogs, a parrot in a huge cage, bundles of golf clubs, hockey clubs, tennis rackets, fishing rods, and goodness only knows what besides; her belongings filled the whole of her own side of the compartment, and most of mine. The last of them was being hustled in as the train was actually moving. As she was depositing them anywhere, and anyhow—I never saw anyone treat her belongings with scantier ceremony—she observed,—

"I cut that rather fine. Don't believe in getting to the station before the train is ready to start—but that was a bit of a shave."

It was a "bit of a shave"; the marvel was that she succeeded in catching the train at all. I—disliking to be bustled—had been there a good twenty minutes before it started, so—although she might not have been aware of it—there was a flavour of something about her remark which was very nearly personal.

It was only after we had gone some distance that the dogs appeared—not a little to my amazement. One of them—which came out of a brown leather hand-bag—was one of those long-bodied, short-legged creatures, which always look as if they were deformed. The other, a small black animal with curly hair, she took out of the pocket of the capacious coat which she was wearing. Directly she placed it on the floor of the carriage it flew at me, as if filled with a frenzied desire to tear me to pieces. While it was doing its best to bark itself hoarse, its owner removed a green cover from the parrot's cage; whereupon the bird inside commenced to make a noise upon its own account, as if with the express intention of urging that sooty fragment to wilder exertions. That compartment was like a miniature pandemonium.

"Don't let them worry you," remarked the mistress of the travelling menagerie.

But as she made not the slightest attempt to stop their worrying me, I did not quite understand what she expected I was going to do. When the black dog got the hem of my skirt into its mouth, and began to pull at it with its tiny teeth, I did remonstrate.

"I am afraid your dog will tear my dress."

"Not she! It's only her fun; she won't hurt you."

I was not afraid of the creature hurting me; but my skirt. The mistress's calmness was sublime. Suffering her minute quadruped to follow—without the smallest effort to control it!—its own quaint devices, she was serenely attaching a new tip to a billiard cue which she had taken out of a metal case. As if she felt that her proceedings might impress me with a sense of strangeness, she proffered what she perhaps meant to be an explanation.

"Always tip my own cue. I've got a cement which sticks; and I like my tip to be just so. If you want to be sure of your cue, tip it yourself."

Presently my liliputian assailant passed from unreasonable antagonism to a warmth of friendship which was almost equally disconcerting. Springing—after one or two failures, on to the carriage seat, it deposited itself in the centre of my lap—nearly knocking my book out of my hands; and, without a with-your-leave, or by-your-leave, but with the most take-it-for-granted air imaginable, prepared for slumber. Perceiving which, the short-legged dog descending, in its turn, to the floor of the carriage, began to prowl round and round me, sniffing at my skirts in a manner which almost suggested that there was something about me which was not altogether nice. All of a sudden the parrot, which had been taking an unconcealed interest in the proceedings, discovered a surprising, and, hitherto, wholly unsuspected capacity for speech.

"Don't be a fool!" he said.

Whether the advice was addressed to me, or to the short-legged dog, I could not say. But it was so unexpected, and was uttered with so much clearness—and was such an extremely uncivil thing to utter—that I quite jumped in my seat. The lady with the billiard cue made a comment of her own.

"That bird's a magnificent talker; and that's his favourite remark."

It proved to be. I do not know how many times that parrot advised somebody not to be a fool before we reached our journey's end; but the advice was repeated at intervals of certainly less than two minutes. And as the creature kept its eyes fixed intently on me, there was a suggestiveness in its bearing as to the direction for which its "favourite remark" was intended, which was in the highest degree unflattering.

When we stopped at my station a girl coming up to the carriage door began showering welcomes on my companion and her creatures with a degree of fluency which pointed to an intimate acquaintance with all of them.

"Hollo, Pat, so you've come!—Hollo, Tar!"—this was to the small black animal. "Hollo, Stumps!"—this was to the short-legged dog. "Hollo, Lord Chesterfield!"—this was to that excessively rude parrot, who promptly acknowledged the greeting by rejoining,—

"Don't be a fool!"

Then, seeing that I was only waiting for the removal of some of the impedimenta to enable me to get out, the girl exclaimed,—

"Are you Molly Boyes?" I admitted that I was. "I'm Bertha Sanford— awfully glad to see you. This is Miss Patricia Reeves— commonly known as Pat. Great luck your coming down together in the same compartment; you'll be as intimate as if you'd known each other for years."

I was not so sure of that. More—I doubted if Miss Patricia Reeves and I ever should be intimate, as I understood intimacy. Still worse, I was disposed to be dubious if Miss Reeves's bosom friend could ever be mine.

A pony phaeton was waiting outside the station, with another girl in it. This proved to be Margaret Sanford. She welcomed "Pat" and "Pat's" etceteras with as much effusion as her sister had done. There was a discussion as to what was to happen. Since the phaeton would hold at most three, somebody would have to walk. Miss Reeves insisted on being the someone; she and Bertha immediately set off at what struck me as being a good five miles an hour. Until then I had supposed myself to be no bad pedestrian for a mere girl; but when I saw the style in which those two were covering the ground I was glad that I had been permitted to ride.

Not that the ride was one of unalloyed bliss. The journey down from town had not been all that I had hoped that it would be; how different it would have been if Philip had been my companion instead of Miss Reeves. And, somehow, the discovery that she was bound for the same destination as I was; and was—plainly—an old and intimate friend, jarred. I do not believe that I am hard to get on with; no one has ever given me any reason to suppose it. And yet, all at once, the fact that the Sanford atmosphere was one in which Miss Reeves was thoroughly at home seemed to hint, with distressing significance, that it was one in which I distinctly should not shine.

The impression heightened as Margaret drove me along. She conversed on matters of which I, for the most part, knew little, and, up to that moment, had cared less. She talked of golf, inquiring, in an offhand sort of way, what my "handicap" was; evidently taking it for granted that, in common with the rest of the world, I had a "handicap." I do not know what I answered; because, as it happened, not only was I without that plainly desirable appurtenance, but I did not even know what she meant. Hitherto golf had not come into my life at all. But fortunately, she chattered on at such a rate that she was able to pay no attention to what I said; so that it did not matter what I answered. It appeared that she had recently been playing a "tie" or a "match" or a "game" or a "round" or a "skittle," or something—I do not know which it was, but I am almost certain it was one or the other—with a Mrs Chuckit—I am sure of the name, because it was such an odd one—in which, it seemed, she had met with an unparalleled series of disasters. From what I could gather she had been "stymied" and "bunkered" and "up" and "down" and "holed" and "foozled" and "skied" and "approached" and "driven," and all sorts of dreadful things. At least, I believe they were dreadful things; and, indeed, from the emphatic way in which she spoke of them, I am convinced they were. One thing of which she told me I am sure must have been painful. She said that she got into a hedge—a "beast of a hedge" she called it; though how, or why, she got into it she did not explain; and that no sooner did she get out of it—"which took some doing"—so it shows it must have been painful—than back she went —"bang into the middle" of it again—which seemed such a singular thing for anyone to do that, had she not been speaking with such earnestness, and such vigour, I should almost have suspected her of a desire to take advantage of my innocence. Then, she admitted, she had lost her temper—which was not to be wondered at. If anyone had thrown me, or "got" me into a hedge, anyhow, I should have lost mine right straight off. The moral of it seemed to be that "the last hole cost her seventeen," though seventeen what—whether pounds or shillings—she did not mention; nor what manner of hole it could have been that she should have been so set on getting it at apparently any price. It was all double Dutch to me. But she rattled on at such a rate that I hoped to be able to conceal my ignorance; for I felt that if she discovered it, I should drop in her estimation like the mercury in the thermometer which is transferred from hot water into cold.

Suddenly, however, she began to ask me questions which sent cold shivers up and down my back. What cleeks had I got? whose "mashie" did I use? did I care for a "heeless" cleek?

I fumbled with the inquiries somehow, until she put one which I had to answer.

"Do you do much with a brassey spoon?"

She looked at me with her grey eyes which made me feel as if I was in the witness-box and she was cross-examiner. I did not do much with a "brassey spoon." Indeed, I did nothing. I had no idea what anyone could do. In fact, until that second I had not been aware that spoons were ever made of brass. And, anyhow, what part spoons of any kind played in the game of golf I had not the dimmest notion. But I was not going to give myself away at a single bound; I was not quite so simple as that. So I thought for a moment; then I answered—

"I suppose that I do about as much as other people."

As a non-committal sort of answer I thought it rather neat; but I was not so clear in my own mind as I should have liked to have been as to what was the impression which it made upon Margaret. She looked at me in a way which made me wonder if she suspected.

Luckily, before she was able to corner me again, we came to the house. In the hall a lady met us whose likeness to Philip was so great that it affected me with something like a shock; she was his replica in petticoats. In his clothes she might easily have passed as his elder brother. It was Mrs Sanford. She took both my hands in hers—standing in front of her relatively I was a mere mite—and looked me up and down.

"There isn't much of you, and you're ridiculously young."

"The first fault I am afraid is incurable. But the second I can grow out of. Many people do."

She laughed, and took me in her arms, literally lifted me off my feet—and kissed me. It was humiliating, but I did not seem to mind it from her. I had a sort of feeling she was nice. As I looked at her I understood how it was that she had two such athletic daughters. Philip had never struck me as being particularly athletic, though he was so big and broad. But as I talked to his mother I began to realise with a sinking heart how little I knew of him after all.

I cannot say that when I got into my bedroom I felt very ecstatic. Without an unusual degree of exertion I could have cried; but, thank goodness, I had sense enough not to do that.

When I went down to tea I found that Bertha and Miss Reeves had arrived —and the luggage, and the creatures. The Sanfords had creatures of their own; dogs and birds galore. Among the latter was one which I afterwards learnt was a jay. It made the most ridiculous noises, so that I felt that Lord Chesterfield was justified in fixing it with his stony gaze; and in observing, with serious and ceaseless reiteration—

"Don't be a fool!"

The conversation immediately got into channels which I would much rather it had kept out of. Bertha began it.

"Molly, you've just come in time. There's going to be a sing-song on the island to-night, and as I'm getting up the programme I hope you'll turn out to be a gem of the first water. What'll you do?" I did not know what a "sing-song" was. Bertha explained. "A sing-song? Oh, a kind of a sort of a concert —informal, free-and-easy, don't you know. All the river people turn up on the island—they bring their own illuminations—then some of us do things to amuse them. Will you give us a banjo solo?"

"I'm afraid I don't play the banjo."

"Not play the banjo? I thought everyone could make a row on the banjo. Can't you play it enough to accompany your own singing?"

"I'm afraid I don't sing."

"Don't sing? Then what do you do?"

"I bar recitations"; this was Miss Reeves.

"I don't care what you bar," retorted Bertha. "I'm going to recite: at least, I'm going to do a sort of a sketch with George Willis."

"I don't call that reciting."

"It wouldn't make any difference if you did."

I was rapidly beginning to learn that these people had a candid way of addressing each other which, to a stranger, was a little alarming.

"The question is, Molly, what shall I put you down for? Will you give us a dance?"

"A dance? I don't know what you mean."

"A cake-walk, or a skirt-twirl, or a few steps—anything."

"Do you mean, will I dance, all by myself, in front of a lot of strangers?"

"Yes, why not? Everybody does if they can."

"I cannot, thank you."

"Then what can you do?"

"I have no parlour tricks."

"No—what?"

"I have no parlour tricks."

I ought to have been warned by the tone in which Bertha put her inquiry; but I did not notice it until it was too late. Directly I had repeated my assertion I realised that I had said something which it would perhaps have been better left unsaid. They all exchanged glances in that exasperating way which some people have when they wish to telegraph to each other something which is not precisely flattering to you. Miss Reeves laughed outright; Bertha drummed with her fingers on her knee; Margaret observed me with her keen grey eyes; while Mrs Sanford spoke.

"Isn't that one of those things, Molly, which one would rather have expressed differently? Because, hereabouts, we rather pride ourselves on our capacity for what you call 'parlour tricks'; and were not even aware that they were 'parlour tricks' in the opprobrious sense which you seem to suggest. I have always myself tried to acquire a smattering of as many of what, I fancied, were the minor accomplishments, as I could; and I have always endeavoured, sometimes at the cost of a good deal of money, to induce my girls to acquire them too. I have never felt that a woman was any the worse for being able to do things for the amusement—if not for the edification—of her friends."

I had not been so snubbed since I had been long-frocked, and to think that it should have been by Philip's mother! I fancy that I blushed in a perfectly preposterous manner, and I know that I went hot and cold all over, and I tried to wriggle out of the mess into which I had got myself.

"I only wish I could do things, but I can't. I never have been among clever people, and I'm so dreadfully stupid. Hasn't Philip told you?"

"Philip has told us nothing, except—you know what. But Philip himself is a past-master of all sorts of parlour tricks. Don't you know so much of him as that?"

Of course I did. I resented the suggestion that I did not. I was commencing to get almost cross with Philip's mother. I was perfectly aware that there was nothing which Philip could not do, and do well, better than anyone else. But it had not occurred to me that therefore his relations, and even his acquaintances, were all-round experts also. And I was not by any means sure that I appreciated the fact now—if it was a fact. It was not pleasant to feel that in what were here plainly regarded as essentials, I should show to such hideous disadvantage. I should practically be out of everything, and no girl likes to be that, especially when her lover's about. Before long Philip would be comparing me to everybody else, and thinking nothing of me at all.

It is possible that my doleful visage—I am convinced that it had become doleful—moved Margaret to sympathy. Anyhow she all at once jumped up and, I have no doubt with the best will in the world by way of making things easier for me promptly proceeded to make them worse.

"Come along, Molly, let's have some tennis. Run upstairs and put your shoes on."

"My shoes? What shoes?"

"Why, your tennis shoes."

"My tennis shoes? I—I'm afraid I haven't brought any tennis shoes."

"Not brought any tennis shoes? But, of course, you do play tennis?"

The question was put in such a way as to infer that if I did not, then I must be a sorry specimen of humanity indeed. But, as it happened, I did play tennis, at least, after a fashion. We had what was called a tennis lawn at home, the condition of which may be deduced from the fact that I had never imagined that it would be inadvisable to play on it in hobnailed boots if anyone so desired.

"Of course I play; but—I haven't brought any particular shoes. Won't these do?"

I protruded one of those which I had on. Margaret could not have seemed more startled if I had shown her a bare foot.

"Those! why, they've got heels."

Miss Reeves went a good deal further.

"And such heels! My dear girl"—fancy her calling me her "dear girl," such impertinence!—"sane people don't wear those royal roads to deformity nowadays—they wear shoes like these."

She displayed a pair of huge, square-toed, shapeless, heelless, thick-soled monstrosities, into which nothing would ever have induced me to put my feet. I said so plainly.

"Then I'm glad that I am not sane. Sooner than wear things like that, I'd go about in my stockings. I don't believe that mine are royal, or any other, roads to deformity, they fit me beautifully; but, at anyrate, yours are deformities ready-made."

I did not intend to allow myself to be snubbed by Miss Reeves without a struggle. She was no relative of Philip's. But she might just as well have been; because, with one accord, they all proceeded to take her part.

"My dear Molly," said Margaret, speaking as if hers were the last words which could be said, "you are wrong. In shoes like yours you're a prisoner. You mayn't be conscious of it; and you won't be till you try others. Then you'll find out, and you'll be sorry that you didn't find out before. I want to be mistress of my feet; I don't want to be their servant. I wear shoes like Pat, and nothing would induce me to wear any other kind—I know better."

"And I," echoed her mother and sister.

There they were, all three displaying—with actual gusto!—shoes which were facsimiles of those worn by Miss Reeves. They were probably the productions of the same expert in ugliness.

"You won't be able to do anything really comfortably till you wear them too; then you'll tell yourself what a goose you were not to have gone in for them ages ago. But you'll find Philip'll soon win you into the ways of wisdom."

Philip would? I should like to see Philip even dare to try. If I could not wear—without argument—shoes to please myself, then—

I imagine that Margaret perceived, from the expression of my countenance, that she had gone a little too far; because she said, in quite a different tone of voice,—

"Never mind about shoes! play in those you have on, and I'll tell Jackson to give the lawn an extra roll in the morning."

If I had been wise I should have taken the reference to Jackson as a hint, and slipped out of playing. But my back was a wee bit up, and I was a little off my balance, so I played. Of course I made a frightful spectacle of myself. It did make me so wild.

Bertha and Margaret said they would play Miss Reeves and me, which I did not like, to begin with. Under the circumstances, I felt that one of them might have offered to take me as a partner. They might have seen that I was commencing to regard Miss Reeves as if she were covered with prickles. Besides which, considering what I imagined I had come there for, and the position which I was shortly to occupy in the family, it did seem to me that they ought not to have paired me with a stranger. But as they evidently preferred to play together, they plainly did not think it worth their while to study my tastes for a moment. So I was as sugary to Miss Reeves as I could be.

"I am afraid you have a very bad partner," I observed.

"I don't mind," she was kind enough to reply. "I expect you're one of those dark horses who're better than they choose to make out."

I tried to be, but I failed ignominiously. I do declare that I am not always so bad as I was then. But, as I have said, I was a little off my balance; and all I could do was make an idiot of myself. Bertha served first; my partner suggested I should take her service. I took it, or rather, I didn't take it. She sent the balls so fast that I could scarcely see them; and then there was such a twist on them, or whatever you call the thing, that I could not have hit them anyhow. I did not hit them, not one.

"What horrid balls," I murmured, when Bertha had made an end.

"You seem to find them so."

My partner spoke with such excessive dryness that I could have hit her with my racket. When it came to her turn to serve she asked me a question.

"Won't you stand up to the net and kill their returns?"

No, I would not stand up to the net and kill their returns. I did not know what she meant, but I knew that I would not do it. And I did not. She herself played as if she had been doing nothing else all her life but play lawn-tennis. She was all over the place at once. I was only in her way, and she treated me as if I was only in her way. I had to dodge when I saw her coming, or she would have sent me flying—more than once she nearly did. It was a painful fiasco, so far as I was concerned; I have a dim suspicion that we scored nothing. When the game was finished she looked me up and down.

"Bit off your game, aren't you?"

"I'm afraid I am," I muttered.

I was too cast down to do anything else but mutter. There was a look in her eyes which, unless I was mistaken, meant temper. And she was such a very stalwart person that I had a horrible feeling that, unless I was very careful, she might make nothing of shaking me.

"Perhaps you're stronger in singles; I should like to play you a single; will you?"

"Thank you, some—some other time."

"Shall we say to-morrow?"

We did not say to-morrow. I would not have said to-morrow for a good deal. Margaret came to my rescue.

"You play Bertha. Molly and I'll look on."

We looked on, while they performed prodigies. I had never before seen such playing. The idea of my associating myself with them was preposterous. As we watched, Margaret was not so loquacious as I should have desired. In her silence I seemed to read disapprobation of the exhibition of incompetence which I had given. Moreover, when she did speak, her remarks took the form of criticisms of the play, approving this stroke, condemning that, with a degree of severity which made me wince. It was impossible to sit beside her for many seconds without realising that she regarded lawn-tennis with a seriousness of which—in that connection—I had never dreamed. Obviously, with her, it was one of the serious things of life.

Suddenly she hit upon a theme which was not much more palatable to me than lawn-tennis had been, in such company.

"Let's play ping-pong, you and me?"

"Ping-pong?" My heart sank afresh. It seemed in that house, that games were in the air. "Wouldn't you rather sit here and watch them playing tennis. I like to watch them."

I would rather have watched anyone play anything than play myself. But Margaret was of a different mind.

"Oh no, what's the fun of it? One gets rusty. Let's do something. Of course ping-pong's not a game one can take really in earnest; but there's a tournament in the schoolroom on Wednesday, and I ought to keep my hand in. Come along and let's have a knock up."

We went along. She did not give me a chance to refuse to go along. She led the way.

"Of course you *do* play?"

"Well—I have played. But I'm quite sure that I don't play in your sense."

"Oh, everyone plays ping-pong—the merest children even. I maintain that it's nothing but a children's game."

It might be. In that case, she would soon discover that I was past the age of childhood.

"Have you brought your bat?" I had not. "It doesn't matter. We've got about thirty different kinds. You're sure to find your sort among them."

A ping-pong board was set up in the billiard-room. On a table at one side were enough bats to stock a shop. I took the one she recommended, and we began.

Ping-pong is a loathsome game. I have always said it, and always shall. At home we played it on the dining-room table. The boys made sport of me. They used to declare in derision, that I played "pat-ball." I should have liked some of them to have played with Margaret. She would have played with them, or I err. I thought the serves had come in with disgusting swiftness at lawn-tennis—they were nothing compared to her serves at ping-pong. That wretched little celluloid ball whizzed over the net like lightning, and then, as I struck at it blindly, expecting it to come straight towards me, like a Christian thing, it flew off at an angle, to the right or left, and my bat encountered nothing but the air. On the other hand, when I served she smashed my ball back with such force that it leaped right out of my reach, or any one's, and sometimes clean over the billiard-table. I had soon had enough of it.

"Hadn't we better stop?" I inquired, when, for the second time in succession, she had smashed my service nearly up to the ceiling. "It can't be very amusing for you to play with me."

A similar reflection seemed to occur to her. Resting her bat on the edge of the board, she regarded me in contemplative fashion.

"What *is* your favourite game?" she asked.

For some occult reason the question made me blush, so far, that is, as my state of heat permitted.

"I'm not good at any, so I suppose I haven't a favourite game. Indeed, I don't think I'm fond of games."

"Not fond of games?" Her tone was almost melancholy, as if my admission grieved her. "That is unfortunate. We're such a gamey crowd—we are all so keen on games."

Her bearing so hinted that I had been the occasion to her of actual pain that it almost moved me to tears.

When I got up into my room to dress for dinner I was a mixture of feelings. It would not have needed much to have made me sneak down the stairs, and out of the house, and back to the station, if I had been sure of getting safely away. I could not say exactly what I had expected, but I certainly had not expected this. Philip had always made such a fuss of me, that, I fear, I had taken it for granted that, under the circumstances, his people would make a fuss of me too. Instead of which they had received me with a take-it-for-granted air, as if they had known me for years and years; and then had promptly proceeded to make me feel so unutterably small, that I was almost inclined to wish that I had never been born.

I hated to be made small. I hated games. I hated—during those moments, in which I was tearing off my frock, I nearly felt as if I hated everything. But just in time, it was borne in to me how wicked I was. It was not their fault if I was a little donkey; it was my own. They were not to blame if I had allowed my education to be neglected, and had not properly appreciated the paramount importance of tennis, and ping-pong, and golf, and all the other, to my mind, somewhat exasperating exercises which came under the generic heading of "games." As I proceeded with my toilette, and surveyed the result in the mirror, my spirit became calmer. At least they none of them looked better than I did. I might not be such an expert, but I certainly was not uglier than they were. And that was something. Besides, I was young, and strong, and healthy, and active. If I set myself to do it, it was quite within the range of possibility that I might become a match for them even at tennis and ping-pong. I did not believe that I was such a duffer as I had seemed.

No one could have been nicer than they were when I went down into the drawing-room; Miss Reeves actually was so nice that she took my breath away. They stared as I entered; then broke into a chorus.

"Well," began Bertha, with that outspokenness which seemed a family characteristic, "one thing's sure and certain—you'll be the beauty of the family. We shall have to show you as an illustration of what we can achieve in that direction. You look a perfect picture."

"A dream of loveliness!" cried Miss Reeves. "Now, if I were a man, you're just the sort of girl I'd like to marry. Even as a mere girl I'd like to kiss you."

She put her hands lightly on my bare shoulders, and she did kiss me—on both cheeks, and on the lips—there and then. It was most bewildering. I had not looked for that sort of thing from her. But Mrs Sanford's words warmed the very cockles of my heart.

"If you are as delightful as you look, my dear, that boy of mine ought to be a very happy fellow."

No woman had ever spoken to me like that before. It filled me with a delightful glow—made me even bold. I went close up to her, and I whispered—

"I should like to make him happy."

Then she drew me to her, and she kissed me—laughing as she did so. It was really a most peculiar position for a person to be in. But I forgave them for making such an object of me at tennis.

After dinner Mrs Sanford said,—

"Bertha, Margaret, and I will go over to the island in the dinghy,—we, being on this occasion, the chief exponents of parlour tricks, and responsible for all the other performers of the same—and then, Pat, you and Molly might follow in the punt."

At Mrs Sanford's mischievous allusion to "parlour tricks" they all looked at me, and laughed; but, by now, I was beginning to get used to their ways: I laughed too. A little while before I should have objected to being again paired off with Miss Reeves, but my sentiments were also commencing to change towards her. Mrs Sanford went on—

"We shall have to see that all things are ready and in order; so that you will have fifteen or twenty minutes before you need appear."

We saw them off—the garden ran right down to the water's edge. Then Miss Reeves proposed that, since there was no need to hurry, we should get into the punt, and dawdle about upon the river till it was time to join them. The idea commended itself to me; although I was regarding the punt—which was moored alongside—with some misgivings. Incredible though it may sound, I had never seen such an article before.

But then I had never before been within miles and miles of the Thames,— except over London Bridge, and that kind of thing. I had never been in a boat in my life, whether large or small, on sea or river. Such was my ignorance, that I had not been aware that women ever rowed—especially in little weeny boats all alone by themselves. The workmanlike manner in which Bertha and Margaret had rowed off with their mother had filled me with amazement,— they had gone off with nothing on their heads, or shoulders, or even their hands. They had a heap of wraps in the bottom of the boat; but it had not seemed to occur to them that it was necessary to put them on. True, it was a lovely evening and delightfully warm, but there were lots of other boats about; and it did seem odd that three ladies should start off in a boat all alone by themselves in exactly the same costume in which they had just been sitting at dinner.

"Hadn't I better put something on?" I inquired of Miss Reeves, who showed symptoms of a desire to hurry me into the punt before I was ready.

"Why," she rejoined. "It'll be hot all through the night. You don't feel chilly?"

"No; I don't feel chilly—but—"

I looked about me at the strangers in the other boats in a way which she was quick to understand. She was shrewd enough.

"My dear Miss Boyes—" she paused. "I mean my dear Molly—I must call you Molly—I really must—up here, one regards the Thames as one's own private river. It's the mode to do—and to dress—exactly as one pleases. In summer, on the upper reaches of the Thames, one is in Liberty Hall. Step into that punt—if it pleases you, just as you are; or if it pleases you, smother yourself in wraps—only do step in. Are you going to pole, or am I?"

"To pole?"

She eyed me quizzically.

"Don't tell me that you don't know what to pole means?"

"But I don't. How should I, when I never saw a punt before this second."

"Dear me, how your rudiments have been neglected. Poling, you uninstructed child, with the stream, and the right companion, on a summer evening, is the poetry of life. Jump inside that boat, and I'll give you an illustration of the verb—to pole."

She gave me one; a charming illustration too. Certainly, lying on the bottom of that punt, amid a pile of cushions while it moved smoothly over those glittering waters, under that cloudless sky, was delicious. And the ease with which she sent us along, just dipping the long pole into the stream, while the gleaming drops of water fell off the shining shaft.

"Well," she asked, "how do you like my illustration?"

"It's lovely! I could go on like this for ever,—just looking at you. It shows off your figure splendidly." She laughed. "And it doesn't seem to be so difficult either."

"What doesn't seem difficult?—poling? It isn't. You only have to put it in, and take it out again. Nothing could be simpler."

Of course I knew that she was chaffing me; and that it was not quite so simple as that. But, all the same, I leaned to the opinion that it was not so very hard. And I resolved that, when Philip came, and he was there to teach me, and to take a genuine interest in my education, that I would try my hand. I suspected that I might look rather decent, poling him along.

It was very jolly on the island. There were crowds of people, some of them gorgeous, some in simple skirts and blouses, but scarcely any of them wore hats,—the men looked nicer than I had ever seen men look before. I came to the conclusion that the river costume did suit men. The "parlour tricks" were excellent; I became more and more ashamed of myself for having spoken of them as parlour tricks. Bertha and Margaret and Mrs Sanford were splendid. I believe that the people would have liked them to have kept on doing things all night long—and no wonder. If I had only been a hundredth part as clever, I should have been as proud as a peacock. Everything would have gone off perfectly, and I should have had one of the pleasantest evenings of my life, if it had not been for my stupidity.

When all was over I found myself in the punt with Margaret. She was kneeling at one end, arranging her music and things. Although it was pretty late there was a full moon in an unclouded sky, so that it was almost as light as day. All at once I discovered that we had got untied or something, and were drifting farther and farther from the land.

"We're going," I exclaimed.

"That's all right," said Margaret. "Pole her clear."

Evidently she, engrossed in affairs of her own, took it for granted that I was no novice; in that part of the world novices seemed to be things unknown. There were lots of boats about us; people were making laughing remarks about our being in the way; the pole was lying in the punt: Miss Reeves had handled it as if it were a feather. Here was an earlier opportunity to try my hand than I had anticipated; but—surely!—until Margaret was disengaged, I could act on her instructions and "pole clear." So I picked up the pole.

Two things struck me instantly; one, that it was much longer than it had seemed; and the other, that it was a very great deal heavier. But I had been so hasty that, before I realised these facts—though I realised them rapidly enough—the end of it was in the water. Down it went with a jerk to the bottom. Had I not hung on to it with sudden desperation it would all of it have gone. I wished it had! For while I clung to it I all at once perceived that, in some mysterious way, the boat was running away from underneath me. It was the most extraordinary sensation I had ever experienced, and so startling! and it all took place with such paralysing swiftness. Before I understood what was really happening—before I had time to scream or anything, I found that I was actually pushing the punt away with my own feet, that I was standing on the edge of it, and splash! I was in the river.

There was no water to speak of. It was quite shallow; only a foot or two deep. I was out again almost as soon as I was in. But I was soaked to the skin. And the worst of it was, that I knew that not a creature there sympathised with me truly. All round me people were laughing outright—at me—as if it were quite a joke. I could not see where the joke came in. Although Mrs Sanford and the girls and Miss Reeves pretended to sympathise with me, I felt persuaded that even they were laughing at me in their heart of hearts. More than once I caught them in a grin.

I did feel so wild with myself when I got between the sheets! All the same, I slept like a top. I seemed to have only been asleep a minute or two when I was disturbed by a knocking at my bedroom door.

"Who's there?" I cried.

"Come for a dip?" returned Margaret's voice.

"A dip?" I shuddered; she had roused me from the loveliest dream. "Where?"

"Why, in the river, child! It's a perfect morning for a swim!"

"In the river?—for a swim?—But I can't swim."

"I'm coming in," she cried. And in she came, rushing across the floor, putting her strong arms underneath my shoulders, raising me from the pillow. "I don't believe you can do anything—you little goose! But you're a darling all the same!"

She kissed me three or four times, then dropped me; scurried back across the floor, and out of the room.

I sighed, and, I believe, I turned over and went to sleep again.

When I got down to breakfast I found that they had all been about for hours. There was a letter from Philip lying on my plate. He wrote to say that he was coming down by the first train.

"You might go and meet him," suggested Mrs Sanford. "Can you drive?"

They all grinned; but I did not mind, not a tiny bit.

"Can I drive?" I retorted scornfully. "Why, I've driven since I was a little thing."

"And pray, how long ago is that? Anyhow, if you can drive you might go to meet him by yourself."

I did—in the pony phaeton; it was lovely. When Philip came out of the station my heart jumped into my mouth; especially when he took his hat off, and kissed me in front of all the people. It was so unexpected.

As I drove him back I told him what an absolute duffer I was, what an utter failure, what an all-round nincompoop. He declared that he did not believe a word of it; which seems, from one point of view, to have been a trifle rude. And he said that, as for my not being able to do things, he would show me how to do them all, and he guaranteed—but I knew there was a twinkle in his eye—that soon I would do them better than anyone else.

And I should not be surprised if he does teach me how to do some things. He has taught me such a deal already.

So, as I observed at the outset, although I am not quite, I am almost perfectly happy. And, after all, that is something. Particularly as I daresay I shall be quite happy before very long.

VIII

THE PRINCESS MARGARETTA

She was not only charming—quite common women are sometimes charming— but there was about her an air of dignity which—I had almost written which was indescribable. She made you feel what an altogether superior person she was, and what an altogether inferior person you were, and yet she did it in a way which really almost made you feel as if she flattered you; paid you a delicate compliment, in fact. I recognised this peculiarity about her from the first.

She made her first appearance on the pier. And an extraordinary sensation she made. Nobody knew who she was, and yet anybody could see that she was somebody. There was, even about the way in which she carried her parasol—my wife noticed it at the time—an indefinable something which marked her out as not being one of the rank and file.

It was one morning when the band was playing that she first appeared. That same night she was at the entertainment in the pavilion. The "Caledonian Opera Company" were there that week, and even the shilling seats were crowded. She was in the second row among the shillings. And by the greatest chance in the world Grimshaw happened to make her acquaintance. He sat in the next seat to her. She dropped her programme; he picked it up; and so the acquaintance was made.

Her behaviour towards him was instinct with the greatest condescension. Grimshaw assured me that he was almost overwhelmed. She really treated him as if he had been her equal; as if he had been an acquaintance of some standing. She allowed him to escort her to her hotel. And she told him all about herself; and, of course, it all came out.

This divinely beautiful woman—I have never heard a word whispered against her beauty, even by the women—was the Princess Margaretta. She had taken a suite of rooms at the hotel—quite a palatial suite, considering— and she had come to stay at Beachington for the season.

I suppose there is no place anywhere where people of rank and position may expect to receive a warmer welcome than at Beachington.

When it was known that the Princess Margaretta was staying at the "Parade Hotel," all the inhabitants of Beachington called upon her, one might say, within five minutes. The inhabitants of Beachington do not, as a rule, call upon visitors. They are rather a higgledy-piggledy lot, are visitors. In general, they are only welcomed by the hotel proprietors, and lodging-house keepers, and the tradesmen and that class of person. But, in the case of a Princess, Beachington society felt that, as a society it had its duties to fulfil, and it fulfilled them. In that statement you have the situation.

The Princess received everybody. I must own that, for my part, I was a little surprised. She received the Pattens, for instance. And the Pattens are nothing and nobody. It was like their impudence to call on a Princess. Patten was only in the Custom House. And as for his wife—we never even speak of his wife. Then she received the Jacksons. It is the belief, at Beachington, that old Jackson used to keep a public-house. It is not only that he suffers from a chronic thirst, but he looks like it. And there were other people. But then, of course, she could not be expected to be able to discriminate at first. She wanted an adviser. I am bound to say that, ere long, she had more advisers than perhaps she cared for. Some people are so pushing.

I assure you that I have never known Beachington livelier than it was that season. The Princess was a widow. There is something pathetic even in the mere state of widowhood. In the case of a young and beautiful woman the pathos is heightened. And the Princess was rich. She owned it with a most charming frankness. It seemed her husband had been an American, and he had added his fortune to her fortune, and the result was a mountain of wealth which weighed the Princess down. She spoke of handing it over to the starving millions, and being free again. As I have said, I had never imagined that Beachington could have been so lively.

I confess that I was taken aback when, one day, Grimshaw dragged me along the parade, past the asphalt, on to the rough ground, where there were no people, and put to me this question,—

"Beamish, do you think it would be impossible for a man to fight a duel nowadays?"

I stared at him. I asked him what he meant. Then it all came out.

Grimshaw was actually making eyes at the Princess Margaretta: Grimshaw is three years younger than I am, and I am fifty-five. He is short and stout, not to say puffy. He is balder than I am, and my wife says that for me to brush my hair is a farce. He lives in unfurnished rooms, for which he pays twenty pounds a year with attendance, and he has nothing but his half pay to live upon.

"Do you think that if I were to fix a public insult upon Crookshanks I could force him to call me out?"

Crookshanks—he calls himself "Surgeon-General" upon his cards; he is a retired army doctor—is about sixty. He has been a widower nearly twenty years. His eldest daughter is herself a widow. She has two children. Mother and children all live with him. He has two other daughters, both unmarried. Between them poor Crookshanks hardly dare call his soul his own. And yet Crookshanks was not only making up to the Princess, but, in Grimshaw's judgment, he was proving himself a dangerous rival.

I told Grimshaw that it was only because Crookshanks was a greater idiot than himself that he was not the greatest idiot in Beachington. I don't stand on ceremony with Grimshaw—I never have done.

"I don't know." Grimshaw mopped his brow. The slightest exertion makes him painfully warm. "If I could only get Crookshanks out of the way, I have reason to believe she cares for me."

I asked him what his reason was. He hesitated. When he spoke his tone was doubtful. I detected it, although he tried to disguise the thing.

"I lent her fifteen pounds. I don't think that a woman would borrow money from a man unless she cared for him. What do you think—eh, Beamish?"

I did not know what to think. I happen to know that Grimshaw's daily expenditure is measured out with mathematical exactness. I wanted to know where he got his fifteen pounds from. This time his tone was unmistakably rueful.

"I had to borrow it myself; and I had to pay a stiff price for it, too. She wanted it for flowers."

Wanted it for flowers! I told him that I thought he had more sense. Russian women are notoriously careless in money matters. Fifteen pounds were nothing to her, while to him—they were fifteen pounds. I promised that he would never see his money again. I left Grimshaw with his heart in his boots. He made no further reference to fighting Crookshanks.

But, the fact is, I soon found out that everybody was making love to the Princess Margaretta. Not only all the unmarried men but, unless rumour lied, some of the married men as well, There were some pretty scandals! Rouse, the curate of St Giles', had a *tête-à-tête* dinner with her in her private sitting-room, and stayed so late that the landlord of the "Parade Hotel" had to tell him it was time to go. I charged Rouse with it to his face. He had the grace to blush.

"The Princess is a member of the Greek Church—a most interesting subject." That is what he said. "I have hopes, Admiral, of winning her to the faith we hold so dear. It is only a passage in one of the Articles which keeps her back. I do not understand exactly how—it seems to be almost a question of grammar—yet so it is. But it would, indeed, be a triumph to win her from the Greeks."

What I objected to most was the conduct of young Marchmont. It was only shortly before that he had asked my permission to pay his attentions to our Daisy. And he had paid his attentions with a vengeance. Yet here he was dangling about the Princess's skirts as though he were tied to her apron-strings. I did not wish to have a discussion with him, for Daisy's sake; but I made up my mind to say a word to the Princess.

My chance came before I expected. She stopped me one afternoon on the Front. I was walking, she was in a carriage. She asked me to get in, so I got in, and away we drove.

"Do you know, Admiral," she began, "yesterday I made such a silly mistake. I called at your house, and I left the wrong card."

"The servant told me something about it. She said that you left a card with the name of 'Dowsett' on it."

"That is so—Dowsett." She leaned back in the carriage. She shaded herself with her parasol in such a way that, while her face must have been invisible to the people on the front, it was visible enough to me. She looked supremely lovely. No wonder all the men were after her—the beggars. "Do you know, Admiral, that, at one time, I had almost made up my mind to enter Beachington under false colours."

I asked her to explain. She did explain.

"You know that we, who, so to speak, are born in the purple, have moments in our lives in which we are conscious that title and honours are—what shall I say?—mere fripperies. One longs, now and then, to step down from the pedestal on which chance, rather than our desert, has placed us, and become—what shall I say again?—one of the masses. I don't know how it may be with others in my position, but it is often so with me. And to such an extent, that at one time I even thought of coming to Beachington as plain Mrs Dowsett. I thought it would be such fun, so obviously ridiculous, you know. I even had cards printed with the name of Dowsett on them. Wasn't it a curious fancy? I suppose one of them got mixed up with my own cards, and, in my silly way, I left it at your house by mistake." She paused, then she added: "My husband's name was Dowsett. He was an American of the finest kind. He was what they call in America, One of the Four Hundred."

"Then, if your husband's name was Dowsett, I presume that your name is Dowsett, too. So that you are Mrs Dowsett after all."

"My dear Admiral! Once a Princess always a Princess. I do not cease to be

111

the Princess Margaretta because, by accident, I chance to have had a husband who was a commoner."

She said this in a way which showed that I had wounded her sensibilities.

Then I tried to bring the subject round to young Charles Marchmont. I got there by degrees. She caught up the hints I dropped with a quickness which confounded me.

"Poor Mr Marchmont! He is so utterly in love with me!"

"In love with you—Charles Marchmont!"

I stared. I almost let out that the young scoundrel was, nominally, engaged to Daisy—my little girl. But I did not choose to give my child away even to the Princess Margaretta.

"He has given me a hundred pounds."

I almost sprang from the carriage seat.

"Charles Marchmont has given you a hundred pounds!"

"I have not told him so, but I have almost made up my mind to devote it to the Russian Jews. It makes one so sad to think of them—don't you think that it makes one sad? All the world knows how deeply I am interested in the sufferings of my unfortunate compatriots. Because they are Hebrews, is that a reason why we should give them stones instead of bread? Oh, no! Are they not my fellow-creatures? But every one in Beachington has made my sympathies his own. It is beautiful!" The lovely creature wiped her lovely eyes. "Every one has showered gifts upon me—gifts of money and of money's worth. Even Mr Rouse has given me five pounds and a ring which was his mother's."

Poor Rouse! I doubt if he had any private means to speak of, and I know that the income from his curacy was only sixty pounds a year.

It is incredible—I am ashamed of myself when I think of it—but before I got out of that carriage, I actually gave her all the money I had in my purse. To the relief of the Russian Jews, I understood that it was to be devoted at the time, though I am free to admit that she did not make an exact statement of the fact. I did not dare to tell Mrs Beamish what I had done. I have never dared to tell her to this hour.

Two nights after Douglas came up to me on the pier. He was beaming with something—possibly with rapture. When he saw me, in the dim light, he rubbed his hands together—in a way he has.

"Congratulate me, Beamish! Congratulate me, my dear Beamish!"

Before I congratulate a man, I like to know what I am expected to congratulate him on. I told him so. He dropped his voice to a sort of confidential whisper.

"She has promised to make me happy."

"She? Who?"

"The Princess Margaretta." He drew himself up. Douglas is a tall, thin man, so perhaps he thought that he would make himself still taller. "The Princess Margaretta, Beamish, that august and most beautiful lady, has, scarcely an hour ago—most auspicious hour of my existence!—promised to be my wife."

I was dumbfounded. I could only stare. Douglas is an old Indian Civil. He was Resident of—somewhere or other, I forget the name of the place. The driest old stick I ever yet encountered. As much fitted to be the husband of a fair young creature like the Princess Margaretta as—as I am.

"Yes, Beamish, I am to be married at last."

And quite time, too, ancient imbecile. I felt inclined to kick him as he stood there, smirking and twiddling his watch-chain.

"I have been making matrimonial approaches towards the Princess Margaretta almost since the moment in which she arrived at Beachington. I felt that such a woman as that must be mine, though, at the same time, I scarcely dared to hope. But the Princess is a woman of the widest sympathies. I am inclined to the belief that it is because I have made her sympathies my own that I have made her heart mine also. I presented her this afternoon with a cheque for a thousand guineas to be devoted to a cause in which she is much interested—the relief of the Russian Jews. It was, perhaps, for a person in my circumstances, a rash thing to do. But I do not regret it, for I am persuaded that it was that spontaneous act upon my part which induced her to say 'yes' to my whispered prayers."

I moved away from him; I could not congratulate him—I could not! I fancy that he was so lifted up in the seventh heaven of his happiness that he never noticed the omission.

On the other side of the pier I came upon Macbride. Macbride is a Yankee —a New England man; as keen and cute, and yet as nice a fellow as you would care to meet. He spends three or four months of every year in England on business, and, during that time, he is continually in and out of Beachington.

He was leaning over the railings, looking down at the sea, when I came up to him.

"Macbride," I said, "did you ever hear anything in the States of a man named Dowsett?"

He knew what I was driving at immediately. That man knows everything!

"The Princess's Dowsett?"

"That's it. I see you know that her husband's name was Dowsett."

Macbride considered a moment before he spoke.

"It's my opinion that there never was a Dowsett."

"Macbride! Why, she told me so herself!"

"I imagine that she may have told you a good many things which belong to that order of fiction which is distinctly a stranger to truth." He was silent; although I could not see his face, I guessed, somehow, he was smiling. "It is my further opinion—I mention it to you, because I think that you are beginning to suspect as much yourself—that the Princess is no better than she ought to be."

I gasped. If she had been doing us! What would Mrs Beamish say? I had staked my reputation on the woman.

"Do you know that she has promised to marry Douglas?"

"I know she has. I also know—from her own lips, so the authority is an unquestionable one—that there is more than one man in Beachington who is under the pleasing impression that she has promised to marry him. For instance, she has more than half promised to marry me. And I, for my part, am more than half inclined to marry her."

"Macbride! when you say that you think she is no better than she ought to be!"

"If you consider, how many women are there who are any better than they ought to be? Where shall you find a perfect woman? And Heaven protect us from her when she's found. Possibly you misconstrue my meaning. When I state that I believe her to be no better than she ought to be, I make a statement which, in my judgment, applies to all the women I ever met, not to speak of all the men. I think—I am not sure, but I think—that I understand the Princess Margaretta. I think, also, that she understands me. There is one advantage gained—a common understanding—especially as I am myself, in some respects, a rather peculiar person." For the first time he stood up, turned, and faced me. "Beamish, the Princess Margaretta is a clever woman. What she wants is a clever man. With a clever man she might be happy, and she might make him happy. Her misfortune has been that, up to now, the men she has encountered have been, generally speaking, fools."

I could not make him out. And I not only could not make him out, but I did not know what to say to him. What can you say to a man who tells you that he thinks a woman is no better than she ought to be, and then, in the very same breath, that he is more than half inclined to marry her? And that when he knows that she has not only promised to marry another man, but, as he more than hints, half a dozen other men besides.

The following morning, just as I was going to start for my morning stroll, the servant came and said that a "gentleman" wished to see me. She hesitated as she said "gentleman," as if she were doubtful if that word exactly applied.

"Admiral Beamish?" enquired the visitor as I entered the room into which the maid had shown him. I told him that I was that individual. "Can you tell me what is my wife's present address? She appears to have changed her lodging. I am Mr Dowsett."

I stared. The visitor was a small, insignificant, sandy-haired, mild-looking individual of about forty years of age. No wonder the servant had hesitated to call him a "gentleman." He carried "small shopkeeper" on him, written large.

"I don't understand you. I fancy there is some mistake," I said.

The stranger eyed me as though the mere tone of my voice filled him with alarm.

"Perhaps so. But my wife told me that she had the honour of your acquaintance, She mentioned your name in her last letter."

"Your wife? Who is your wife?"

"My wife is Mrs Dowsett."

"Dowsett?" A cold shiver went down my back. I had heard the name before. "Is it possible that you are referring to the Princess Margaretta?"

"The—who?"

"The Princess Margaretta—who, as all the world knows, is staying at the 'Parade Hotel'?"

"I hope not—I do hope not. I hope she's not gone so far as the Princess Margaretta."

The little man wrung his hands together as if he were positively suffering pain.

"The Princess did say that her late husband's name was Dowsett. Perhaps

115

you are a relation of his?"

"Her late husband! I'm her present husband, if it's Mrs Dowsett. But perhaps you wouldn't mind telling me what kind of party the Princess Margaretta is—I mean to look at."

I told him. I described the Princess's many charms. I spoke of her glorious hair, her great blue eyes, her irresistible smile, her exquisite figure, her bearing of great lady. I did not do her justice—who can do a beautiful woman justice by a mere description?—but I apparently did her sufficient justice to enable him to recognise the picture I had drawn. When I had finished, that little man dropped into a chair with what sounded to me very like a cry of anguish.

"It's Eliza!" That is how he referred to the Princess Margaretta—the, as she had given me to understand, near relation to the Romanoffs, the reigning Russian family. "She's done it again! And worse than ever!—After all she promised!"

When I understood what his broken exclamations might mean, I began to perspire.

"I fear that you and I, sir, are at cross purposes. May I ask you to explain! And, first of all, be so good as to tell me who you are."

"That's me." He took from his pocket a card, a common tradesman's card, on which was printed "James Dowsett. Grocer and General Provision Merchant," with an address at Islington. "That's me," he repeated with an air of positive pride, "that's who I am. And I'll do you as good a tea at one and ten as you'll get anywhere in London, though I say it."

"And do you mean to tell me," I gasped, "that the Princess Margaretta is not a widow, not—not a relation of the Romanoffs, but—but a small grocer's actual wife?"

"Not such a small grocer's as you might think. I could give you a banker's reference which perhaps would startle you. It isn't always them, you know, who carry things off with the biggest air who are the biggest."

"But," I cried, "are you aware, sir, that the person whom you assert to be your wife, has, here in Beachington, laid claim to Royal rank?"

The little man's air of modest pride disappeared with even comic suddenness.

"Not to Royal rank? Not quite to Royal rank, I hope?"

"But I say yes—I say yes. She told me with her own lips that she was a near relation to the Russian Czar."

Mr Dowsett began again to wring his hands.

"Oh, Eliza, what have you done?"

"If the person you refer to as 'Eliza'—great powers, what a name!—is the person who calls herself the Princess Margaretta, then she has been guilty of the most impudent fraud of which I ever heard, and proved herself to be a swindler of the purest water."

Mr Dowsett stared, or, rather, glared at me. He drew himself to his full height—five foot three inches. He turned pale with rage; he actually shook his fist in my face.

"Don't you call my wife a swindler, you—you old villain!"

I was astounded.

"May I ask, Mr Dowsett, what language you would apply to a person who, being a grocer's wife, calls herself a widow, in possession of a large fortune, a Princess in her own right, and a near relative of the reigning Czar?"

Mr Dowsett looked at me, as if he were at a loss for words. Then, to my surprise and my disgust, he began to cry. Mr Dowsett appeared to be a man of variable moods.

"You sha'n't call her a swindler, you sha'n't! She's no more a swindler than you are. It's all them—them dratted books."

"Dratted books, Mr Dowsett? What do you mean?"

"It's them penny novelettes and the stories in the fashion papers, and that stuff. She gets reading about things, and then she thinks she's the things she reads about. I'll tell you what she said to me not very long ago. 'Jimmy,' she said—I'm Jimmy—'let's pretend that I'm a duchess. I've been reading about such a beautiful duchess. Let's pretend I'm her.' So we did, just her and me. I called her 'Your Grace,' and all. We kept it up for nearly a month. Then she said, 'Jimmy, I'm tired of being a duchess. I've been reading such a lovely story about a lone, lorn orphan. Let's pretend I'm a lone, lorn orphan, whom you picked up out of the streets, for a change.' So we pretended that she was a lone, lorn orphan who'd gone through enough to make your hair go grey. But, there! I don't know what we haven't pretended she was."

That any man could be capable of such childish imbecility seemed to me almost incredible. But then man's capacity of imbecility is incredible. Consider how a man of my standing had been induced to receive a grocer's wife as a Royal Princess!

"May I ask, Mr Dowsett, how you came to allow your wife to come to

Beachington unaccompanied by her husband?"

"Well, sir, it was this way. I was more than usually busy this year, and Eliza was anxious for a change, and she begged me to let her go, so I let her go."

"And do you mean to tell me that she has given you no hint of what she has been doing since she came?"

"Lor' bless you, she's written to me every day, regular. The best letters ever you saw—that funny! How I have laughed at them, oh lor'!" Mr Dowsett seemed inclined to laugh even at the recollection. "But, to tell you the truth, I didn't know what was true in them and what was make-believe. She did say that she told every one that she was a Princess, and that every one took her for one; but I never thought for a moment she was in earnest. Though goodness knows that she's clever enough, and beautiful enough for one, isn't she, sir?" I didn't tell him what I thought; though I felt that in the truth of that lay my excuse. "She wouldn't give me her address. She said it would spoil the fun. So I sent my letters to the post-office."

"Did you, indeed? There appear to be some curious husbands and wives in existence nowadays, but scarcely a more curious couple, I apprehend, Mr Dowsett, than you and the—lady whom I know as the Princess Margaretta. Although you do not know her address, I do. So, with your permission, we will pay an immediate visit to the Princess Margaretta."

When we pulled up in front of the "Parade Hotel," the little man gave a little start.

"My gracious! Is she staying here? She did mention once that she was stopping at the biggest hotel in the place. But I thought that was her fun. Oh, Eliza, what have you done?"

As he went into the hotel Grimshaw was coming out. He seemed to be in a state of considerable agitation. He addressed me almost at the top of his voice.

"Beamish, you will find Crookshanks lying senseless on the landing. When he comes to, tell him that I shall be perfectly ready to give him the satisfaction of a gentleman."

He went striding off, without giving me a chance to request him to be a little more explicit. We did not find Crookshanks lying senseless on the landing. We met him coming down the stairs, with his handkerchief to his nose. He looked at us askance.

"Is Major Grimshaw downstairs?"

He put the question to me in a sort of anxious whisper.

"Grimshaw's just gone out."

"You are quite sure he's gone?

"Certainly. He just now passed me."

"Thank you. I—I was afraid he might be waiting down below."

He continued sneaking down the stairs, as if a weight had been taken off his mind. I had expected better things of Crookshanks. But perhaps those three girls of his have knocked the heart all out of him.

Unannounced I entered the Princess Margaretta's sitting-room. I wanted to take her unawares. I took her unawares. Quite a dramatic little scene seemed to be taking place within. Old Douglas and Mr Macbride appeared to be indulging in that kind of conversation in which one does not care to indulge in the presence of a lady.

When the Princess saw who had come in with me, she came dashing forward. She gave a little cry of joy.

"Oh, Jimmy!" She actually threw herself upon his breast in the presence of us all. "You dear, I'm so glad you've come. I'm tired to death of being the Princess Margaretta."

The little grocer seemed to be as happy as a king when he had her in his arms, as though he asked for nothing more.

Macbride declared that he had suspected something of the truth all through. But I doubt it. She had been "playing" at being the Princess Margaretta—to think of that minx's brazen impudence! Every one got back his own again. I even got back the contents of my purse. But when he was presented with the bill at the hotel that grocer must have stared.

To my mind Beachington has never been the same since the incident of the Princess Margaretta.

IX

THE END OF HIS HOLIDAY

I

"That's a fine girl!"

The lady thus tersely referred to by Mr Harry Davison was followed into the room by a gentleman who was as noticeable as herself. As they searched for a vacant seat they were attended by the glances of the breakfasters. Chance had it that they found an unoccupied table which was close to that at which Mr Davison was seated. Mr Lintorn finished his breakfast, eating it steadily through, while Mr Davison, eating nothing, stared at the lady. Having discussed the meal, Mr Lintorn, fitting his eyeglass into its place, eyed the new-comers.

"I thought so."

"Thought what?"

Mr Lintorn paused before replying. He rose from his chair. An odd smile was on his face.

"They're some people I knew in the Riviera."

With a little nod to his friend, he moved towards the new arrivals. Left alone, Mr Davison observed Mr Lintorn's proceedings with surprise. He thought he perceived that that gentleman was not received with too effusive a welcome. It pleased Mr Davison to perceive it. But Mr Lintorn seemed in no way discomposed. Breakfasters finished and rose and went, but he stayed on. Mr Davison stayed too. He got up at last and began to walk about the room, lingering once or twice in the vicinity of the little table. Still Mr Lintorn declined to take the hint. In the end he had the courage of despair.

"Er, excuse me, Lintorn: er—"

There he ceased. He was Nottinghamshire born and bred, a handsome, sunny-faced lad scarcely out of his teens, with the flush of health upon his cheeks; but assurance was not his strongest point. Scarcely had he opened his mouth than he was overwhelmed by the fear that he was making an ass of himself. He became a ruby. Then the young lady did an extraordinary thing; she helped him over the stile.

"Mr Lintorn," she spoke English with quite a charming accent, "will you not permit us to know your friend?"

It was said with such a pretty little air that the request was robbed of singularity. Mr Lintorn, to whom, indeed, the proposition seemed a little unexpected, acceded to the lady's wishes.

"M. de Fontanes, Mdlle. de Fontanes, permit me to introduce to you Mr Davison."

Mr Davison's awkwardness continued, although the lady was so gracious. Perhaps her exceeding graciousness only increased his sense of awkwardness; it is so with some of us when the grass is green. They left the hotel together, this quartet; together they even wandered on the sands. Behind, the old gentleman with Mr Lintorn; in front, mademoiselle with Mr Davison. Under these circumstances, despite his awkwardness, Mr Davison seemed to enjoy himself, for when they parted he turned to Mr Lintorn.

"Lintorn, she's a goddess!"

Mr Lintorn, through his eyeglass, surveyed his friend. Then he lit a cigarette. Then he pointed to a lady, who could boast of some sixteen stone of solid figure.

"Another goddess," he observed.

"That monstrosity!"

"Perhaps some people do prefer them lean."

"Lean? You call Mdlle. de Fontanes lean? Why, she's as graceful as a sylph!"

"I shouldn't be surprised. What is a sylph?"

"Did you see such eyes?"

"Yes; often."

"Where?"

"In other people's heads."

"Lintorn, you're a brute!"

On that they parted. They joined forces again at dinner. Afterwards they went to the Casino. There was a little ball that night. The place was crowded. M. de Fontanes and his daughter were there. Mdlle. de Fontanes behaved towards Mr Davison like an old-time friend. She danced with him, not once nor twice, but three times running; and, oddly enough, between the dances they lost her father. Looking for him occupied a considerable amount of time; and still they could not find him. At the end of the search the young lady was compelled to seat herself while Mr Davison procured her an ice. As he was engaged in doing so, someone touched him on the shoulder. It was Mr Lintorn.

"Take care," he said, his hand upon the other's arm.

"What do you mean?" asked Mr Davison. He was heated with pleasure and excitement. Mr Lintorn eyed him fixedly.

"Take care; you're spilling that ice."

The fact was correctly stated. Mr Davison was holding the plate in such a manner that the half-melted mass was dripping over the edge. Still it was scarcely necessary to stop him in order to tell him that; the more especially as it was the stoppage which was the cause of the ice being spilt.

Mr Davison saw Mdlle. de Fontanes home. Under the circumstances he could scarcely help it. When a lady is alone—we need not lay stress on such incidentals as youth and beauty—where is the man who would not proffer her his escort through the perils of the midnight streets? The night was fine, the breeze was warm; they lingered first in the gardens of the *établissement* to look upon the sea. Then they strolled gently through the Boulogne streets. They had told each other tales—unspoken tales—by the time they reached the Rue des Anges, but perhaps she understood his tale better than he did hers.

The lady paused. She addressed her cavalier,—

"This is our apartment. I am afraid my father will scold me."

"Scold you! Why?"

"You see, I am all he has, and so—I wait upon his pleasure. I am so seldom away from him that, when I am, even for a little time, he misses me. But will you not come in? Perhaps your presence may save me from my scolding."

Mr Davison was not in the mood, nor was he the man, to say "No" to such an invitation. He went in to save her from her scolding. They found the old gentleman in the *salon*, seated, in solitary state, in front of a table on which were a couple of packs of cards. His manner in greeting his daughter was more than a trifle acid.

"Well? You have come! It is good of you, upon my honour. I have not waited quite two hours—yet."

"I am so sorry."

She put her arms about his neck, her soft cheek against his rough one. He disengaged himself from her embrace.

"Permit me! I am not in the vein!"

"Father, you see that Mr Davison is here. Mr Davison, my father is justly angry with me. I have kept him waiting two hours for his *écarté*."

Mr Davison advanced to the old gentleman with outstretched hand.

"Let me pay forfeit in Mdlle. de Fontanes' stead: play with me."

The old gentleman touched the extended palm with the end of his frigid fingers. He looked the speaker up and down.

"Do you play *écarté?*"

"I ought to; I have played it my whole life long."

"Then," said the old man, with beautiful irony, "you should be a foeman worthy of my steel."

They sat down. But the young lady did not seem easy.

"Is it not too late to play to-night? I am already guilty of detaining Mr Davison."

Mr Davison repudiated the idea with scorn.

"Too late! Why, sometimes I sit up playing cards the whole night long."

"After that," murmured the old man softly, "what has one left to say?"

They played, if not all night, at least until the tints of dawn were brightening the sky. The stakes were trifling, but, even so, if one never wins, one may lose—in time. When Mr Davison rose to go he had lost all his ready money and seventeen pounds besides. This he was to bring to-morrow, when he was to have his revenge.

Mdlle. de Fontanes let him out. In the hall, before she opened the door, she spoke to him.

"I wish you would promise me not to play with my father again."

"Promise you! But why?"

"Do not be offended. You are a younger man. You do not play so well as he, my friend."

The "friend" came softly at the end. But Mr Davison chafed at the under-estimation of his powers.

"You think so because I have not won to-night. Let me tell you, for your satisfaction, that I was not afraid of meeting any man at the 'Varsity, and there are some first-rate players there."

The lady smiled.

"At the 'Varsity? I see." She opened the door. The dawn streamed in. "Good-night."

As Mr Davison strolled homewards he saw before him in the air, not a pack of cards, but a woman's eyes.

II

Mr Davison saw Mr Lintorn again at the eleven o'clock breakfast that morning.

"Find her father?" was Mr Lintorn's greeting to him as he took his seat.

"Find her father? Whose? Oh, Mdlle. de Fontanes'! No; I had to see her home."

"Hard lines!"

Mr Lintorn waited until the second course was served before he spoke again.

"It took you a long time to see her home?"

"I don't understand you."

"I sat up for you until nearly two, and you weren't in then."

"It was very good of you to sit up for me, I'm sure."

Mr Lintorn, adjusting his eyeglasses, looked his friend fixedly in the face.

"Davison, if you will allow me, on this occasion only, to play the part of mentor, you will have as little to do with the de Fontanes as you conveniently can.

"What the deuce do you mean?"

"Nothing; only a word to the wise—"

"Considering that they are not my friends, but yours—"

"Who said they were my friends?"

"You introduced me."

"I introduced you? The like of that!"

The pair sallied forth together to see the bathers. Who should they chance upon but M. and Mdlle. de Fontanes. Mademoiselle had bathed. She looked radiant. Unlike the average woman, who finds the ordeal of emerging from the sea a trying one, the sea had but enhanced her charms. They were quite a family party. M. de Fontanes even unbent so far as to express a hope that the two Englishmen would dine with them that same evening. They were but in a temporary apartment; he could not promise them much, but they should have something to eat. Mr Davison accepted with effusion. Mr Lintorn, a little to his friend's surprise, after what had passed between them, accepted too.

Mr Davison spent the rest of the day in looking forward to his dinner. It was to be at seven. As a matter of course, he was dressed at six. Yet, owing to Mr Lintorn, it was half-past seven before they reached the Rue des Anges. Mr Davison was perspiring with rage. Mdlle. de Fontanes received them. Her father was standing, looking black, behind. Mr Lintorn was the first to enter the room.

"I pray your pardon, but Mr Davison has not yet reached an age at which punctuality at dinner is esteemed a virtue."

The thing was gratuitous.

"I assure you, Mdlle. de Fontanes—" burst out Mr Davison.

The young lady cut him short.

"I forgive you," she said. "It is so nice to be young."

During dinner Mr Davison scarcely spoke a word. His feelings were too strong for speech—at least, at such a gathering. The young lady, observing his silence, commented on it in what seemed almost a spirit of gratuitous malice.

"I am afraid, Mr Davison, we do not please you."

"Mdlle. de Fontanes!"

"Or perhaps you are not so eloquent as Mr Lintorn—ever?"

"No, never."

Mdlle. de Fontanes spoke so hesitatingly, and in such low tones, that only Mr Davison caught the words she uttered next.

"Perhaps—there is a certain manner—which—only comes with age."

"You seem to think that I am nothing but a boy. I will prove to you that at least in some things I am a man."

She looked up at him and smiled. His cheeks were flushed, his eyes were bright. To make up, perhaps, for his lack of conversation, he had been drinking all the time. When they re-entered the *salon* the card-table was arranged for play. Mr Davison went up to it at once.

"M. de Fontanes, I hope for my revenge."

Mdlle. de Fontanes went to his side and whispered him,—

"I asked you!"

"But I had promised. Besides, I wish to show you that *écarté* is one of the things in which you underrate my age."

M. de Fontanes sat down. There was a curious look upon his face.

"Mr Lintorn, you and I are old antagonists. Who was it used to win?"

"Invariably you."

"Ah, then it is your turn now!"

"Perhaps."

They played gallery. In spite of his prediction, fortune, as a rule, was with their host. The stakes were trifling, his losses small, yet it was curious to see the irritation with which Mr Lintorn saw his francs forsake him. He was playing with M. de Fontanes. The old gentleman scored the king. Suddenly Mr Lintorn, throwing his cards on the table, rose to his feet.

"It is enough!" he said.

His opponent looked up in not unnatural surprise.

"How?"

"You have won, and you will win certainly." He turned to the lady. "Mdlle. de Fontanes, you must excuse me. I have letters to write."

Without another word he left the room. A pause of blank amazement followed his disappearance. M. de Fontanes sat like a figure carved in stone.

"Is Mr Lintorn ill?" his daughter asked.

Mr Davison took upon himself to answer.

"He must be, or else mad. I believe he always is half-mad. But never mind! I'm glad he's gone. Now, M. de Fontanes, you have to reckon with me. For revenge! Your daughter doubts if I can play *écarté*. I will show her that her doubts are vain."

He drank two glasses of Maraschino, one after the other, emptying each at a draught. Placing the liqueur case beside him on the table, he sat down again to play. And they played on, and on, and on, hour after hour. Mr Davison continually lost. Fortune never varied; it was against him all the time. As his losses increased, he insisted on increasing the stakes. At last they were playing for really considerable sums.

"Fortune must turn!" he cried. "I never saw such cards in all my life! And, when it turns, I want to have a chance, you know."

So he persisted in raising the stakes still higher. And he drank! He emptied the flask of Maraschino, and began upon the Kummel, and would have emptied that if his host's daughter had not, probably in a moment of abstraction, removed the case of liqueurs from the table. He was in the highest spirits, and lost as though losing were a pleasure. And mademoiselle leant over his shoulder and whispered in his ear.

But at last her father declared that play must cease.

"You have had bad fortune," he observed.

"Extraordinary!" exclaimed Mr Davison; his utterance was a little thick. "Extraordinary! Never had such bad fortune in my life before. It isn't fair to judge of a man's form from the play tonight? What do I owe you? A heap, I know."

"A trifle," M. de Fontanes looked through his tablets. "Three thousand seven hundred and fifty francs."

"Three thousand seven hundred and fifty francs! Why, that's a—that's a hundred and fifty pounds! Great snakes!"

The magnitude of the sum almost sobered him. M. de Fontanes smiled.

"You must try again for your revenge."

As before, the lady escorted the guest downstairs, "assisted" him would, on the present occasion, perhaps, have been the better word. The touch of her hand at parting increased his sense of intoxication. The cool air of the early morning did not tend to lessen it. He went staggering over the cobblestones. On the quay he encountered a solitary figure—the figure of a man who was strolling up and down and smoking a cigar. Mr Davison, with a burst of tipsy surprise, perceived that it was Mr Lintorn.

"Lintorn! I thought you were writing your letters."

Mr Lintorn quietly surveyed him.

"Did you? How much have you lost?"

"How do you know I've lost?"

"Why?" Mr Lintorn shrugged his shoulders. "The man happens to be a cheat."

"Don't—don't you say that again!"

"Why not? You would have seen it yourself if you had had your wits about you. He was cheating all the time."

"You—!"

Mr Davison struck at his friend. Mr Lintorn warded off the blow. Mr Davison struck again. The man was drunk and bent upon a row. It was impossible to avoid him without actually turning tail and fleeing. So Mr Lintorn let him have it. Mr Davison lay on his back among the cobble-stones. Mr Lintorn advanced to his assistance. The recumbent hero greeted him with a volley of abuse. Seeing that to persist would only be to bring about a renewal of hostilities, Mr Lintorn strolled off to the hotel alone, leaving Mr Davison to follow at his leisure.

III

The next morning Mr Davison did not put in an appearance at breakfast. So Mr Lintorn went to look for him in his room. He knocked at the door.

"Who's there?" growled a voice within.

"Lintorn. May I come in?"

Without waiting for the required permission he entered. The hero was still in bed. There was that look about him which is noticeable in the ordinarily sober youth who has enjoyed the night before not wisely, but too well. And his eye—outside the actual organ—was a beautiful black. Mr Lintorn started at sight of these signs of mourning.

"Davison, I had no idea—"

"You had no idea of what, sir? What do you mean by entering my room?"

"I cannot express to you how ashamed of myself I feel. I—I had no idea that I had hit so hard."

Mr Lintorn felt—too late—that this was one of those delicate subjects which are best avoided. But the words were spoken.

"Look here, Mr Lintorn: I chanced to stay in the same hotel with you at

Nice, and it has suited me since, as a traveller, to adapt my movements to yours. Beyond that, you are a perfect stranger to me. You are, at best, but a chance acquaintance. Be so good as to consider that acquaintance dropped."

Mr Davison spoke, or intended to speak, with the dignity and the hauteur which are appropriate to the travelling man of fashion, who has spent six weeks abroad. But such a character is difficult to maintain when one has "hot coppers" and a black eye, and is lying in bed. None the less Mr Lintorn perceived that the present was not a favourable moment for argument. He fixed his glass in his eye, gave Mr Davison just one look, bowed, and left him to his dignity.

Mr Davison rang for his shaving-water, and the waiter who brought it was so indiscreet as to notice the gentleman's condition—the condition, that is, of what has been called his optic.

"Mais, monsieur est blessé!"

Mr Davison's knowledge of French was not peculiar for its extent, but it was sufficient to render him aware that the man exaggerated the actual fact.

"Get out!" he shouted.

The man got out, having learned, it is to be hoped, a lesson in tact. When Mr Davison began to shave he found that his hand was shaky. His temper was ruffled, his head ached most dreadfully. The looking-glass revealed with terrible distinctness the state of his eye; it was really not surprising that the waiter had found it impossible to avoid making his little observation. In shaving—not, by the way, in his case an absolutely indispensable operation— he cut a gash about an inch and a half in length on the most prominent part of his chin. This, ornamented with a strip of yellow sticking-plaster, did not, so to speak, harmonise with the rest of his appearance. It did not harmonise with his temper, either; he was in a mood to cut the throat of the first man he met.

When he had completed his toilet he sat down and penned the following note:—

"Mr Davison presents his compliments to M. de Fontanes. He encloses notes to the value of three thousand seven hundred and fifty francs—the amount of his overnight losses at *écarté*. As such a sum is larger than Mr Davison cares to lose, he would be obliged by M. de Fontanes giving him his revenge at the earliest possible moment—say this evening at eight o'clock."

Mr Davison felt this was a communication which any man might be proud of having written; that it conveyed the impression that he was not a lad to be trifled with, and that it would give M. de Fontanes and his daughter to understand that, sooner or later, he would be quits, and more. Before enclosing the notes it was necessary to have the notes to enclose. That involved sallying forth to get them. So he sallied forth, patched chin, black eye, and all, to the banking-house of MM. Adam et Cie. Those gentlemen were so good as to honour his cheque to the extent he required—not, however, without commiserating him both on the state of his chin and the state of his eye. Having received his notes, he sent his letter. Then he returned to the hotel to wait for a reply. It came.

"MON BRAVE.—Ce soir, à huit heures, chez moi. Mille remercîments.

"DE FONTANES."

Although M. de Fontanes spoke such fluent English, it appeared that he preferred to trust to his own language when it came to pen and paper.

On the stroke of eight Mr Davison made his appearance in the Rue des Anges. His entry made a small sensation. Mdlle. de Fontanes, advancing to meet him, stopped short with a little cry.

"Mr Davison! Oh, what is the matter! Are—are you ill?"

Mr Davison turned the colour of a boiled beetroot.

"I do not understand you," he said.

The father's tact was finer than the daughter's.

"On the stroke of the hour!" he murmured, extending his hand to greet his guest, as though guests with patched chins and black eyes were everyday occurrences.

They sat down to play. Before they commenced Mr Davison delivered himself of a few remarks.

"You must understand, M. de Fontanes, that I have lost more than I quite care to lose. Therefore, I cannot afford to play for trifling stakes. I suggest with your permission, that we commence with five-pound points."

"Five-pound points!" cried mademoiselle. Her distress seemed genuine.

"I said five-pound points."

Mr Davison's manner towards the daughter of the house was scarcely courteous. Perhaps he resented the surprise she had shown at his appearance.

"Five pounds—or fifty."

M. de Fontanes smiled at the board as he murmured this liberal agreement with his guest's suggestion.

It was not the drink that night, but the cards! The younger player never touched a king. Never had a man such luck before. In so short a space of time as to make the whole affair seem like a conjuring trick, his debt to M. de Fontanes had entered its second century. He appeared to grow bewildered, as, indeed, in the face of such a run of luck an older player might easily have done. He got into such a state that he would have been unable to play the cards even if he had had them, and he never had them.

"This—this is awful!" he groaned. "At this rate I shall be able to do nothing even if luck turns. What do you say to doubling the stakes?"

Mdlle. de Fontanes was reclining in an easy-chair, ostensibly reading a book; in reality following the game. She sprang to her feet.

"I forbid it!" she cried. "Father, I forbid it!"

"Do not disturb yourself, my child. I am in all things moderate. The stakes are high enough—for me."

Mr Davison's losses increased. He never scored a trick. He was making a record in bad luck. His lips were parched, his hands trembling.

"That makes three hundred pounds," said M. de Fontanes, reading his tablets.

"Three hundred pounds!" repeated the young man, a little hoarsely, perhaps.

"It shall not be!"

The interruption came from Mdlle. de Fontanes. She advanced to the table. She laid her hand upon the pack of cards which Mr Davison was about to deal. Her father looked up at her interrogatively.

"I say it shall not be. I will not have it, father. Mr Davison, you owe my father nothing; he cheats you all the time."

M. de Fontanes rose. His tall figure seemed to tower to an unusual height.

"I care not. I tell you, Mr Davison, you owe my father nothing—not a sou —! He cheats you all the time!"

Mr Davison staggered to his feet, his eyes opened, as it were, by a sudden flash of lightning. He threw the pack of cards, which he was holding, into the old man's face.

There was silence. Then the old man's lips moved.

"To-morrow," he muttered, so that the words were scarcely audible, and left the room.

When he was gone, the lady addressed the gentleman:

"You, too, had better go."

Mr Davison went. Mdlle. de Fontanes was left alone. She did not escort him down the stairs. And this time, as he walked through the night to his hotel, it was not a woman's eyes, but a pack of cards which he saw before him in the air.

IV

The next morning—another morning!—at a very early hour, Mr Davison entered Mr Lintorn's bedroom. The latter gentleman was still engaged in his toilet.

"Lintorn, I am an ass!"

"The fact," said Mr Lintorn placidly, and as though there had been no unpleasantness of any kind between them, "does not surprise me so much as the statement of the fact."

"I've behaved like an ass to you."

"You have."

Mr Lintorn wiped the soap off his razor; he had a steadier hand than Mr Davison.

"I've behaved like an ass all round."

"I can believe it easily. Indeed, you are, in general, an ass. You're a nice fellow, but you are an ass. You'll grow out of it in time, but you'll have to do a deal of growing first." Mr Lintorn glanced at his friend, who was pacing round the room. "How's your eye?"

"Oh, hang my eye! Lintorn, how much do you think I've lost within the last three nights? Five hundred pounds!"

Mr Lintorn whistled.

"How pleasant it is to be rich and young."

"But I'm not rich. With the exception of five thousand pounds left me by my aunt to help me along while I'm reading for the bar, I've scarcely a penny in the world."

"Davison, you don't mean that?"

"I do mean it. And the worst of it is, it's not been fairly lost. That old rogue's been rooking me all through."

"Oh, you've discovered that, have you? After trying to murder me for warning you."

Then Mr Davison told his tale. How Mdlle. de Fontanes had interrupted the game, and exposed her father's pernicious practices. Mr Lintorn expressed much admiration of the lady's conduct.

"She looked like a goddess then, if you like. I should like to have seen her."

"She did look like a goddess; but I don't know that you would have liked to have seen her. She made me feel uncommonly small, I do know that."

"That's of course! but that's so easy."

While Mr Davison was thinking of a retort with which to crush his friend —for even a worm will turn—there came a tap at the door. A waiter entered.

"A lady to see M. Davison."

"A lady! To see me! What's her name?"

"She does not give her name. It is a young lady—a pretty young lady." It was the waiter who had found it impossible to avoid commenting on Mr Davison's appearance. It was plain he had not learnt his lesson yet. "She attends in the *salon*."

The waiter disappeared.

"Bet you a guinea," cried Mr Lintorn, "that it's Mdlle. de Fontanes. Davison, I've almost finished shaving; I'll take this business off your hands if you like."

"Thanks; I'm much obliged. This time I will not trouble you."

It was Mdlle. de Fontanes. When Mr Davison appeared she was standing in the centre of the room. A thick black veil was before her face. That waiter must have had keen eyes to detect the prettiness beneath it. A little packet was in her hand. Opening it, she turned out its contents on the table. There was a little heap of notes and gold.

"That is the money which my father has won from you."

This was her greeting as the young gentleman entered the room.

"Mdlle. de Fontanes!"

There was a pause. Mr Davison looked from the lady to the money, and from the money to the lady. With a little movement she lifted her veil.

He saw her face; it was pale, with the look upon it which follows a sleepless night.

"Did you think that we would keep it?" She put out her hand and touched his sleeve. "Did you think so badly of us, then, as that?"

He thought that he had never seen her look so pretty. There was something in her voice which caused "a choking in his throat.

"But I cannot take the money. Especially—if you will forgive me, Mdlle. de Fontanes—especially from you."

She sat down. For a moment she covered her face with her hands. Suddenly she rose.

"Do not make my burden heavier than it is already. Mr Davison, my father cannot help but cheat. It is a disease. In the common things of life he is the most honourable of men—the best of fathers. But with the cards, night after night, since he must play, I play with him, and he cheats me."

She fell on her knees by the side of the table. Burying her face in her hands, she cried as though her heart would break. Mr Davison could only whisper—

"Mdlle. de Fontanes."

She looked up at him.

"Say you forgive me," she cried.

"Forgive you! I! What have I to forgive?"

"For taking you home that night; for letting you know my father; for letting you know me."

Mr Davison fumbled with a compliment.

"That—that is an honour for which I—I ought to thank you."

She rose. She regarded him intently, the tears still stealing from her eyes. Never had he felt so uncomfortable before a woman's gaze. It seemed to him that he was passing through all the colour phases of the rainbow.

"So you forgive me, truly?"

"If—if there is forgiveness needed."

"If you forgive me"—she came close to him, he felt her hand steal into his —"kiss me, Harry."

He kissed her as though she were a red-hot coal. Never did a travelled young man of the world so kiss a pretty woman yet! And when he had kissed her there was silence. Then, slipping her hand into the bosom of her dress, she drew out a locket, to which was attached a narrow black ribbon.

"Keep this in memory of a chance acquaintance. Look at it sometimes, and, in looking, think of me. And, in thinking of me, do not think of me as one who plundered you, but as one who—"

She paused. She looked down. But he was the most awkward of men. When she looked up again her face was fiery red. She drew herself away from him, and when she spoke her tone was changed.

"So, Mr Davison, you quite perceive that you owe my father nothing. You two are quits. But there is one thing you must promise me—you will not fight him."

"I do not understand."

"Oh, it is simple. He will challenge you. After what passed last night he is sure to challenge you. But, however that may be, you must say 'No.'"

"If you wish me to, I promise. But in England we don't fight duels."

"No? Not even at the 'Varsity?"

She nodded to him and smiled. And in a moment she was gone. Mr Davison found Mr Lintorn still engaged in putting the finishing touches to his costume. The expression of his countenance was a vivid note of interrogation.

"Well, was it she?"

Mr Davison said "Yes."

"I should have won that guinea."

Mr Davison narrated the interview. When he had finished, Mr Lintorn reflected.

"Odd! Something of the same sort happened to me. It was at Mentone I first encountered the de Fontanes. On two or three evenings I played *écarté*. I lost; but not five hundred pounds. Two or three days afterwards the sum which I had lost came to me enclosed in an envelope. Not a scrap of writing was with it, but the address was in a feminine hand; I always suspected it came from the lady. When I again inquired for the de Fontanes they were gone. But my curiosity was piqued. I did not forget them. So I renewed the acquaintance when I saw them here."

"If he challenges me, what shall I do? I promised not to fight him. Besides, the thing would be a rank absurdity."

"Stand to your promise. I tell you what to do. There's a boat leaves for Folkestone in an hour. Let's go by it together."

"But wouldn't that look like running away?"

"It would be running away."

Mr Davison did not quite like this way of putting it, but he went. They travelled together. On the boat Mr Davison remembered the locket. He opened it. It contained a portrait of the giver. As he eyed it, he observed in that curious vernacular which is an attribute of some examples of modern youth,—

"By Jingo! aren't those French girls goers?"

But Mr Lintorn was an older man. His range was wider.

"Don't judge of a nation by an individual. Mdlle. de Fontanes is unique; the product, I should say, of a very singular experience."

Actually, Mr Davison kissed the portrait.

"I will always keep it," he said.

X

THE GIRL AND THE BOY

I

Archie Ferguson's smoking-room. He and I its only occupants. We had been to a meeting of the Primrose League which had been held at the neighbouring county town. Knocking off the ash from his cigar, he broke an interval of silence by asking me a question.

"Did you notice a woman who, just as we were leaving the hall, came up and shook hands with me in rather an effusive way?"

"A good-looking, well-dressed woman, with rather an effusive smile? I wondered who she was."

"She's a Mrs Bennett-Lamb. The weight-carrying man who was standing at her side was Mr Bennett-Lamb. Perhaps you know the name. She and her husband have been the owners of a good deal of the public-house property in London which is worth owning. They're the proud possessors of some of it still. They've made a heap of money. Some of it they've spent in buying a place near here—Oakdene. It's on the cards that their daughter—they've only one, and she's an uncommonly pretty girl—will make a first-rate match. In which case, no doubt, they'll try to graduate for county honours."

He flicked off another scrap of ash before he spoke again.

"It was Mrs Bennett-Lamb who found the money with which to start the firm. The way in which she found it was curious. It's a queer story. I'll tell it you, if you like. It's a rather good one."

I lit another cigar; and smoked it while Ferguson told his story.

*　　*　　*　　*　　*

At that time Mrs Bennett-Lamb was a chorus girl at the Frivolity Theatre. In those days only pretty girls were allowed to appear on the Frivolity stage. The management's standard of beauty was a high one. It drew all London. And the prettiest of the whole crowd was Ailsa Lorraine. Whether Ailsa Lorraine was or was not her real name I am unable to tell you; I have reason to know that nowadays her husband calls her Peggy; but that was the name by which she was known on the programme. Miss Lorraine was engaged to be married—to Joe Lamb. Where the "Bennett" comes from Mr and Mrs Bennett-Lamb only know. It is certain that then the present J. Bennett-Lamb, Esquire, was plain Joe Lamb. Not to put too fine a point upon it, Joe Lamb was a grocer's assistant—and not a flourishing specimen of his kind. In fact, the more he considered his position and future prospects the more despondent he became.

One Sunday afternoon he went to tea at Miss Lorraine's. While they were enjoying the meal he gave utterance to the feelings which filled his bosom.

"We've been engaged for more than two years," he began.

"Two years!" the tone in which she echoed his words were intended to indicate surprise. "It doesn't seem anything like so long as that, does it, Joe?"

"It does to me. It seems every bit as long. In fact, I don't mind telling you that it seems longer."

Neither the words nor the manner in which they were spoken suggested a compliment, as the lady appeared to think. There was a rueful look upon her pretty face and a mist dimmed her eyes as she asked him a question in return.

"Does that mean that it has seemed so long because you're tired of being engaged to me?"

"It does; that's just exactly what it does mean."

"Joe!"

"Now don't jump up like that! You nearly upset the tray, and I've hardly touched my third cup of tea. What are you up to? Crying?"

"I'm sure, Mr Lamb, if you wish to release me you're perfectly at liberty to do so at once; and you need never see nor speak to me again. There's no fear of my bringing an action against you for breach of promise of marriage."

"Whatever are you talking about?"

"I'm sure if you'd even dropped so much as the slightest hint you'd have seen the last of me long enough ago; and I certainly wouldn't have worried you to come to tea."

"What have I said or done to start you off like this?—just as I was beginning on a fresh round of toast!"

"How dare you say you were tired of being engaged to me!"

"So I am."

"Joe—Joe Lamb!"

"It's gospel truth. I want you for my wife; that's what I want."

The lady's face perceptibly brightened. The tone of her voice was altered also.

"Joe! What extraordinary ways you have of expressing yourself. Will you kindly explain exactly what it is you mean?"

"I've been engaged to you more than two years, and you're no nearer being my wife than you were at the beginning. If anything, you're further off. And I'm sick and tired of waiting; that's what I mean."

"If you'd only said so at first."

"I did; didn't I?"

"I thought you meant something quite different."

"I can't help what you thought. I know what I meant."

"Poor Joe! So you want us to be quick and get married, do you?"

"Of course I do; what else do you suppose I got engaged for? But we can't marry on ten bob a week."

"Hardly."

"And that's all I get, living in. I asked the governor yesterday to give me thirty bob and let me live out. He said all he'd give me was a week's notice."

"The wretch!"

"As for bettering myself; I dare say I've spent five shillings on paper, stamps and envelopes, and nothing's come of it. We don't want to get married and have you keep on the stage."

"We certainly don't. I have a voice in that matter. When I marry I leave the stage for good; I don't marry until I do. I hate the theatre; that is, I don't mind being in front of the curtain, looking on; but I hate being behind. I only go there because I don't know any other way of earning two pounds a week. I've no delusions about the stage like some of the girls have. But, tell me, Joe, can't you think of any way of earning more?"

"There's one way."

"What's that?"

"Emigrating."

As she repeated the word again the expression on the lady's face grew rueful.

"Emigrating!"

"Going to Africa or Canada or one of those places where a fellow has a chance."

"But you'd have to leave me behind."

"That's the worst of it."

"We mightn't see each other again for years."

"We mightn't."

There was a pause. The lady had seated herself on the arm of the chair on which her lover sat, and was smoothing his hair with her dainty little hand.

"Joe, would you like to do that?"

"I'd sooner do anything—anything! I'd sooner sweep a crossing; I'd sooner be a shoeblack. I hear that some of them shoeblacks earn six and seven shillings a day when there's plenty of mud about."

"I don't think I should care for you to be a shoeblack, even when there's plenty of mud about. I'd almost rather you did anything than that."

"But there's nothing I can do."

Another pause; this time a longer one. Joe Lamb sat with his hands thrust deeply into the pockets of his Sunday trousers; a frown upon his brow. The lady continued to smooth his well-brushed hair.

"Joe, suppose I were to see my way to earn some money."

"You! Are they going to raise you to fifty shillings, and give you a line to speak: 'The carriage waits,' or something of that sort?"

She suffered his ungraciousness to pass unheeded.

"Suppose I were to see my way to earn, say, five thousand pounds."

Mr Lamb, withdrawing his head from the neighbourhood of the lady's caressing hand, sat bolt upright in his chair with a start.

"Five—what?"

"I know a public-house which is to be bought cheap, if bought at once. Never mind how I know, but I do. We could get it for five thousand pounds and have plenty over to go on with. You and I might work the business up and in two years sell it for twice as much as we gave for it. Joe, what do you think?"

"I think—it's no use my telling you what I think, because you wouldn't like it. You might as well talk about buying the moon."

"I'm not so sure of that. I believe I could earn the money if I liked."

"You earn five thousand pounds! Well! I don't want to say anything—not a word; but might I just ask how you propose to set about it?"

"By bringing an action for breach of promise of marriage."

"What!"

"I shouldn't be surprised if I got at least five thousand pounds by way of damages."

Joe Lamb, who had risen from his seat, was staring at her with, on his countenance, an expression of increasing stupefaction.

"From whom?—from me?"

"The idea!" She laughed, as if the notion tickled her. "In the first place, I shouldn't dream of suing you, even if you were to prove false; and you know very well that you're not worth half as many farthings if I did. No; I propose to obtain my five thousand pounds from Sir Frank Pickard."

"Who's Sir Frank Pickard?"

"He's a young gentleman—a very young gentleman, just turned twenty-one, who's fallen head over heels in love with me."

The lady was looking down at her skirt, as she smoothed it with the tips of her fingers, with an air of the most extreme demureness. Mr Lamb's face, as he regarded her, was rapidly assuming the hue of a boiled lobster.

"So you've been encouraging him, have you?"

"I have been doing nothing of the kind. So far, I haven't spoken to him a single word. I've declined to receive his presents—even his flowers."

"So he's been sending you presents, has he!—and flowers."

The lady sighed, as if she found the gentleman a little trying.

"My dear Joe, all sorts of people fall in love with me to whom I have never spoken in my life, or they say they do. They send me flowers and presents, and all kinds of things, which I always refuse to accept, although some of the other girls call me a goose for my pains. I can't help their falling in love with me, can I?"

She looked up at him with an air of innocence which was almost too perfect to be real. So far from it appeasing him, he began stamping up and down the room, clenching and unclenching his fists as he moved.

"A nice sort of thing for a man to be told by his young woman! You shall leave that confounded theatre this week!"

"To do so is part of my plan. I shall hand in my notice to-morrow—that is, if I am engaged to Sir Frank Pickard by then."

"What?"

"Joe! don't be silly! Why are you glaring at me like that? Won't you understand? Already, in three separate and distinct letters Sir Frank has asked me to marry him."

"Has he?"

"Though, of course, I've paid no sort of attention to his insane request."

"I should think it was insane!"

"I don't fancy I use the word in quite the same sense in which you do. However, I've been making inquiries about him. I find he's of a very old family, and tremendously rich. His father is dead. He's the only child of his mother; she can't prevent his doing anything he chooses to do, and she wouldn't if she could. She idolises him. During his minority the income has accumulated, until now he has at his command a perfectly enormous sum of ready money. Five thousand pounds is nothing to him, or ten either. My idea is to ask him to call on me to-morrow, and then to get him to repeat in person the proposal which he has already made by letter. Having accepted him, I shall see that he puts it all down in black and white, so that everything is quite ship-shape. And then I shall hand in my notice at the theatre."

During the lady's remarks Mr Lamb's countenance was a panorama of disagreeable emotions.

"And where do you suppose I shall be while all this is going on?"

"You'll be at the shop."

"Not much I sha'n't. I'll keep on hanging about your front door until I catch sight of your fine gentleman; and then I'll break his neck."

"Don't be silly. After we're engaged and everything is signed and sealed and settled I shall begin to behave in a fashion which will soon make him as anxious to break his promise as he was to make it."

"I bet he will! You wait till I get within reach of him, that's all."

"You will not appear upon the scene. You would spoil all if you did. I shall manage everything."

"I fancy I see myself letting you do it! You've got some pretty ideas of

142

your own!"

"You'll find by the time I've finished that I've some very pretty ones indeed. You don't know what a treasure you possess. When Sir Frank begins to show signs of wanting to back out of his promise I shall begin to talk about my injured feelings; to which, however, he'll find it possible to apply a soothing plaster in the shape of—well, say five thousand pounds."

"You're a nice piece of goods, upon my word! I ask you again where do you suppose I shall be while all this is going on?"

"And I tell you again, you'll be at the shop. You open so early and close so late, and get out so little on week-days, that you never get a chance of seeing me even after I leave the theatre. Possibly by next Sunday, when we shall have a chance of seeing each other again, it will all be settled."

"By next Sunday?"

"Exactly. I mean to keep things moving. Possibly by next Sunday I shall be within reach of the money which will enable us to marry and ensure our future happiness. Think how delightful that will be! We can't marry on ten shillings a week; after we're married I don't mean to stay on at the theatre, and so keep up a home for us both; and as for your emigrating—the chances are that we might never see each other again. And, anyhow, it might be years before you earned even a tenth part of five thousand pounds. So do be reasonable. I'm sure if you think it over you'll see perfectly well that my way is by far the best."

It was some time before Mr Lamb was reasonable—from the lady's point of view. It is doubtful if to the end he saw as plainly as she would have liked him to, that her way was the best. But at that period of her career she had a way about her to which few men were capable of offering a prolonged resistance. Joe Lamb was distinctly not one of those few. By the time they parted she wrung from him what she told him plainly she intended to regard as his approbation of her nefarious schemes. So soon as his back was turned she wrote a stiff, formal note, in the third person, in which she informed Sir Frank Pickard that Miss Ailsa Lorraine would be at home to-morrow—Monday—afternoon at three o'clock and might be disposed to see him if he desired to call.

"It's not exactly a nice sort of thing to do," she admitted to herself, as she secured this epistle in an envelope. "But it's the sort of opportunity which never may occur again; it seems wicked to throw it away. Especially as poor dear Joe never will be able to get the money by himself. I am convinced that he's just the sort of man to take advantage of a chance if he has one. And I love him well enough to get him one. And that's the whole truth in a nutshell."

II

On the Monday afternoon a hansom drew up at the door of the by no means pretentious house in which Miss Lorraine had her quarters. Out of it stepped Sir Frank Pickard. He bore with him upstairs what seemed to be a by no means insignificant portion of the contents of a fair-sized shop. In one hand he carried a magnificent bouquet, a large basket of splendid fruit, a big box of bonbons and a mysterious case which, as a matter of fact, was filled with various kinds of gloves. In the other were unconsidered trifles in the shape of bottles of perfume, silver knickknacks, a writing case, and other odds and ends. His arms were filled with parcels of different shapes and sizes which contained he alone knew what. Under the circumstances it was not surprising that he found it a little difficult to know what to do with his hat. As he entered Miss Lorraine's sitting-room he was in a state of some confusion. Plumping the contents of one of his arms on the nearest chair, whence they mostly proceeded to tumble on to the floor, he removed his hat in a fashion which was rather dexterous than elegant. As if conscious that he was not making his first appearance under the most propitious conditions, his cheeks were a beautiful peony red.

Miss Lorraine had risen to receive him. She had on her best frock—a frock which she specially reserved for high-days and holidays. Although she had made it herself, it could not have become—or fitted—her better had it been the creation of one of the world's great dressmakers. At least, such was the instant and unhesitating opinion of Sir Frank Pickard. He felt that he had never seen a more perfect example of feminine beauty—of all that was desirable in woman; he was convinced that he never should. He was trembling from head to foot; as some boys still do tremble when, for the first time in their lives, they are head over heels in love. Miss Lorraine, on the other hand, was both cool and calm—an accident which enabled her to perceive that her visitor was very much the reverse. She looked him up and down, inclining to the opinion, as the result of her inspection, that he was not an ill-looking boy. He was fairly tall, broad-shouldered, carried himself well, and looked a gentleman. She told herself that, had her affections not been pre-engaged, it was extremely possible that she might have regarded him in quite a different kind of way. But her heart really was Joe Lamb's; and she never for a moment contemplated the feasibility of transferring it to anybody else.

The lady was the first to speak.

"You are Sir Frank Pickard?"

The visitor had been afforded an opportunity to disencumber himself of his parcels, and therefore ought to have become more at his ease. But the simple truth was that the sight of the lady embarrassed him more than the parcels had done. His heart was thumping against his ribs; he seemed to be giving way at the knees; his tongue clave to the roof of his mouth. However, he managed to stammer out something; though it was only with difficulty that he could articulate at all.

"It's awfully good of you to let me come and see you."

The lady smiled—a smile which might have been described as of the glacial kind.

"Will you sit down, Sir Frank?"

He sat down, on the extreme edge of a chair, as if fearful of occupying too much of it at once. He looked—and no doubt was—excessively uncomfortable. Placing herself in the only arm-chair the room contained, she observed him with an air which was at once both cruel and condescending.

"You have written me one or two notes, Sir Frank?"

He stammered worse than ever. Not only did he find the question an awkward one, but it seemed to him that the lady was even more bewitching in the arm-chair than she had been when standing up. As he realised—or thought he realised—her charms still more clearly, his few remaining senses were rapidly deserting him.

"I—I'm afraid I did."

"In which you asked me, a perfect stranger, to be your wife?"

"I—I'm awfully sorry."

"You are sorry? Indeed. Do you mean that you are sorry you asked me to be your wife?"

He gasped. There was something in her tone, something in the way in which she peeped at him from under the long lashes which shaded her violet eyes, something in her attitude, in the quality of the smile which parted her pretty lips, which set every fibre in his body palpitating. What did she mean? What could she mean? Was it possible that she meant—what he had scarcely dared to hope she ever would mean?

In his stuttering eagerness his words tumbled headforemost over each other.

"Of course what I meant was that I know perfectly well that I never ought to have written to you like that. It was frightful cheek, and—and the sort of thing I ought to be kicked for. But as for being sorry that I asked you to be my wife—!" The boy's feelings were so intense that for the moment his breath entirely failed him. When he continued, tears were actually standing in his eyes. "Oh, Miss Lorraine, if you only knew what I have felt since I first saw you. I have been to the theatre every night; I have waited at the stage door to see you come out—"

"So I understand. It was very wrong of you."

"I had to do something—I couldn't help it. I didn't know anyone who'd introduce me; you wouldn't answer my letters; you refused my presents—"

"Certainly; under the circumstances they were so many insults."

"I didn't mean them for insults—I swear I didn't. I wouldn't have insulted you, or allowed anyone else to insult you, not—not for all the gold of the Indies."

"Sir Frank, the question I put to you was, are you sorry that you asked me to be your wife? That is, did you really wish me to be your wife, and do you wish it still?"

"Wish it! I'd give all I have if you'd be my wife; you'd make me the happiest fellow in the world!"

"If you truly mean that—"

"Put me to the test and see if I mean it!—say yes!"

"I do believe that you mean it; so I will say yes. One moment, Sir Frank!" Rising from his chair the young gentleman showed symptoms of a desire to express his feelings in a style which the lady might have found slightly inconvenient. "A girl in my position cannot be too careful. If you care for me as you say, you will see that even better than I do." That was rather a bold stroke of Miss Lorraine's, and a clever one. For it made an irresistible appeal to the boy's quixotic nature. "Remember, you and I are still almost strangers. Nevertheless, you have asked me to be your wife; and I have consented. Will you write a few lines, setting forth the exact position of affairs, on this sheet of paper?"

She pointed to paper, pens and ink, which were on the centre table. The youngster did hesitate. There was a matter-of-fact air about the fashion in which the lady made her suggestion which, even to his eyes, rather blurred the romance of the situation. But his hesitation did not endure. He was like wax in her hands. Presently he sat down and wrote on a sheet of paper the words which—without his being altogether conscious of the fact—she had put at the point of his pen.

"You understand, Sir Frank," she remarked, as she folded up what, from her point of view, was an invaluable document, and slipped it in the bodice of her dress, "this engagement of ours must be no hole-and-corner affair. You must not conceal it from your mother!"

"Of course not. I never have concealed anything from her in my life, and I certainly don't mean to start concealing from her that I'm engaged to be married."

"You must introduce me to her."

"Rather! I shall be only too delighted, if you'll let me. She already has some idea of how it is with me. I wrote to her that I'd fallen head over heels in love. She always has said that she'd like me to marry young; when she hears that I'm to be married right away she'll be delighted."

Miss Lorraine was not so sure. But she did not say so. She was becoming momentarily more convinced that this really was a remarkable young man.

"When do you think you can introduce me to your mother? I should like it to be as soon as possible."

She was thinking of the following Sunday, and of her provisional promise to Mr Lamb.

"Next Wednesday, if that wouldn't be too early."

"Not at all. Wednesday would suit me perfectly."

"That's awfully good of you; because, in that case, I shall be able to introduce you not only to my mother, but, as it were, to everybody else as well. You see, the village people are holding their annual flower show on Wednesday, at my place in Sussex; I've lent them one of my fields. And my mother's got a house-party, and that kind of thing, to do honour to the occasion. I think it would be even better if you could come to-morrow, that's Tuesday. And then by Wednesday you'll know the whole houseful; and then at the flower show I could introduce you to the village people, they're nearly all my tenants. If you'll say yes, I'll run down at once and let my mother know you're coming."

"To-morrow will suit me even better than Wednesday, thank you."

"And of course you'll stay the rest of the week, and over Sunday."

"You'll be tired of me long before then; and your mother also."

"Not she! My mother doesn't tire so easily. And as for me, I shall never be tired of you—never!"

The lady was of a different opinion, but she did not say so.

When they parted it was on the understanding that Sir Frank Pickard was to go and prepare his mother's mind for the coming of his lady love upon the morrow; and the lady was left in the possession of more valuable property than she had previously owned, if all that she had ever had in her life had been lumped together.

As she contemplated her new belongings, and reread what was written on the sheet of paper which she took out of her bodice, she made certain inward comments.

"Some girls would marry him straight off, perhaps most girls, and forget that there ever was a Joe. And if I did marry him he should never have cause to regret it, nor to be ashamed of me; nor his mother either; nor his friends. If I liked, I could make as good a Lady Pickard as anyone. But, fortunately or unfortunately, I don't happen to be that particular kind of girl. I'd rather be Mrs Joe Lamb, with five thousand pounds in my pocket, than Lady Frank Pickard, with fifty thousand pounds a year."

She smiled a very peculiar smile, which, if anything, rather enhanced her charms. She made a very pretty picture as she turned Sir Frank's promise of marriage over and over between her fingers.

III

It is not on record how exactly Lady Pickard received her son's communication. It may be taken for granted that it was not with feelings of ecstatic delight. To hear that he proposed to present her with a daughter-in-law to whom he had spoken only once in his life could hardly have filled her breast with the proud consciousness of his peculiar wisdom. Nor, probably, was her estimate of his character heightened when she learned that the lady in question was a chorus girl at the Frivolity Theatre. It is within the range of possibility that the reception of the news was followed by what, for her, was a very bad half-hour. There is even reason to suspect that she then and there retired to her own apartment, and, for a time at least, was the unhappiest woman in England. No mother likes, unexpectedly, to discover that the son whom she has idolised has suddenly shown signs of being a hopeless idiot.

But Lady Pickard was a cleverer woman than her boy, at that time, imagined. When, after a few dreadful minutes, the first stress of the shock began to fade away, she commenced to perceive, however dimly, that the situation might not, after all, be so terrible as it actually appeared. She realised, also, that there were two or three facts which she would have to bear in mind.

In the first place, her son was his own master. Whom he would wed, he could wed; no one might say him nay. In the second, considering his position, and his sex, he had been on the whole a tolerably fair specimen of his kind; he was not, at bottom, such an absolute idiot as his own conduct had so uncomfortably suggested. She felt sure that there was something to be said about the girl, or he would not have chosen her. She had reason to know that his taste, as regards women, was fastidiousness itself. If he had asked her to his home she entertained a pleasant conviction that, superficially at anyrate, she need not fear any shocking scandal. He would bring no woman there of whose conduct, appearance, or manners there was any serious risk of his being ashamed. Of so much she felt persuaded. In her heart she was still persuaded that, where women were concerned, his judgment might, in the long run, be implicitly relied upon. Since there was positively no means of postponing the lady's threatened visit, she was far too wise to risk a public rupture with her son, with the accompanying scandal. It was just as well that she had such an assurance.

As for the future—well, her son was not yet married to Miss Ailsa Lorraine. All sorts of little accidents might intervene. Some one or other of them might yet induce him to change his point of view. It was conceivable that she might never quarrel with her boy at all, and still be rid of the lady.

She, of course, had not the dimmest notion of the fact that, for reasons of which she could not have the faintest inkling, there was not the slightest danger of Miss Ailsa Lorraine ever becoming Lady Pickard.

Various friends of her own were coming to stay with her during the week of the flower-show—that great event of the village year. On the Tuesday, carriage after carriage brought visitors from the station to the house. As the afternoon drew on nearly every bedroom in the big, old place had its occupant. It was glorious weather. Tea was being served out of doors. The people were, for the most part, in the best of tempers, and the highest spirits. Frank Pickard was very far from being the most miserable person there. On the contrary he was brimming over with health and happiness. So happy, indeed, was he, that, boy-like, he seemed quite incapable of concealing from anyone the cause of his contentment. Not altogether to his mother's satisfaction, he blurted out to everyone who cared to listen to the tale of his good fortune in being able to persuade a feminine paragon to promise to be his wife. Soon all were aware that, shortly, the lady was to be presented to them in person. Frank would have liked her to have come by an earlier train— indeed the earliest. But, instead, the lady had chosen to travel by what was almost the latest, one so late, in fact, that it necessitated putting off the already late dinner to permit of her being among the other guests at table.

"I'm frightfully sorry," he explained. "But, of course, if she couldn't come any earlier, she couldn't; we shall have to make the best of it. Hullo!—who's this?"

The drive to the house wound along one side of the lawn on which the guests were assembled for tea. As he spoke, there appeared on the drive a waggonette—a village waggonette—an ancient, dilapidated vehicle, which was the property of Mr Goshawk, the local flyman. On the box were two figures—a man and a woman. As Sir Frank spoke, the conveyance stopped. The woman climbed down from the box to the body of the vehicle, from which she presently emerged, carrying, as best she could, several brown-paper parcels, and a cardboard hatbox. The driver appeared to remonstrate.

"Don't you trouble about those, miss," he was heard to remark. "I'll take them up to the house."

The woman's reply was still more audible. "There aren't any flies on me; not much you don't. The odds are that if I once lose sight of my belongings I shall never see them again. I know you cabmen. Thank you very much; but if it's all the same to you, what's mine I'll stick to."

Hampered by her various possessions, she scrambled as best she could over the wire fencing on to the lawn. With one or other of her miscellaneous properties bumping against her at every step, she came striding towards the tea-drinkers. It chanced that young Brock was the first person she came to. He was engaged in a *tête-à-tête* with Florence Stacey of such an engrossing kind that he was not even aware of the advent of the waggonette. His first intimation of the stranger's approach was obtained from Miss Stacey.

"I do believe she's coming to you," she cried. Rising from his seat, Brock turned to see what was meant, and almost in the same instant found himself in the stranger's arms, that dexterous person managing to throw them about him without shedding a single parcel.

"Hullo, Frank, old boy," she exclaimed. "You're looking a bit of all right, upon my word. Catch hold of some of these, there's a good chap; I've had about enough of them."

Before the astounded Brock—who, at that stage of his existence, would not have been seen carrying even so much as a pair of gloves!—could realise what was happening, he found himself in possession of half-a-dozen large and untidy brown-paper parcels of different shades, and a shabby, old cardboard box, tied round with what looked like a clothes-line. It is true that, so soon as he had them he dropped them, but, as he was often told afterwards, that was the moment of his life at which he ought to have been photographed. He would have made a striking picture. So soon as his feelings permitted, he demanded an explanation.

"What do you mean by going on like this? Who are you? I don't know you. And my name's not Frank."

The newcomer remained unabashed.

"All right, old man; no harm done; keep your hair on."

She regarded him fixedly, as if he were some strange specimen which she was endeavouring to place, the unfortunate Brock showing a marked disposition to retreat from her immediate neighbourhood. At last it seemed she arrived at the conclusion that there had been some slight misunderstanding.

"Well, if I wasn't mistaking you for somebody else! It's lucky I didn't kiss you in front of the crowd, wasn't it?" Stanley Brock's inflamed countenance hinted that he thought it was. The lady only smiled. She proceeded to explain still further. "You're a nice-looking boy, especially in those nice white calico clothes"—the "calico" clothes in question were of linen duck—"but you're not my boy; now that I look at you right in front I see that you're not my boy. My boy's as nice-looking as you are, and perhaps a little nicer; no offence, my rosy lad." This was possibly a delicate allusion to Brock's complexion, which was becoming momentarily more ensanguined. "My boy's Sir Frank Pickard. You see, although I'm going to be his wife I've only seen him once; and then I scarcely had what you might call a real good look at him. Seems queer, doesn't it? Ours is a romance, ours is—one of the good old-fashioned sort. I'm Miss Ailsa Lorraine, and I was, up to yesterday, in the chorus at the Frivolity. He fell in love with me from the front row of stalls; that's how it is, you see. They tell me Sir Frank Pickard lives here. You don't happen to know if he's anywhere about just now?"

Frank Pickard's sensations during this scene were of a kind which, although they were never forgotten, he never cared—or dared—to recall. He would have found it difficult to diagnose them, either then or at any other time. When, in after years his thoughts recurred—as they sometimes would—to that moment, what he remembered chiefly was the burning desire which seized him that the ground might open, and he sink into it and be hidden from the sight of all for evermore.

The whole thing was such a bolt from the blue. A moment before he had been telling everyone what a charming person he had won for his wife—how she combined in her person all those attributes which go to make up the perfect woman. With his mother he had dwelt upon the fact of her refinement; had specially pointed out that, though she was only a chorus girl, she was still a high-bred lady. On questions of refinement and breeding he was conscious that his mother esteemed his judgment.

And now, all at once, he found himself confronted by a young woman who was attired in a costume which suggested, more than anything else, a caricature of the tasteless vulgarity to which a certain sort of female could attain. She wore—on that blazing summer's day—a fantastically-cut, ill-fitting dress of scarlet satin—very long behind and very short in front—which was edged and trimmed with some weird material in light green. A black silk petticoat—with ragged edges—was more than visible; as also were her openwork light blue silk stockings, terminated by a pair of cheap, brand-new mustard-coloured shoes. On her bedizened hair was a monstrous picture hat, which bade fair to take the earliest opportunity of toppling forward over her eyes. The fingers of her ungloved hands were covered with gaudy—but worthless—rings; half a dozen bracelets and bangles of silver, and more than dubious gold, were on either wrist; a preposterous chatelaine dangled from a still more ridiculous belt; while her neck was imprisoned by a two-inch-high collar of imitation pearls. To complete the picture, her cheeks were rouged and powdered; her eyebrows pencilled, and her eyes kohled; her lips carmined. In spite of all her efforts she had been unable to conceal the fact that she was pretty; but, under the circumstances, her prettiness seemed to make the matter worse.

Frank Pickard stared at her as if she were some creature born of a nightmare. Was this the dainty damsel whom he had been worshipping from a distance and who had seemed still daintier when he had been brought into close neighbourhood with her yesterday? What hideous metamorphosis had taken place in her between this and then? If he could only have taken to his heels and run!

He was not to escape so easily. Having received no answer from Stanley Brock, she repeated her inquiry.

"I say, old man, look lively! Didn't you hear me ask you if Sir Frank Pickard was anywhere about?"

Mr Brock moved his hand in a sort of vague half-circle, which comprised the spot on which the gentleman in question was standing as if rooted to the ground.

"There is Sir Frank Pickard."

With that genius for blundering which Miss Lorraine seemed to have all at once developed, swinging round, she grasped by both her hands the nearest gentleman, who happened to be General Taylor, one of Lady Pickard's oldest and most particular friends.

"Why, Frankie, I don't take it to be very kind of you not to be taking any notice of me at all. Scotland Yard! you're not Frankie! You're old enough to be his grandpa!" She returned to Stanley Brock; as if the fault were his. "What are you giving us? This isn't my Frank! I'm not collecting fossils just yet, if it's all the same to you."

What the General felt—and his friend the hostess—history does not recount. Silence had settled down on the assembly which was more eloquent than any ribald laughter could possibly have been; it was the silence of stupefaction. It meant that everyone was on tenterhooks as to what was the next thing which this extraordinary person—who had dropped from the clouds—would do or say. Screwing his courage to the sticking point, Frank did his best to rescue his friends from an impossible situation. Advancing towards the dreadful stranger, he addressed her with what one is bound to admit was a voice which trembled.

"Good afternoon, Miss Lorraine."

She looked at him with a glance which was both impudent and mischievous.

"Miss Lorraine! What ho! So you've turned up at last; and now you have turned up you don't seem over hearty. I say, Frankie dear, I wish you'd give me a hand with my baggage. These brown-paper parcels contain pretty nearly everything I've got in the world; my evening dress is in this one. Such a oner! you wait till you see it, you'll stare! Being tumbled about anyhow on the grass won't do it any good. Help me to put the whole lot of it straight, there's a dear."

She was stooping over her collection of miscellaneous rubbish with the apparent intention of piling it into something like a symmetrical heap. Frank showed commendable presence of mind.

"If you will walk with me up to the house, we will send a servant down, and have it all placed in your room."

Miss Lorraine showed no desire to associate herself with his plan to remove her, at anyrate, temporarily, from the scene.

"I'm not going to walk up to the house with you, not much I'm not. Where I am I'll stay. Look here, Frank, if these people are your friends you introduce them to your future wife; I don't like being among a lot of folks and not know who's who. It don't seem sociable. And where's your mother? You promised to introduce me to the old lady the very first chance you had."

The "old lady" thus delicately referred to—who was herself of opinion that she was still very far from being old—cast at her son such a glance that he became immediately conscious that compliance with Miss Lorraine's request was altogether out of the question. He ingeniously shirked it.

"Won't you have some tea? You must be tired—you came by an earlier train than we expected."

"That's how it turned out. I'll tell you how it was. This dress, you see, that I've got on, it isn't my own, it belongs to a lady who's a friend of mine. I asked her to lend it to me directly I knew I was coming down here, and she said she would; but we're not the same figures, you know, and I knew it'd want a good bit of altering, taking in here and letting out there; your friends'll understand how sometimes one lady's dress has to be pulled about before it can be got to fit another, and I thought it wouldn't be finished before the train I told you of. But it turned out after all that there wasn't so much difference in our waists as I'd supposed, she was only three-quarters of an inch—"

Frank made a gallant effort to curtail what bade fair to be some extremely intimate personal details.

"Did you say you'd have some tea?"

"I didn't say anything about it, that I know of. I can't say that I care for tea, not as a general rule; but I don't mind having a drop if there's nothing better going. Hullo, where's the old lady off to?—and the old chap I mistook for you?"

The "old lady" and the "old chap" were Lady Pickard and General Taylor. The pair were making a dash for cover.

"Why, they're all going!"

They all were. Following her ladyship's lead the entire company was showing a disposition to seek safety in flight. Frank stammered an explanation.

"You see, they had their tea before you came; I expect they've all got something to do."

Miss Lorraine feigned indifference, even if she felt it not.

"Oh, they can go for all I care. It makes no odds to me. If my company isn't good enough for them I'm sure I don't want to keep 'em. Besides, if we're left alone it'll give you a chance to say some of those pretty things which are nearly dropping off the tip of your tongue. I say, Frankie, don't you think I'm looking simply sweet?"

What "Frankie" answered the chronicles do not state.

IV

"Frank, is this an intentional outrage of which you have been guilty? Or is it an insolent practical joke which you have planned to play at the expense of your mother's friends?"

For the first time in his life Frank Pickard saw his mother really angry. Of the reality of her anger, as he confronted her in her boudoir, to which he had ascended in obedience to an urgent summons, there could be no doubt. He was conscious that her anger was justified. He was ready enough to admit it.

"It is neither, mother. Only—I don't understand."

"What don't you understand?"

"How the Miss Lorraine I saw yesterday has become transformed into the Miss Lorraine you saw just now."

"My dear Frank, I don't wish to hurt your feelings—although you have shown yourself indifferent as to mine—"

"Mother!"

"So I will not probe too deeply into the matter of what you call 'transformations,' and similar mysteries; I merely wish to know how long you propose to allow that person—whose presence, even in the immediate neighbourhood, is a monstrous insult both to your acquaintances and to me— to continue on these premises."

"I should like you, first of all, to believe that this is not the person I saw yesterday."

"Do you desire me to understand that this is not the person you asked to be your wife?"

"She is, and she is not. I assure you that I should never have extended that

155

invitation to the person you have seen to-day. At present, I can't explain. I don't understand myself. A trick has been played on me. Before I have finished I will find out exactly how it has been done; and why, and by whom it has been played."

"And in the meantime, while you are examining the intricacies of a puzzle which is simplicity itself to all but you, do you propose that the young woman shall continue an inmate of this establishment?"

"I do not. On the contrary, I have requested General Taylor to get rid of her at once."

"Frank!"

"Mother, I am not the fool I seem to be. I assure you that the girl I fell in love with, and whom I asked to be my wife, was not like the one you have seen. I have already been putting two and two together. I am beginning to suspect that I have been the victim of some sort of conspiracy. The only thing I can do is to free myself from it as soon as I possibly can."

"But how do you intend to be rid of the girl? You don't imagine that she will take herself off at your mere request—or General Taylor's?"

"I am inclined to fancy that this is about to resolve itself into a question of money. I have instructed the Genera! to offer her any sum within reason for my release, and for the return of a certain document which she obtained from me yesterday."

"Frank!"

"You see, mother, it is necessary to take immediate action; at any cost I must free you from the risk of again encountering this person, not to speak of the others. Had I more time for consideration, I might take other steps. As it is, I don't think that the General will have so much difficulty as he perhaps anticipates."

For once in a while, rather late in the day, Frank Pickard's judgment was not at fault; General Taylor had no difficulty whatever. The General had an interview with the lady in question in the library, having deemed it desirable to fortify himself for it by a preliminary glass of sherry. As it turned out, however, as a fortifier the sherry was completely wasted; he had no resistance to encounter.

He opened proceedings with what was distinctly a professional tone and air.

"I am a soldier, Miss—eh—Lorraine, and therefore accustomed to come to the point without any sort of circumlocution. I will therefore at once put to you the question for which I have solicited the favour of this interview. How much do you require to leave this house at once; to release Sir Frank Pickard from his engagement to marry you, and for the surrender of the written undertaking which you extracted from him yesterday?"

Some ladies would have resented both the form in which the inquiry was couched, and the manner in which it was put. The General thought it extremely possible that, in this case, resentment might take a shape which was at once active and unpleasant. He was mistaken. The lady, as soon as the inquiry was addressed to her, answered, with the most matter-of-fact air in the world,—

"Five thousand pounds."

The General stared. He was genuinely taken aback by the magnitude of the demand, and by the prompt calmness with which it was made.

"Five thousand pounds! Monstrous! Do you take Sir Frank Pickard for a fool?"

The lady smiled.

"I don't think, General, that, if I were you, I should ask too many questions like that—it might be awkward for everyone concerned. The sum I have named is my lowest figure; my very lowest. As I believe the lawyers put it, it is named without prejudice. Unless I receive a cheque for that amount during the next fifteen minutes by that clock on the shelf, the figure will be raised. And as, also, if I am to remain for dinner there is not much time for me to put on my other frock—a startler, General, I give you my word!—I shall be obliged if you will not keep me a moment longer than you can help."

The General stared still more. It burst on him, with the force of an electric shock, that his young friend had placed himself in a very peculiar position indeed. Some remarks, in good, plain Saxon, were exchanged. As a result, the General interviewed his principal. After a period of time, which probably did not much exceed the fifteen minutes she had named, the lady quitted the house she had so recently entered as an invited guest, with her brown-paper parcels, and her cardboard bonnet-box, but without that sheet of paper on which Sir Frank Pickard had placed a formal undertaking to make her his wife.

That same night when, at last, Joe Lamb was enabled, by the closing of his master's shop, to get out into the streets to obtain what, comparatively speaking, was a mouthful of fresh air, he received a boisterous salute from a female in gorgeous and fantastic attire.

"Hullo, Joey! How goes it, my gay young pippin?"

He showed signs of objecting both to the address, and the person from whom it came.

"Don't holler at me like that; who are you? Why—if it isn't Peggy! What's the meaning of this Guy Fawkes show?"

"Crummy, isn't it? It's earned me that."

She held out in front of him a slip of paper. He took it in his fingers.

"What's this?—a cheque?—payable to you!—for five thousand pounds! Peggy, what does this mean?"

"It means that what I told you of 's come off, and before next Sunday, too. It means that I've been engaged to be married since I saw you; and now I'm disengaged again; and I've been paid five thousand pounds for allowing myself to be disengaged again. It was this rig-out did it. You remember that scene at the Frivolity, where the costers were supposed to take their donahs to Hampstead Heath on a bank holiday? This was one of the costumes which the girls wore. The sight of it was enough for Sir Frank Pickard and his aristocratic friends. I could have got ten thousand if I'd liked, but I was satisfied with five. Joe, that means that you needn't emigrate; and that we can be married whenever you like."

They were married within the month.

*   *   *   *   *

When Sir Archibald Ferguson had finished the story which is here set down, I regarded him for some moments in silence.

"That's not a bad yarn; but—how come you to be so well acquainted with the intimate details?"

Before he answered he rolled his cigar over and over between his fingers as if considering. Then he stood up in front of the fireplace and, from that vantage post, beamed down at me.

"I'll tell you. Open confession is—occasionally—good for the soul. I can trust you. I have taken the liberty to alter the names of some of my characters. The Frank Pickard of my story is—yours truly, Archie Ferguson."

"No?"

"Yes. Seems incredible, doesn't it, that a staid and happily-married man of many years' standing, with a big family of strapping sons and daughters, should have been that particular kind of idiot. But it's true; I was. It only demonstrates—what perhaps does not need demonstration—that because a youngster shows himself to be a first-class fool as a youngster, you mustn't take it for granted that he's going to continue to be a fool his whole life long."

"But how came you to be so well posted in the lady's part of the story?"

"That's not the least queer part of it. When Mr and Mrs Bennett-Lamb first established themselves here I felt—funny. I didn't know what I might expect. But one day we were going up by the same train to town. She invited me into her compartment. I didn't quite like going, but—I did. We had the compartment to ourselves. After the train had started she told me her side of the story, exactly as I have told it you. She told it uncommonly well— uncommonly. And by the time the train reached town I was more than half inclined to the opinion that the five thousand pounds had been judiciously expended. Fact! She has made her husband a first-rate wife, and been an excellent mother to his child. In fact, she's an all-round clever woman."

"So," I admitted, with a degree of candour which I am not sure that he altogether relished, "I should imagine."

XI

A MUTUAL AFFINITY

I

"What the—blazes!"

George Coventry sat with an open envelope in his hand. It was an ordinary white envelope—"business" size—of not too fine a quality. It was addressed: "George Coventry, Esq., Hôtel Metropole, Brighton." The address was type-written.

"Dun!"

That was the one word which had crossed his mind when he first glanced at the exterior of this missive. When he took it up his suspicions were strengthened. It was fat and bulky.

"Contains either a writ or a bill in several volumes."

He laid it down again. He looked at it ruefully as he puffed at his pipe. Then, gathering together his courage with a sigh, he opened it. It was at this point he emitted the above exclamation,—"What the—blazes!"

The envelope was full of crinkly pieces of paper—bank-notes. There were ten of them. Each was for a thousand pounds. Mr Coventry stared at them with bewildered amazement.

"Someone is having a joke with me! Bank of Elegance, for a fiver!"

But they were not on the Bank of Elegance. Mr Coventry fancied that he knew a genuine bank-note when he saw one. After examination, he concluded that if these were forgeries, then he was not so good a judge as he thought he was. He took a five-pound note from his pocket-book for the purpose of comparison.

"Right uns, as I'm a sinner! Then, in that case, it strikes me they've been sent to the wrong address."

In his desire to establish the genuineness of the notes, he had temporarily overlooked a sheet of paper which he had drawn with them from the envelope. This he now examined. It was a single sheet of large post. On it these words were typewritten,—

"The accompanying bank-notes (£10,000) are forwarded to Mr George Coventry, to enable him to pay the losses which he has experienced during the Brighton races."

When Mr Coventry read this, his bewilderment, instead of being diminished, was considerably increased. There was no signature, no address, no clue to the sender. One type-writer is like another, so that there was no clue in the words themselves. Someone, of infinite faith, had entrusted £10,000 to the guardianship of a flimsy envelope and of a penny stamp. Mr Coventry had flattered himself that no one knew—as yet—of the particularly tight place that he was in. Here was proof positive that he had been guilty of self-deception indeed.

He stuffed the notes into his pocket-book. He put on his hat. He went across the road to the pier. He had a problem to solve. Who had chosen so curious a method of sending him so princely a gift? He was prepared to stake his little all—that was left—that it was none of his relations. If the donor was one of his "friends," how basely had he libelled the large and miscellaneous circle of his acquaintances! And yet, a stranger? It would needs be an eccentric stranger who would send an anonymous gift of £10,000 to an unknown person, to enable that unknown person to pay his bets. This thing might have happened in the days of the fairies, but surely the wee folk are gone!

"Would—would you lend me your arm? I—I am afraid I have hurt my foot."

Mr Coventry was standing at the head of the flight of steps which led to the landing-stage. The Worthing boat was just gone. There was a crowd of people to see it start. Although he was one of them, Mr Coventry had not the faintest appreciation of what the small excitement was about. The sound of a voice apparently addressing him recalled him to himself. He looked down. On the step immediately beneath him was a little woman dressed in black.

"I—I beg your pardon? Did you speak to me?"

"Would you help me to a seat? I have twisted my ankle."

The little woman was young. Her big brown eyes seemed to Mr Coventry as though they were filled with tears. She was leaning against the rail. She seemed in pain.

"Let me carry you to a seat."

Then, before all the people, in that impetuous way of his, he lifted her in his arms and bore her to a seat. She said nothing when he placed her there. Perhaps she was too surprised at his method of proceeding to be able to find, at an instant's notice, appropriate words to fit the occasion.

"I'll fetch you a bath-chair."

He fetched her one with a rapidity which did credit to his agility and to the chairman's. The little woman was placed within it. She murmured an address in the Steyne. The procession started. Mr Coventry walked beside the chair. He asked if her foot was better. She said it was. He asked if she was sure it was. She smiled, a little faintly, but still she smiled; she said that she was sure. The Steyne was reached. He saw her enter the house. He raised his hat. He walked away.

It was only when he had gone some little distance that a thought occurred to him.

"I ought to have asked her her name."

He hesitated for a moment as to whether he would not go back and supply the omission; but he perceived, on reflection, that this would be absurd. He told himself that he would call, perhaps that afternoon, and inquire how her foot went on.

That afternoon he called at the house in the Steyne. A person, evidently of the landlady type, opened the door. He handed in his card with, pencilled on it, the words: "I venture to hope that your foot is better." A reply came to the effect that he was requested to walk upstairs. He walked upstairs. He was shown into what was undeniably a lodging-house sitting-room. As he entered, someone was lying on a sofa; it was the little woman in black.

"It is very kind of you to call, Mr Coventry. I ought to have thanked you for your goodness to me this morning, but you were gone in a moment."

Mr Coventry murmured something. He hoped that her foot was better.

"Oh, it is nothing. Only I think that I had better rest it a little, and that is rather a difficult thing for me to do; rest means interference with my work." Perhaps because he seemed to hesitate, she added: "I am a teacher of music."

"Then I am afraid that your accident will be hard on your pupils."

She laughed. "The worst of it is, there are not many of them. I cannot afford to offend the few I have." She changed her tone. "I cannot think how it was I was so awkward, Mr Coventry. I was coming up the steps when my foot slipped, and—there I was. It was such a silly thing to do."

Mr Coventry explained that it was the easiest thing in the world to twist one's ankle. Further, that a twisted ankle sometimes turned out to be a serious matter. Possibly the lady knew this without his telling her, yet she seemed grateful for the information.

The gentleman's visit, considering the circumstances, extended to what seemed to be an unnecessary length, yet neither appeared particularly desirous to bring it to a close. Before they parted they were talking like old friends. She had told him that her name was Hardy—Dora Hardy. She had imparted the further information that she was an orphan—alone in the world. They talked a great deal about, it must be owned, a very little, and they would probably have had as much to say even if the subject matter had been still less. Such conversations are not dependent upon subjects.

The next day he returned to inquire after her foot. It seemed better, but was not yet quite recovered; its owner was still upon the couch. That visit was even longer than the first had been. During its progress Mr Coventry became singularly frank. He actually made a confidant of the little woman on the couch. He told her all his history, unfolded the list of his follies—a part of it that is, for the list was long. Some folks would have said that he was adding to the crowning folly of them all. He told her of his recent disastrous speculations on what, doubtless in the cause of euphony, is called "the turf." He even told of the ten thousand pounds!

It must be allowed that Miss Hardy seemed to find the young gentleman's egotistical outpourings not devoid of interest. When he spoke of the contents of the mysterious envelope she gave quite a little start.

"I don't understand. Do you mean to say, Mr Coventry, that yesterday morning you received £10,000 from a stranger?"

"I do. In ten bank-notes of a thousand pounds each."

"But it's ridiculous. They can't be genuine."

"Aren't they? See for yourself. If they're not, then I never saw a genuine bank-note yet."

He took an envelope from his pocket. He gave it to Miss Hardy.

"Is this the envelope in which they came?"

"It is."

"And are these the bank-notes?"

"They are."

She took out the rustling pieces of paper. Her eyes sparkled. She laughed;

it sounded like a little laugh of pleasure.

"Bank-notes! Ten of them, for a thousand each! You beauties!" She pressed them between her little hands. "Think of all they can buy. Ten thousand pounds!" She laughed again; this time in her laughter there was the sound of something very like a sob. "Why, Mr Coventry, it's—it's like a fairy tale. Some people never dream that they will be able to even handle such a sum—just once."

"It is a queer start."

Mr Coventry rose from his chair. He stood with his back to the fireplace. The little woman followed him with her eyes.

"Come, Mr Coventry, you know very well from whom they came."

"I wish I did."

"Think! They came from that rich old uncle you have been telling me about."

"He would see me starve before he gave me a fiver. I know it is a fact."

"Is there nobody of whom you can think?"

"Not a soul! I don't believe there's an individual in the world who would give me a hundred pounds to keep me from the workhouse."

There was a pause. The gentleman looked at the lady; the lady looked at him. She kept folding and unfolding the notes between her dainty fingers; a smile parted her lips.

"Mr Coventry, I know from whom they came."

"Miss Hardy, you don't mean it! From whom?"

"They came," with a rapid glance she looked down, then up again, "from a woman."

"A woman!" Mr Coventry looked considerably startled. "What woman?"

"Ah, there it is!"

Mr Coventry still looked startled.

"I suppose, Miss Hardy, you are simply making a shot at it."

"It looks to me like the act of a woman. Think! Is there a woman possible?"

Mr Coventry looked even disconcerted.

"It—it can't be. It—it's quite impossible."

"I thought there was. Mr Coventry, here are your notes. I don't wish to intrude upon your confidence."

"But, I—I assure you, the—thing can't be."

"Still, I fancy, the thing is, and so, I see, do you. Mr Coventry, if it is not stretching feminine curiosity too far—in my case you have piqued it—might I ask who is the woman?"

"There isn't one; I assure you there isn't. But I'll tell you all about it." Mr Coventry fidgeted about the room, then sat down on the chair he had just vacated. "Have—have you ever heard of a Mrs Murphy?"

"Had she anything to do with Mr Murphy?"

"You mean the iron man? It's his widow. She's—she's stopping at the Métropole just now."

"Isn't she rich?"

"Awfully, horribly rich. In fact my—my uncle wrote to me about her."

"You mean Sir Frederick?"

"Yes, old rip! I wrote, asking if he could let me have a few hundreds, just to help me along. He wrote back saying that he couldn't, but that he could put me in the way of laying my hands on several hundred thousands instead. Then he spoke of the widow."

"I see; go on."

Mr Coventry had stopped. He seemed to be a little at a loss.

165

"Then, somehow or other, I—I got introduced to her."

"Did you, indeed? How strange!"

"Don't laugh at me, Miss Hardy. The woman's my aversion. She's old enough to be my mother, or—or my aunt, at any rate."

"One's aunt may be younger than oneself."

"She isn't, by a deal. She's a hideous, vulgar old monstrosity."

"You appear to have a strong objection to the lady."

"I have. It—it sounds absurd, but she's always after me. She must mistake me for her son."

"For her son? You look twenty-five, and I thought I saw in one of the papers the other day that Mrs Murphy was in her early thirties."

"She looks fifty, if a day. She can't have sent me all that money."

"As to that, you should know better than I. She might, if she took you for her son."

"If I thought she had, I—I'd send it back to her."

Mr Coventry had recommenced fidgeting about the room. Miss Hardy's suggestions seemed to have seriously disturbed him. That young lady continued to trifle with the bank-notes. As she trifled she continued to smile demurely.

"Hasn't another rich woman been stopping at the Métropole?"

"You mean the American?"

"Was she an American?"

"Rather! Sarah Freemantle. Got five millions—pounds—of her own, in hard cash."

"Has she been stopping at the hotel since you've been there?"

"I believe she has, though I wasn't aware of it till she had gone."

"Haven't you ever seen her?"

"Never; which is rather queer, because she's often been at dances which I've been at. But I hate Americans."

"Do you, indeed? How liberal-minded!"

"Don't laugh at me. You—you don't know how worried I am."

"Some people wouldn't feel worried because £10,000 fell into their lap from the skies. Here, Mr Coventry, are your precious notes."

"I'll send them back to her at once."

"Her? Whom? Mrs Murphy? Don't you think you are rather hasty in jumping at conclusions? Suppose, after all, they didn't come from Mrs Murphy?"

"I'll soon find out, and if they did—"

"Well, if they did? I thought you mentioned some rather pressing obligations which you had to meet."

"Confound it! I know I've been a fool, but I'd rather be posted than owe my salvation to a woman's money."

"All men are not of your opinion, Mr Coventry."

The lady's tone was dry. The young gentleman had a tendency in the direction of "high-falutin."

Among his morning's letters on the morrow the first which caught his eye was a missive enclosed in an envelope which was own brother to the one which had contained the notes.

"Another ten thousand pounds," he wailed.

But he was mistaken. Only a sheet of paper was in the envelope. On the sheet of paper two words were type-written:

"Buy Ceruleans."

Mr Coventry endeavoured to calm himself. Constitutionally, he was of an excitable temperament. The endeavour required an effort on his part. When he could trust himself to speak, he delivered himself to this effect:

"What in thunder are Ceruleans? And why am I to buy them?"

He examined the paper; he examined the envelope; he observed that the postmark was "London, E.C."—that could scarcely be regarded as a tangible clue.

The remainder of his correspondence was not of an agreeable tenor. Everybody seemed to be wanting money; moreover, everybody seemed to be wanting it at once. He went downstairs with, metaphorically, "his heart in his boots." On the way down he encountered an acquaintance. Mr Coventry stopped him.

"I say, Gainsford, what are Ceruleans?"

"Ceruleans?" Mr Gainsford fixed his eyeglass into his eye. "Ceruleans?"

Mr Gainsford thrust his hands into his breeches pockets. "What do you know about Ceruleans?"

"I don't know anything, only some fool or other has been advising me to buy them."

Mr Gainsford eyed Mr Coventry for some moments before he spoke again.

"Coventry, would you mind stepping into my sitting-room?" Mr Coventry stepped in. "I should be obliged if you would tell me who has been advising you to buy Ceruleans. I give you my word that you shall not suffer through giving me the name of your informant. I don't know if you are aware that I am a member of the London Stock Exchange."

"I can't give you the name of my informant, because I don't know it myself. I have just had that sent me through the post. From whom it comes I know no more than Adam."

Mr Coventry handed him the paper on which were the two type-written words, "Buy Ceruleans." Mr Gainsford eyed this very keenly. Then he applied an equally keen scrutiny to Mr Coventry himself.

"Odd! Very odd! Very odd indeed!"

He paused, then continued with an air of quite judicial gravity,—

"Ceruleans, Mr Coventry, is Stock Exchange slang for an American mine which has just struck oil. The fact of its having done so is known, as yet, in England, to only one or two persons. Until you showed me that sheet of paper, I was under the impression that it was known only to one other person beside myself. Whoever sent you that piece of paper is in the know. Your correspondent has given you a recipe for a fortune."

"What do you mean?"

"What I say. Get into the market before the rush begins, and—ah! you might take what some people would call a snug little fortune in less than a couple of hours. Mr Coventry, I am going up to town at once. Come with me, and I will put you in the way of doing the best day's business that ever you did in all your life."

Mr Coventry went up to town with Mr Gainsford. When the young gentleman returned that night to Brighton, he was quite a man of means. On the return journey he just got into the station as the train was starting. He made a dash at the first carriage he could reach. He was settling himself in the corner, and the train was rapidly quickening, when a voice saluted him.

"Mr Coventry!"

He turned. At the other end of the compartment was Mrs Murphy.

"How nice! I was just thinking that I was going to have the carriage all to myself, and you know that I am not fond of my own society."

At that moment, Mr Coventry could not have even hinted that he was fond of hers. The lady went on—her volubility was famous,—

"I have been dabbling on the Stock Exchange."

Mr Coventry did not heed her. He was reflecting that the train did not stop till it reached its journey's end, and how about a smoke on the way? Her next words, however, caused him to prick up his ears.

"I have done wonderfully well. In fact, I have made what to some, less fortunately circumstanced than myself, would be quite a fortune. I have been buying Ceruleans. Do you know what Ceruleans are?"

Did he? Didn't he?

"Ceruleans! Then—it was you—"

He stopped, petrified. The lady seemed amused.

"It was I what?"

Mr Coventry took out a well-stuffed pocketbook.

"Mrs Murphy, allow me to return you these."

A broad smile was upon the lady's face as she took what the gentleman gave her; but when she perceived what it was she held, the broad smile vanished.

"What is it you are returning me? I was not aware—why, they're bank-notes for a thousand pounds each! Mr Coventry! What do you mean?"

The expression of her face, the tone of her voice, were alike expressive of the most unequivocal amazement. But, disregarding these signs, Mr Coventry pursued a line of his own.

"It was very good of you to send them me—though I hardly realise what it was which could have caused you to suppose that I was a fit subject for your charity. At the same time, I hope it is scarcely necessary for me to point out that it is quite impossible for me to take advantage of your generosity."

"Mr Coventry! What on earth do you mean?"

The lady's manner was altogether unmistakable, but Mr Coventry rushed at his fences.

"I can only say that I hope that you will find a more worthy object of what

I cannot but call your eccentric liberality."

Mrs Murphy, as she sat, bank-notes in hand, endeavouring to grasp the gentleman's meaning, would not have made a bad study for a comic artist.

"Mr Coventry, will you be so good as to take back your property?"

The lady held out the notes. The gentleman waved them from him.

"My property! I presume you mean your property?"

"Mr Coventry, what do you mean by giving me these bank-notes?"

"Rather, Mrs Murphy, I think I am entitled to ask what you meant by giving them to me?"

"Pray, Mr Coventry, are you mad?"

"I can only presume that you thought I was mad."

"Thought you were mad! I am beginning to think so now."

"You flatter me. And—then there's the tip for Ceruleans. I—I confess that I have taken advantage of it; but had I known what I know now, I would sooner first have died. I have not yet received the whole of my gains—indeed, I have only received a portion as a favour from a friend. Here, Mrs Murphy, is a cheque for £5,000."

Mr Coventry thrust another slip of paper into the astonished lady's hand. She kept her presence of mind admirably upon the whole.

"I suppose, Mr Coventry, that you are a gentleman?"

"I suppose I was until you taught me otherwise."

"Then, as a gentleman, perhaps you will keep silence while a lady speaks."

Mr Coventry shrugged his shoulders.

"I see that I have here ten notes of a thousand pounds each. Am I to understand that someone has made you a present of £10,000?"

"Mrs Murphy, pray don't dissemble!"

"I have not the slightest intention of what you call dissembling. If you suppose I was the donor, you are under a great delusion. I don't think I ever gave any living creature even ten thousand pence; I have far too just a sense of the value of money."

It was Mr Coventry's turn to look astonished.

"Then if—if it wasn't you—"

"Who was it? That I cannot tell you. Someone, I should say, with more money than sense."

"But—but the tip for Ceruleans?"

"I have not the least notion what you're talking about. But I may tell you this: I myself only received what you call a 'tip' for Ceruleans this morning."

"The—the deuce you did!"

"Possibly you are aware that one of the chief holders of Ceruleans is a lady?"

"A lady!"

"That lady happens to be my friend. This morning she called on me while I was having breakfast. During that call she gave me the information on which I acted."

"Who—who is this lady?"

"I don't know that it is a secret; the lady is Sarah Freemantle."

"Sarah Freemantle!"

"She is staying in Brighton, you know—or perhaps you don't know—because she has actually gone and hidden herself away in one of the back streets, as if, as I tell her, she were hiding from her creditors. Her creditors! Why, she's worth untold millions!"

Mr Coventry was silent. Mrs Murphy sat and watched him. He was quite worth looking at. George Coventry has been pronounced by a high authority to be the handsomest man in England. Oddly enough, he was not only handsome, but he looked good and honest too; and he was without an atom of conceit. In the eyes of some people it was an extra recommendation that he was not exactly wise.

When Mrs Murphy had looked at the young gentleman quite two minutes, she moved up to his end of the carriage.

"Mr Coventry, here is your property. You are fortunate in having such a friend."

Without a word Mr Coventry placed the cheque and the notes within his pocket-book.

"After all, I am not sure that I would not have liked to have been that friend myself."

Mr Coventry fidgeted.

"You—you are very good."

"Do you think so? I should like to be good—to you."

Mr Coventry shivered. Was this woman making love?

"I married my first husband, Mr Coventry, to please my mother. When I marry again I mean to please myself."

"What—what time is this train due in Brighton?"

"Never mind what time the train is due in Brighton." She smiled.

Some men, who are about to pop the question, delight in the shyness of the maiden. Was it possible that she delighted in the shyness of the youth?

"George—I may call you George. Mayn't I call you George?"

"Have you any objection to my smoking a pipe?"

"Smoke if you please. Do what you please. My only desire is to give you pleasure."

She laid her gloved hand softly on his arm.

"You haven't such a thing as a match about you?"

"George, before you begin to smoke, turn round and look at me."

Mr Coventry's head was turned round the other way; he was blowing through the stem of his pipe.

"George!"

If the lady had been a gentleman we should have written that he put his arm about her waist.

"Thunder! my pipe won't draw!"

The gentleman sprang to his feet with startling suddenness; but the lady was equal to the occasion. Before he knew it she had taken him with both her hands, and drawn him on to her knee.

"You silly thing!"

While Mr Coventry was wondering if the skies had fallen, she had kissed him on the lips.

Just then the train reached Brighton.

II

Mr Coventry chartered a fly to the Steyne. He drew up at the house in which lived the little woman with the foot. The person who opened the door informed him that Miss Hardy was in. He rushed upstairs without waiting to be announced. The little woman was seated writing at a table. At his entrance she rose with a start—as well she might.

"Miss Hardy, I—I want to speak to you."

"Mr Coventry."

As the lady stood facing the gentleman she turned a little pale, or perhaps it was a curious effect of the lamplight shining in her face. As for the gentleman's complexion, any suggestion of pallor was ridiculous. A ripe tomato was the best comparison which could have been applied to him.

"I beg ten thousand pardons, but I—I've been with that Murphy woman in the train!"

The girl said nothing. Her big brown eyes were fixed upon her visitor's countenance. In them was a look of not unjustifiable inquiry.

"I—I daresay you think that I'm mad; but I'm not. The fact is, Miss Hardy, I've had a stroke of luck!"

"I am glad to hear it."

"Is that all?"

"What else would you have me say?"

The intensity of the gaze which the gentleman kept fixed upon the lady she must have found a little trying. All at once he went forward. He brought his hand down heavily on the little table at which she was standing.

"Dora, I love you!"

The remark was sudden. The girl for a moment was silent, as if she could scarcely believe her ears. Then a wave of vivid red went up all over her, so that it even dyed the roots of her hair. In her eyes were tears.

"Mr Coventry!"

"Dora, I love you!" If she had had eyes to see, which may be doubted, she might have seen that he was trembling. His words came from him like a flood. "I don't ask you to say that you love me; I know you can't; but I do ask you to say that one day you will try!"

The girl was trembling too.

173

"Mr Coventry, I—I cannot think you are in earnest."

"You know I am."

As she looked into his eyes—and she did look, as though there was fascination in his glance—she could scarcely doubt that at least he thought he was. She tried to smile; the effort was a failure.

"But it's—it's so absurd. You know nothing of me. We are strangers. You only saw me the day before yesterday for the first time in your life."

"What does that matter? I know a man who met a girl upon the Friday and married her upon the Monday."

"Absurd!"

"Some men would be able to do this sort of thing in style; I can't. I know that this sort of thing comes to a man once in his life, and then in an instant. I know that I love you; I know that there will never be another woman to me like you. Some men do not take long to find out these things, you see!"

There was a pause. Then she at last looked down.

"I thought you mentioned something about pecuniary complications."

"This morning I had a hint from a friend; it has brought me in a fortune! There will be enough to settle up with, and something over to start again. And, Dora, I can work."

"Mr Coventry, do you clearly understand that I am a nameless nobody, who has to give music lessons for a living?"

"I understand that you are the woman whom I love!"

She turned her back to him. She moved across the room; she stood trifling with the fringe of the curtains.

"This is the maddest thing of which ever yet I heard."

He could hear that her voice was trembling.

"You know, Dora, I'm not asking you to say at once that you will be my wife. I daren't, and that's the fact; but I'm asking you one day to try to say you will. I want something to keep me going. I want something to save me from that woman Murphy."

"I believe 'that woman Murphy,' as you politely term the lady, is at the bottom of the compliment—I suppose I must call it so—which you have paid to me."

There was a curious intonation in the voice from the curtains.

174

"She has been making love to me. I couldn't stand that when I loved you, Dora!" The gentleman was creeping round the table. "Say that you will try!"

"Suppose I do?"

"Dora!"

She would not let him stay. They parted, this queer pair! He dined, not at his hotel, but at a restaurant on the Front; dined well! When he left it was with that good digestion which waits on appetite. He walked as if he walked on air. He certainly had the gift of making history quickly.

When he reached the hotel, an acquaintance stopped him at the door.

"The great Sarah is here."

"The great who?"

"Sarah! Miss Freemantle! The five-times millionaire."

Mr Coventry looked a trifle bored.

"I'm not interested in the lady."

"The deuce you aren't! I am; and, by Jove, I wish she were in me!"

"I'm sorry for you. Come in and have a smoke."

As they crossed the hall, someone was coming down the stairs. The acquaintance drew Mr Coventry a little aside.

"Here she is!" Mr Coventry glanced up. "That's Miss Freemantle, the little woman in black. She's not a bad-looking little thing."

Mr Coventry looked at the lady referred to. It was Dora Hardy! As she descended the staircase, she leant on Mr Gainsford's arm. On the gentleman's other side was Mrs Murphy. As he saw her, she saw him. The young lady dropped the gentleman's arm. She ran down the stairs with her hand stretched out.

"Mr Coventry!"

"Dora!"

She laughed—and blushed. She turned to her companions.

"I don't think I need trouble you after all, Mr Coventry will see me home."

Before Mr Coventry had realised the situation he found himself in the open air with the lady. They turned, perhaps instinctively, towards Hove. It happened, that night, that that part of the Front was almost deserted. They

175

walked some little distance before the gentleman recovered the use of his tongue.

"Dora—what—what cock-and-bull story was that fool telling me?"

"I really cannot say."

"He—he said that you—you were the great Sarah."

"So I am. Don't I look it?"

The gentleman stopped dead. He groaned.

"What—what a fool I've been!"

"You flatter me."

They resumed their promenade. Her hand stole towards his.

"George, are you sorry you said you loved me?"

"Dora, is—is it a joke?"

"No, George, it's not a joke, it's a romance."

"What—what have I done?"

"Made me happy. Isn't that enough to do?"

They stopped again, under a gas-lamp. It was fortunate so few persons were about.

"George, I have a confession to make. It was not you who fell in love with me, it was I who fell in love with you."

"Dora!"

"It is true. It was at Lady Brentford's ball. I saw you there for the first time. I fell in love with you—at sight. You see, when your turn came, you did not make up your mind more rapidly than I had done. It was a case of Goethe's mutual affinity! I saw you at other houses. I went to them on purpose to see you, but I took care never to be introduced to you."

"Why?"

"You know that I am the great Sarah, George. But when I found that you had come to the very hotel at which I was stopping, I formed a little plot. I changed my quarters, I dropped the Freemantle, and became Miss Hardy. Then—*then* I thrust myself right into your path, and—and it was all soon over. Are you sorry, George?"

"Sorry! But—but about those notes?"

"You goose! They came from me. I knew you had been betting, and I knew that you had lost. I didn't want to lose you for a pound or two. But when you told me that you would not owe your salvation to a woman's money—not knowing who the woman was—why, then I sent you the 'tip' for Ceruleans instead. It was the best thing that I ever did, for it brought me you."

Mr Coventry took off his hat. He wiped his brow. He seemed to be turning matters over in his mind.

"I shall always call you Dora."

"Call me what you please."

"Darling!"

XII

MAGICAL MUSIC

I—APOSTLE SPOONS

Miss Macleod passed the newspaper to her nephew. "Look at that," she said. She had her finger on an advertisement. He looked at it. This is what he read:—

"A clergyman, having a large family entirely dependent on him, is compelled to sacrifice a unique set of apostle spoons. Twelve large, twelve small, silver-gilt, in handsome case. Being in urgent want of money, a trifle will be accepted. Quite new. Would make a handsome present. Approval willingly. Letters only, Pomona Villa, Ladbroke Grove, W."

"What do you think of it?" inquired the lady.

The Rev. Alan smoothed the paper with his hand.

"Not much," he ventured to remark.

"Put on your hat and come with me. I'm going to buy them."

"My dear aunt!"

"They will do for a wedding present for Clara Leach. Other people can marry, if you can't."

The Rev. Alan sighed. He had been having a bad quarter of an hour. He was a little, freckled, sandy-haired, short-sighted man: one of those short-sighted men whose spectacles require continually settling in their place on the bridge of the nose. Such as he was, he was the only hope of an ancient race— the only male hope, that is.

The Macleods of Pittenquhair predated the first of the Scottish kings. Fortunately for themselves they postdated them as well.

For a considerable portion of their history, the members of that time-honoured family had been compelled, in the Sidney-Smithian phrase, to cultivate their greatness on a little oatmeal—for want of cash to enable them to indulge in any other form of cultivation. But in these latter days they had grown rich, owing to a fortunate matrimonial speculation with a Chicago

178

young lady whose father had something to do with hogs. The lady's name was Biggins—Cornelia P. Biggins—the P. stood for Pollie, which was her mother's name, the "front" name came from history. The particular Macleod who had married her had been christened David. He devoted a considerable portion of his wife's fortune to buying up the ancient lands of the Macleods, in the neighbourhood of Pittenquhair and thereabouts. In his person he resolved that the ancient family glories should reappear—and more. But in these cases it is notorious that man only proposes—his wife never bore him a child. To make matters worse, he only outlived Mrs Macleod six months, so that he never had a decent chance to try his luck again.

David had a brother. Being a childless man, and desirous to restore the ancestral grandeur, one would have thought that he would have left his wealth to his brother, who wanted it if ever a man did yet. But, unfortunately, Alan was not only an irredeemable scamp—which might have been forgiven him, for David was by no means spotless—but also the two brothers hated each other with a truly enduring brotherly hatred. Nor had Alan improved matters by making public and unpleasant allusions to hogs and swine, not only on the occasion of David's marriage, but on many occasions afterwards. So it came to pass that when David was gathered to his fathers, his brother's name was not even mentioned in his will. All his wealth was left to his sister Janet.

In course of time Alan died abroad—very much abroad, and in more senses than one. Then, for the first time, Janet appeared upon the scene. She paid for her brother's funeral, and took his only child, a boy, back with her to England. The child's mother, who was nothing and nobody, had died—charitable people said, murdered by her husband—soon after her infant's birth. So his aunt was the only relation the youngster had.

Janet was a spinster. She had ideas of her own, and plenty of them. Her dominant idea was that in her nephew the family sun should rise again in splendour. But alas for the perversity of fate! The boy passed from a public school to the university, and from the university—after a struggle, in which he showed himself, in a lymphatic sort of way, as obstinate as one of Mrs David's father's pigs—into the church. This was bad enough for a son of his father, and the heir to Pittenquhair and ten thousand pounds a year, but what followed was infinitely worse. He became a ritualist of the ritualists—more Roman than the Romans—and the motto which he nailed to the mast was "Celibacy of the clergy"!

Her nephew's conduct almost drove Miss Janet mad. Two wives she might have forgiven—but none! In season and out of season she preached to him the duty of marriage; but what she regarded as a duty he regarded as a crime. She spoke of an heir for Pittenquhair; his thoughts were of something very different indeed. To speak of disinheriting him was to pander to his tastes. The income from his curacy was seventy pounds a year—and he lived on it. The money sent him by his aunt he surrendered to the Church and to the poor. What availed it to preach of disinheritance to a man who behaved like that?

And yet, in his own peculiar way, he was a good nephew to his aunt. He was the meekest, ugliest, shyest, awkwardest of men. His curacy was at a place on the Suffolk coast called Swaffham-on-Sea. From these wilds he was perpetually being summoned by his aunt to attend on her in her house in town. Although—possibly because he was that kind of man—these visits were anything but occasions of pleasure, he generally obeyed the summons. On the present occasion it was the second day of his stay under his aunt's hospitable roof in Cadogan Place. From the moment of his arrival she had continually reviled him. She had suggested as wives some two-score eligible young women, from earls' daughters to confectioners' assistants. She had arrived at that state of mind in which, if he would only marry, she would have welcomed a cook. In his awkward, stammering way, he had vetoed them all. Then she had rated him for an hour and three-quarters by the clock. Finally, exhausted by her efforts, she had caught up the paper in a rage. The Rev. Alan watched her in silence as she read it, fingering a little book of prayers he had in his waistcoat pocket.

All at once she had thrust the advertisement sheet of the paper underneath his nose, with the exclamation—

"Look at that!"

He looked at it, and had read the advertisement reproduced above.

"Don't sit there like a stuck dummy," observed Miss Macleod, whose English, in her moments of excitement, was more than peculiar. "Go and get the thing that you call a hat! Hat!" Miss Macleod sniffed; "if you had appeared in the streets in *my* days with such a thing on your head, people would have thought that Guy Fawkes's day was come again."

The Rev. Alan was still studying the paper.

"But, my dear aunt, you are not seriously thinking of paying any attention to such an advertisement as that?"

"And why not? Isn't the man a clergyman?"

"I can't think that a priest—"

"A priest!" cried Miss Macleod, to whom the word was as a red rag to a bull. "Who spoke about a priest?"

The Rev. Alan went placidly on—

"—under any circumstances would advertise apostle spoons for sale."

"Who asks you what you think? Put on your hat and come with me."

"There is another point. The advertisement says 'letters only'; there is evidently an objection to a personal call."

As Miss Macleod grasped her nephew by the shoulder with a sufficiently muscular grasp, the Rev. Alan put on his hat and went with her.

II—UNDER THE SPELL

They walked all the way—it is some distance from Cadogan Place to Ladbroke Grove. There was not much conversation—what there was was not of a particularly cheerful kind. The day was warm. The lady was tall, the gentleman short. Miss Macleod was a first-rate pedestrian; the Rev. Alan was not good at any kind of exercise. By the time they reached their journey's end he was in quite a pitiable plight. He was bedewed with perspiration, and agitated beyond measure by the rather better than four miles-an-hour pace which his aunt would persist in keeping up.

Pomona Villa proved to be a little house which stood back at some distance from the road. Just as they reached it the door was opened, shut again with a bang, and a gentleman came hastening out of the house as though he were pressed for time. He was a tall, portly person, with very red whiskers, and a complexion which was even more vivid than his whiskers. He was attired in what might be called recollections of clerical costume, and was without a hat. He appeared to be very much distressed either in body or in mind. Just as he laid his hand on the handle on one side of the gate, Miss Macleod grasped it on the other. Brought in this way unexpectedly face to face, he stared at the lady, and the lady stared at him.

"She's at it again!" he cried.

"Sir!" exclaimed Miss Macleod. She drew herself up.

"I beg your pardon." The gentleman on the other side of the gate produced a very dirty pocket-handkerchief, and mopped his head and face with it. "I thought it was a friend of mine."

"Is this Pomona Villa?" asked Miss Macleod.

The bare-headed man looked up and down, and round about, and seemed as though he were more than half disposed to say it wasn't. But as the name was painted over the top bar of the wooden gate, within twelve inches of the lady's nose, he perhaps deemed it wiser to dissemble.

"What—what name?" he stammered.

"I've come about the apostle spoons."

"The apostle spoons! Oh!" The bare-headed man looked blank. He added in a sort of stage aside—"Letters only."

"Perhaps you will allow me to enter."

Miss Macleod did not wait for the required permission, but pushed the gate open, and entered. Her nephew followed at her heels. The bare-headed man stared at the Rev. Alan, and the Rev. Alan at him—one seemed quite as confused as the other.

"Can I see the spoons?" continued Miss Macleod.

"Eh—the fact is—eh—owing to distressing family circumstances—eh—it is impossible—"

What was impossible will never be known, for at that moment the door was opened, and a woman appeared.

"If you please, mum, Miss Vesey says, will you walk in? She's upstairs."

Miss Macleod walked in, her nephew always at her heels. The bare-headed man stared after them, as though he did not understand this mode of procedure in the least.

"Up the stairs, first door to the right," continued the woman who had bade them enter. As, in accordance with these directions, Miss Macleod proceeded to mount the stairs, the woman, who still stood at the open door, addressed herself to the bare-headed man at the gate. Her words were sufficiently audible.

"You brute!" she said, and banged the door in his face.

Seemingly unconscious of there being anything peculiar about the house or its inhabitants, Miss Macleod strode up the stairs. The Rev. Alan, conscious for himself and his aunt as well, crept uncomfortably after. The first door on the right stood wide open. Miss Macleod unceremoniously entered the room. Her nephew followed sheepishly in the rear.

The room was a good-sized one, and was scantily furnished. One striking piece of furniture, however, it did contain, and that was a grand piano. At the moment of their entrance the instrument stood wide open, and at the keyboard was seated a young lady.

"I am Miss Vesey," she observed, without troubling herself to rise as the visitors entered.

Miss Macleod bowed. She appeared about to make some remark, possibly with reference to the apostle spoons; but before she could speak, Miss Vesey went on,—

"That is my father you saw outside—the Rev. George Vesey. He's a dipsomaniac."

Miss Macleod started, which, under the circumstances, was not unnatural. Her nephew stared with all his eyes and spectacles. Miss Vesey was a fine young woman, about nineteen years of age. The most prominent feature in her really intellectual countenance was a pair of large and radiant black eyes.

"I'm engaged in his cure," she added.

"I have called," remarked Miss Macleod, perhaps deeming it wiser to ignore the young lady's candid allusion to her father's weakness, "with reference to an advertisement about some apostle spoons."

Miss Vesey, still seated on the music-stool, clasped her hands behind her head.

"Oh, that's one of his swindles," she said.

"One of his swindles!" echoed Miss Macleod.

"He's agent for a Birmingham firm. He finds it a good dodge to put in advertisements like that. Each person who buys thinks she gets the only set he has to sell; but he sells dozens every week. It's drink has brought him to it. But I'm engaged in curing him all round. The worst of it is that when I begin to cure him, he runs away. He was just going to run away when you came to the gate."

"If what you say is correct," said Miss Macleod grimly, "I should say the case was incurable—save by the police."

"Ah, that's because you don't understand my means of cure: I'm a magician."

"A magician!"

There was a pause. Miss Macleod eyed Miss Vesey keenly, Miss Vesey returning the compliment by eyeing her.

Miss Macleod was a woman of the day. Openly expressing unbelief in all the faiths that are old, she was continually on the look-out for a faith that was new. She had tried spiritualism and theosophy. She had sworn by all sorts of rogues and humbugs—until she found them out to be rogues and humbugs, which, to her credit be it said, it did not take her long to do. Just at that moment she was without a fetish. So that when Miss Vesey calmly announced that she was a magician, she did not do what, for instance, that very much more weak-minded person than herself, her nephew, would have done—she did not promptly laugh her to scorn.

"What do you mean by saying you're a magician?" she inquired.

"I mean what I say. I have my magic here."

Miss Vesey laid her hand on the piano.

"I suppose you mean that you're a fine pianist."

"More than that. With my music I can do with men and women what I will. I can drive the desire for drink out of my father for days together; I can make him keep sober against his will."

Miss Macleod turned towards her nephew.

"This is my nephew. Exercise your power upon him."

"Aunt!" cried the Rev. Alan.

Miss Vesey laughed.

"Shall I?" she asked.

"You have my permission. You say you can do with men and women what you will. He will be a rich man one of these fine days. Make him marry you."

The curate's distress was piteous.

"Aunt! Have you any sense of shame?"

"Suppose I try," observed Miss Vesey, her face alive with laughter. "I'm sure I'm poor enough, and I'm already connected with the clergy."

"Aunt, I entreat you, come away. If you will not come, then I must go alone. I cannot stay to see the Church insulted."

Miss Macleod turned to Miss Vesey.

"Will you let him go?"

"Certainly not," laughed the young lady. "If only to pay him out for being so ungallant."

The Rev. Alan—literally—wrung his hands.

"This—this is intolerable. Aunt, it is impossible for me to stay. You—you'll find me there when you get home."

The Rev. Alan, in a state of quite indescribable confusion, turned towards the door. But before he could move a step, Miss Vesey struck a chord on the piano.

"Stay!" she said.

The curate seemed to hesitate for a moment, then turned to her again. He seemed to be under the impression that he owed an apology to the pianist. "I —I must apologise for—for my seeming rudeness. I know that my—my aunt only meant what she said as—as a joke; but, at the same time, my respect for my sacred office"—at this point the little man drew himself up—"compels me, after what has passed, to go."

Miss Vesey struck a second chord.

"Stay!" she said again.

Before the agitated believer in the propriety of the unmarried state for clergymen could say her yea or nay, she cast her spells—and her hands— upon the keyboard of the instrument, so that it burst out into a concourse of sweet sounds. The Rev. Alan was, in his way a born musician. The only dissipation he allowed himself was music. The soul of the mean-looking, wrong-headed little man was attuned to harmony. Good music had on him the effect which Orpheus with his lute had on more stubborn materials than curates—it bewitched him. Miss Vesey had not played ten seconds before he realised that here was a dispenser of the food which his soul loved—a mistress of melody. What it was she played he did not know—it seemed to him an improvisation. He stood listening—entranced. Suddenly the musician's mood changed. The notes of triumph ceased, and there came instead a strain of languorous music which set all the curate's pulses throbbing.

"Come here!"

Miss Vesey whispered. The curate settled his spectacles upon his nose. He looked around him as though he were not sure that he had heard aright. And the command was uttered in such half-tones that he might be excused for supposing that his ears had played him false.

"Come here!"

The command again. Again the Rev. Alan settled his spectacles upon his nose. He gazed at the musician as if still in doubt.

"I—I beg your pardon? Did you speak to me?"

"Come here!"

A third time the command—this time clearer and louder too. As if unconsciously he advanced towards the pianist, hat in one hand, handkerchief in another, his whole bearing eloquent of a state of mental indecision. He went quite close to her—so close that there would be no excuse for saying that he could not hear her if she whispered again.

Again the musician's theme was changed. The languorous melody faded. There came a succession of wild sounds, as of souls in pain. The curate's organisation was a sensitive one—the cries were almost more than he could bear.

"Pity me!"

The voice was corporal enough. It was Miss Vesey, once more indulging in a whisper. Again the curate was at a nonplus. Again he went through the mechanical action of settling his spectacles upon his nose.

"I—I beg your pardon?" It seemed to be a stereotyped form of words with him.

"Pity me! Pity me! Do!"

The words were a cry of anguish—quite as anguished as the music was. The Rev. Alan looked round the room, perhaps for succour and relief. He saw his aunt, but at that moment her face happened to be turned another way.

"If you need my pity, it is yours."

The words, like the lady's, were spoken, doubtless unintentionally, in a whisper.

"If you pity me, then help me too!"

"If I can, I—I will!"

"You promise?"

"Certainly."

Although the word was a tolerably bold one, it was by no means boldly spoken; probably that was owing to the state of confusion existing in the speaker's mind.

The theme was changed again. The piano ceased to wail. A tumult of sound came from it which was positively deafening. The effect was most bewildering, especially as it concerned the Rev. Alan. For in the midst of all the tumult he was conscious of these words being addressed to him by Miss Vesey.

"Help me with your love!"

The instant the words were spoken the tumult died away, there was the languorous strain again. The curate was speechless, which, all things considered, was perhaps excusable. An idea was taking root in his brain that the musician was mad, at least mad enough to be irresponsible for the words she used. If that were so, then, unlike the generality of lunatics, she had a curious aptitude for sticking to the point.

"Love me, or I die!"

"My—my dear young lady!" stammered the curate.

"You will be my murderer!"

The accent with which these words were spoken was indescribable, as indescribable as the music which accompanied them. It may be doubted if, as he heard them, it was not the Rev. Alan himself who was going mad. The heat and agitation brought on by the pace at which his aunt had marched him from Cadogan Place, the extraordinary manner of his reception at Pomona Villa, the still more extraordinary things which had happened to him since he had got inside; all these, put together, were quite enough to make him uncertain as to whether he were standing on his head or his heels. And then, for him, a staunch believer in the theory, and the practice, of the celibate priest, to have such language addressed to him, after five minutes' acquaintance, by a total stranger! and such a pianist! and a fine young woman! No wonder the Rev. Alan put his hand up to his head under the impression that that portion of his frame was leaving him.

"If you do not marry me," continued this extraordinary young woman, in tones which harrowed his heart—and yet which were not so harrowing as her music, by a very great deal, "I shall die before your eyes."

The Rev. Alan still had his hand to his head. He looked round him with bewildered, short-sighted eyes. Curiously enough his aunt still had her face turned in the opposite direction.

"I—I'm sure—" he stammered.

"Of what?"

"I—I shall be happy—"

"Happy!"

The music ceased, and that for the sufficiently good reason that the pianist rose from her seat and flung her arms about the curate's neck. He said something, but what it was was lost in the ample expanses of Miss Vesey's breast.

"Madam," she cried, addressing Miss Macleod, "your nephew has promised to marry me! He has said that he will be happy."

Miss Macleod, who did not happen just then to be looking in the opposite direction, smiled grimly. Owing to the peculiarity of her physical configuration everything about her was grim—even her smile.

"I am glad to hear it," she observed.

The Rev. Alan struggled himself free from the lady's powerful embrace. His distress was tragic in its intensity.

"This—this is some extraordinary—"

"Happiness!" cried the lady, and again she clasped him in her arms. "Your happiness is mine! It has been my life-long dream to be married to a clergyman; is not my father one already?"

At that moment the father referred to entered the room.

"What's this?" he cried, as a father naturally would cry on seeing his daughter with a stranger in her arms.

The young lady, however, promptly relieved his mind.

"Father, let me present to you my future husband."

"I—I do protest," screamed the frenzied curate.

"You do protest, sir! What do you protest?" The father's voice was terrible, so was his manner. Apparently all his paternal instincts had not been destroyed by dipsomania. "You come to this house, sir, a perfect stranger, sir; you assault my daughter, sir; you take her in your arms."

This was, perhaps, strictly speaking, a perversion of the truth; but at this moment Miss Macleod offered her interposition.

"You need be under no concern. My nephew is a gentleman. I was a witness of his proposal. If he behaves as a dastard to your daughter, I will deliver him to your righteous vengeance then. In the meantime, perhaps you and your daughter will accompany us home to luncheon. We can arrange the preliminaries of the marriage during the course of the meal."

III. —A CURIOUS COURTSHIP

"Miss Bayley, I am in a position of the extremest difficulty."

Miss Bayley was not only the Rev. Alan Macleod's parishioner; she was, so to speak, his co-curate, at Swaffham-on-Sea. That delightful village boasted of a rector who found that the local air did not agree with him, so he spent most of his time in the South of France. The Rev. Alan was, therefore, to all intents and purposes, the head and front of all Church matters in the neighbourhood. Unfortunately the greater part of the population—what there was of it—was dissenting, and that part of it which was not dissenting was even worse—it was Episcopalian!—the lowest of the low! The curate, therefore, found himself in the position of the sower who sows his seed in barren soil. His congregation not unfrequently consisted of two—the verger and Miss Bayley.

The curate had returned to Swaffham, and it was this faithful feminine flower of his flock he was addressing now.

"Oh, Mr Macleod, I am so sorry! Can I help you? Is it spiritual?"

The curate shook his head. He had not fallen quite so low as that. The idea of his coming to a person in petticoats for help in spiritual matters struck him as too absurd. He could scarcely excuse Miss Bayley.

"Can you think that I, your priest, should come to learn of you?"

Miss Bayley looked down.

"I was wrong," she murmured. She told herself that she ought to have remembered that none of the curates ever was half so cocksure about that kind of thing as the Rev. Alan. But then, she was so anxious to lend him a hand in anything.

"An error owned is half atoned."

He meant this for a little pleasantry—but he was an awkward man, even when he trifled. He hesitated. He was conscious that he had come for assistance in a matter quite as delicate as anything which appertained to Church government.

"Miss Bayley." He cleared his throat. "I—I have an aunt." The abashed Miss Bayley signified that she had heard him mention that fact before—which she had, about half a dozen times a day. "She is not one of us." Miss Bayley sighed; she felt that she was expected to sigh. "She is of the world worldly. Her thoughts are fixed on temporalities. Being possessed of great riches, to which I am the natural heir, the continual desire of her life is that I—I should marry."

The Rev. Alan stammered a little at the end. Miss Bayley perceptibly started. That was the continual desire of her life too. She wondered if it was going to be gratified at last.

"That you should marry? Oh, Mr Macleod!"

"I need not tell you that, in such a matter, her desire would not weigh with me in the least. The true priest is celibate."

Miss Bayley's heart fluttered—she did not go with him so far as that.

"But—if she were to disinherit you?"

"Do you know me so little as that? Nothing would please me better than that she should."

He clasped his hands in a kind of ecstasy. The lady, whose father was the parish doctor, and who knew what it was to have to dress on nothing a year, was almost tempted to think that the curate was a fool. But as she could scarcely express the thought aloud, she was wise enough to hold her peace. The gentleman went on rather awkwardly. The travelling was getting difficult, in fact.

"To—eh—such lengths has—eh—she—she—allowed her desire to—eh— carry her, that—eh—it—it has resulted in—eh—involving me in—eh— complications of an excessively disagreeable kind."

Miss Bayley's imagination realised the worst at once.

"Are you engaged?" she cried.

"She—she says I am."

"She says you are!" The lady was on the verge of tears—the blow was sudden. "Mr Macleod, I have something which I have to do upstairs."

She felt that if she stayed in the room she might disgrace herself by crying before his face. The Rev. Alan was dismayed at the idea of her leaving him.

"Miss Bayley, I do entreat you not to go. You do not understand me in the least. *I* do not say I am engaged; quite—quite the other way."

"Oh, Mr Macleod!"

The affair might have its comic side for a looker-on, but it was tragic enough for her. If she did not get this man, whom could she get? At Swaffham-on-Sea eligible bachelors were as rare as snow in summer. Besides —women attach themselves to poodle dogs!—she really liked the man.

The curate continued:

"The—the circumstances really are, I think, the most extraordinary I ever heard of. I should be almost induced to believe that it had all happened in a dream were it not for a letter that I have in my pocket."

"From whom is the letter?"

"From—from Miss Vesey."

"Is that the lady you are engaged to?"

"En—engaged to? I hadn't made her acquaintance ten minutes before she said I had proposed to her."

"She would not have said so unless you had."

"Miss Bayley, do you not know me better than that? Nothing was further from my mind! The proposal came from her."

"I have heard of women proposing to men! And I suppose you accepted her?" She was strongly tempted to add, "You are imbecile enough for anything!" But even in that hour of her trial she refrained.

"I can only assure you that I had no such intention in any words. I may have used words which came from me unawares, owing to the state of confusion I was in on receiving such a proposition from a total stranger."

Miss Bayley turned away. She thought she saw exactly how it was.

"I can only offer you my congratulations. I do not know why you enter into all these details. When is the marriage to be?"

"Marriage!"

"Yes, marriage! I hope you will send me a piece of cake! Oh, Mr Macleod, I never thought you would behave to me like this!"

Miss Bayley fairly succumbed. She buried her face in her hands and ran crying from the room. Mr Macleod, left behind, was thunderstruck. He realised what any man, with even a little knowledge of the world, would have seen from the first.

"She loves me! What have I done?" He sank in a chair and he too buried his face in his hands. Presently he rose again. "Poor, pure soul! She is the best woman in the world!" He twisted his hands together with a nervousness which was peculiarly his. "I have done wrong in the sight of God and man!"

How he got out of the house he never knew; but he did get out, and through the front door too. He set off walking towards the rectory, where in the absence of the rector, he lived rent free. He had not gone twenty yards from the house when a gloved hand slapped him smartly on the shoulder.

"Alan!"

He turned. There was Miss Vesey and her father. He could hardly believe that it was, but it was. The lady was brilliantly attired, perhaps as a set-off to her father. That worthy gentleman resembled nothing so much as what, in former days, they would have called a broken-down hedge parson. He was evidently meant for a clergyman, sartorially. That is, the conception was clear enough, it was the result which was unsatisfactory.

"Your hand, my son!"

He held out his hand after the manner of the fathers in old comedy. But unfortunately he did not wait for the curate to give him his hand, he seized it, and shook it up and down—pump-handle fashion. And while the father was engaged in this edifying performance, the daughter flung her arms about the curate's neck.

"My beloved!" she cried.

If there was any there to behold, they beheld what they had never seen before—the curate embraced as a curate never had been embraced in public, at Swaffham-on-Sea.

"Let me go!" he stammered.

And in due time the lady let him go. Under the circumstances he kept his presence of mind very well—for him.

"You—you'll find the rectory about a quarter of a mile in front of you, just round the bend in the road. If—if you'll excuse me, I have a most important visit I must make."

Miss Vesey's father slapped him heartily—too heartily!—upon the back, again after the fashion of the comedy fathers.

"Don't put yourself out for us, my boy! Don't neglect your duties, as is too often the case with the young. Tell us where the bottles are, and we'll make ourselves snug till you come in."

The curate did not tell them where the bottles were; in fact, there was only a solitary bottle of cod-liver oil in the house, and probably the speaker's thoughts did not incline that way; but they went on to the rectory alone. Miss Vesey waved her parasol, and kissed her glove to him so long as she was in sight. He stood watching them till they were round the bend in the road, then he re-entered the doctor's house.

This time he passed through the back door, straight into the kitchen. "Lauk, sir!" cried the maid-of-all-work; "who'd a thought of seeing you?"

The Rev. Alan addressed her in a fever of excitement.

"Tell Miss Ellen I must speak to her at once."

He went into the parlour, and the maid-of-all-work went upstairs. Presently she returned with a message.

"If you please, sir, Miss Ellen's compliments, and she's got a headache."

Mr Macleod was pacing up and down the room, very much in the manner of the carnivora about feeding time at the Zoo.

"A headache!"

He took his note-book from his pocket. Tearing out a page he scribbled on it these two or three strongly-worded lines.

"I entreat you to see me, if you ever called yourself my friend. It is a matter of life or death; almost, I would venture to say, of heaven or hell.—A. M."

The maid-of-all-work bore these winged words above. The result was presently visible in the form of the lady herself. She entered with the air of a martyr, conscious of her crown.

"You are my priest. I have come."

"It is not as a priest I have summoned you, Ellen, but as a friend."

The use of the Christian name was perhaps unintentional, but the lady marked her sense of the familiarity at once.

"Sir!"

Her lip curled, possibly with scorn. His answer was sufficiently startling. "Ellen, I entreat you to be my wife."

"Your wife, Mr Macleod! Are you mad?"

"I am—nearly! I shall be quite if you don't accede to my request at once."

"I think you are mad now. How dare you insult me! when from my bedroom window I just saw you kissing that creature in the street."

"I kissed her!—She kissed me."

"It's the same thing."

"It's not!" Which was true enough—it was a different thing entirely. "Ellen, can you not see that I was never more in earnest in my life. If you do not marry me, something tells me that that woman will, and for all I know that wretched parent of hers may be the occupant of a dissenting pulpit; he looks disreputable enough for anything. What with her and her father, and my aunt, I am as a reed in their hands. I do entreat you—be my wife."

The offer was not put in the most flattering form. Still, it was an offer.

"If you really want me—" began Miss Bayley.

"Want you! I want nothing so much in all the world."

"And if you think I can be of use to you in the parish—"

"Parish! it's not the parish I'm thinking of, it's—it's that wretched woman."

Miss Bayley did not like this way of putting it at all.

"I will consider what you say, Mr Macleod, and will let you have an answer—say in a month."

"In a month!" the curate was aghast. "I want your answer now. Ellen, I do entreat you, if you do not wish to see me disgraced in the face of all the world, promise to be my wife."

"But, Mr Macleod, you do not even pretend to care for me."

"Care for you! I care for you more than I ever cared for any woman yet."

"Then in that case"—the lady was a little coy—"it shall be just as you will."

At this point the ordinary lover would have taken her in his arms, and here would follow a number of crosses denoting what we have seen termed "osculatory concussions." But the Rev. Alan was not an ordinary lover at all. He continued his frenzied pacing round the room.

"It is not enough to promise to be my wife, you must be my wife."

"Mr Macleod, what do you mean?"

"Miss Bayley—Ellen—those two persons are at the rectory, awaiting my arrival at this moment. She is a disreputable woman, he is a ruffianly man. They are quite capable of coercing me into some dreadful entanglement from which I may find it impossible to release myself. My only hope lies in an immediate marriage."

"I do not understand you in the least."

"Then let me endeavour to make myself quite plain. I will not return to the rectory; you will put on your hat and jacket and come up at once with me to town. I will get a special licence. And we will be married before anyone has an inkling of what it is that we intend."

"Mr Macleod, is it an elopement you propose?"

"Ellen, it is."

The little man was shaking like a leaf.

"I never heard of such a thing in my life."

"Nor did I dream that I should make such a proposition to a living woman —but needs must when the devil drives."

The lady began to cry.

"Alan, I must say you have not a flattering way of putting things."

"What avails flattery at such a moment as this. For Heaven's sake, don't cry. I have heard you say yourself that you don't believe in long engagements."

"Yes—but when one has not been engaged five minutes!"

"What matters five minutes or five years, when one has once resolved? It seems to me that when there is nothing to gain by waiting—but everything to lose—the sooner one marries the better."

There was something in this; she told herself that he was not such a nincompoop after all when he was driven to bay—poor, dear little man! Amidst her tears she thought of other things. A regular marriage would involve a trousseau. She was quite sure that she should get no money out of her father for that—for the best of reasons, he had none to give. And then she knew her curate. She thought it quite possible that if that other woman—the brazen hussy!—did once get him in her hands, he might at any rate be lost to her. Better a good deal than to run the risk of such an end to all her hopes as that!

The end of it was that the Rev. Alan Macleod and Miss Bayley went up together by the next train which left the neighbouring station—eight miles off—for town.

IV.   —HIS AUNT EXPLAINS

Shortly after his marriage Alan Macleod received the following curious letter from his aunt,—

"NEPHEW ALAN,—Don't talk fiddlesticks about giving up the Church because you're married, though *I* never could understand why you ever became a parson, unless it was because your father was the devil's own.

"I meant all along that you should marry the doctor's daughter. Of course, as a Macleod of Pittenquhair, you might have had the best in the land, but then—what a Macleod you are! Have you ever heard of the Irishman's pig? They pull him by the tail when they want him to follow his snout. That is what I have done with you. I heard all about the girl and about your philanderings together, and how you thought it was the Church she worshipped, when the curate was the object of her adoration. Don't you ever believe about single young women worshipping the Church when there's a bachelor inside it! I heard she was a decent body, so I said that, sooner than leave you, the last of the Macleods of Pittenquhair, a barren stock, the girl should have you.

"The thing was how—with you and your 'celibate-priest' stuff and nonsense. But Providence helps those who help themselves—so 'Miss Vesey' tumbled from the skies.

"I saw her first at a thought-reading *séance*. She did some very funny things, and she plays the piano like an angel. She certainly had a gift that way, for, with the aid of her music, she played all sorts of tricks on the fools who were there. I thought to myself, what tricks she might play on you if you came within her range! Then, all of a sudden, the whole thing was hatched in my brain. I made her acquaintance. I took her home to supper. Afterwards, inspired by the largest quantity of champagne I ever saw a woman drink, she told me all about herself. She was the most candid young woman I ever met.

"She was married—to an unfrocked parson. But, according to her own

196

account, she was more than his match. A perfect limb! And as clever as she was wicked—one of those wicked women who are born, not made, for she was not yet twenty-one. I told her all about you. I said that if, through her, you married the doctor's daughter at Swaffham-on-Sea, she should have five hundred pounds upon your wedding-day. She came into the scheme at once. So we arranged it all together.

"Among other things, her husband was one of those scamps who pose, in the advertisement sheets, as distressed clergymen whose large families depend for sustenance on their being able to dispose of some article or other at one-third of its cost price. Just then his line was apostle spoons—which he bought for five shillings and sold for twenty. I was to summon you up to town. I was to bully you about your marriage. And then, when I had thoroughly upset you—which, I explained to her, it was the easiest thing in the world to do—I was to call your attention to his advertisement of the apostle spoons. I was to march you off then and there to buy them. When I had got you into her house I was to leave the rest to her.

"She was to pose as her husband's daughter, which she was young enough to be—in years, at any rate. She said that if I brought you to her in a state of agitation and confusion bordering on imbecility—which I undertook to do—and if you were the sort of man I had described to her, within half an hour she would induce you to use language which might be construed into an offer of marriage. Then, with her husband's aid, she would so drive you to distraction as to send you flying into Miss Bayley's arms as into a harbour of refuge.

"I need not describe to you how she succeeded—though we had neither of us bargained that you would be *quite* the fool you were. When I heard of your eloping with the doctor's daughter the instant 'Miss Vesey' put in an appearance on the scene, I owned that I had at last attained to one article of faith—an implicit belief in the infinite capacity for folly to be found in the human animal in trousers.

"It is unnecessary, under these circumstances, to say that I congratulate you upon your marriage. I hope that your wife will be a sensible woman, and present you, without loss of time, with a son—or, better still, with half a dozen, so that I may have an opportunity of finding at least *one* among them who shall not be *quite* such a fool as his father.—Your affectionate aunt,

"JANET MACLEOD (of Pittenquhair)."

When Miss Macleod's nephew had finished reading this letter, he wiped the perspiration from his brow. Then he wiped his glasses. Then he sat thinking, not too pleasantly. Such a letter was a bitter pill to swallow. Then, not desirous that his aunt's epistle should be read by his wife, he tore it into strips, and burned them one by one. He told himself that he would never forgive his aunt—never! and that, willingly, he would never look upon her face again.

But to so resolve was only to add another to his list of follies. Within twenty-four hours of his marriage—fortunately for him—his wife had proved that the grey mare was once more the better horse. Now she had got her man, at last, the strong vein of common sense that was in her came to the front. When Miss Macleod came to see her, she received her with open arms; and, as a matter of course, where she led her husband followed.

To one thing Alan had been constant—to the doctrine of the "celibate priest." According to him, a "priest" married was not a "priest" at all. Immediately after his marriage, therefore, nobody offering the least objection, he quitted the "priesthood." He is now a gentleman of leisure. Probably with a view of providing him with some occupation his wife bids fair to come up to his aunt's standard of a sensible woman, and to present him with half a dozen sons.

There is, therefore, no fear of the Macleods of Pittenquhair becoming—like certain volcanoes—extinct, at least in the present generation.

XIII

A RUNAWAY WIFE

I. **—FLIGHT**

The quarrel which had begun about nothing, had become a raging storm. She faced him with clenched fists and flashing eyes.

"Perhaps you would like me to leave you!—to go, and relieve you of my presence! Our marriage has been a mistake. If you like, I will do my best so that the mistake may go no further. You have only to say the word, and I will go out of this house, never to return to it. Is that what you wish?"

He laughed. It was as if he had struck her across the face.

"Consult your own wishes, as you are in the habit of doing, pay no regard to mine. I can only say that if you wish to go, you are at perfect liberty to do so—I shall be content."

"Do you mean that?"

"Unlike you, I am in the habit of meaning what I say."

She drew a deep breath, as if she were choking.

"Then you wish me to go? To leave your house?"

"Don't I tell you to have regard only to your own desires—as it is your usual custom? But if you will have it, I tell you quite frankly that if you propose to continue to play the *rôle* of termagant, I would much rather you did it in some other house than this. If I can have nothing else in my home, I should like to have peace."

"Then you shall have it."

"Thank you. Will you be so good as to let me have it at your earliest convenience?"

He turned to leave the room. She stopped him.

"Understand, Frank, that if you don't withdraw what you have said before you leave the room, I shall take your words literally, and act upon them to the letter."

"I understand that perfectly."

"I shall go."

"Then go! I do beg, my dear wife, that you won't stand upon the order of your going. Tomorrow is Christmas Eve, so that it's just the time for a little excursion. I hope you'll have a happy Christmas."

"I hope that your Christmas will be happier than mine is likely to be."

"That is very good of you, I'm sure." He flared into sudden passion. "How fond you are of striking an attitude—your life is one continued pose. Do you suppose that I think you will go? Do you imagine that I don't know you better. You'll talk, talk, talk! and you'll pose, pose, pose! but you're as likely to go as I should be likely to fetch you back if you did go—unluckily for me!"

He was gone, laughing as he went. His laughter was the final straw. That was what he thought of her! He set her down as simply a humbug; a windbag; a spouter of big words, which were all sound and had no meaning. She might threaten to go; he knew that her threats were but phrases. And he had laughed at her! Very good, he should see! He should learn if she was a person to be laughed at! She might have forgiven him much—everything—but his contempt. He would discover, quickly, if she was a doll, a puppet, an automaton, who could be made to gabble anything by pulling a string.

She did not stop to think—being dimly conscious that if she did she might be impelled to listen to the whisperings of common sense; but, while her rage was still hot within her, she tore upstairs; put on something—she scarcely knew what; rushed to the station, and within a quarter of an hour was seated in a train which was flying along the rails to London. Then, when it was too late, and the thing was done, past undoing, she began to consider what the situation really was.

She had the compartment to herself. On the seat in front of her was the copy of the Christmas number of an illustrated paper, which some passenger had left behind. It lay open at a page which caught her eye. She took it up. There were two full-page pictures, one was entitled "The First Christmas." A young husband clasped a young wife to his breast, while they regarded each other with looks of love. The second was called "The Last Christmas." The husband, grown old, was seated in an arm-chair, with bent back, and bowed head. The wife, her hair as white as snow, knelt on the floor beside him, her arms about his neck. They were as happy in each other's embrace as in the days of long ago, and their love was just as young. Edith's eyes filled with tears. That was how she had meant it should be with Frank and herself; their love should continue, showing no signs of the wear and tear of age, to the end. But—

What was she doing? Running away from the best husband in the world, and the home of which she was so proud. Was she mad? or was she dreaming? She started to her feet in a sudden burst of comprehension. That instant her passion was gone; her vision was clear; she saw. And, from what she saw, she put up her hands to veil her eyes. To-morrow was Christmas Eve. Her mother and sister were coming, and some of Frank's relations'. There was to be a family gathering, to spend the first Christmas in the home of the newly-married couple. How she had looked forward to it, and prepared, and made all sorts of plans. But there were still many things to do, various arrangements to complete. There was not a minute to spare, she would be fully occupied up to the very moment of her guests' arrival. Instead of being busied with the multitudinous details which awaited her attention she was tearing up to town. Why? With what purpose in view? On what errand? She alone could tell; and she had not the remotest idea.

She looked out of the window, wondering whereabouts she was. She would get out at the first station at which they stopped; if fortune favoured her, she might catch a train back at once; she would return before her flight had been discovered. How the train must have flown—it was Brentwood they were passing! Why did it fly through the station? She realised, with a shock, that it was the express which she had caught. That it did not stop till it reached town. What was she to do? She endeavoured to collect her thoughts! The train reached Liverpool Street about six. There was not another back till nine. What was she to do during the intervening three hours—at night, in London, all alone? Discovery was inevitable. She would have to make what explanation she could. She remembered Frank's words—that if she went he would not want her back again. Was it possible that he had meant what he had said? The horror of the thought.

Something else occurred to her. She opened her purse to look for her ticket. It was there right enough—first, single, to Liverpool Street. Why had she taken single? She recalled, with a flush of shame, how, even at the booking-office window, she had told herself that the mere fact of her requiring a single ticket to London was sufficient proclamation to the world of what it was she meant to do. She must have been insane indeed! Well, the only thing that remained for her was to stultify herself as soon as she reached town, and to get another single ticket to take her back again.

All at once a horrible fear assailed her. She shuddered as with cold. She looked at her purse. Then sank back again against the cushions, a picture of dismay. All the colour had gone from her cheeks, her hands trembled. Was it possible that she had been so mad as that? Such an utter fool? It was incredible. Ridiculous though her conduct had been, she could not have behaved with quite such blind insanity.

It was some seconds before she regained sufficient self-control to enable her to submit her purse to a fresh examination. This time she went through it slowly, and with method. Only to discover that her worst fears were realised. It contained one of her visiting cards—"Mrs Frank Bankes, The Chestnuts, Tuesdays, 4 to 6." Would she ever be there again on Tuesdays to receive her guests? The bill for the Christmas present which she had bought for Frank; when he had discovered her absence would he find that present? Would he dream of how she had schemed and schemed to buy for him the very thing which she believed he wanted? Would she realise with what a halo of love she had meant to enshrine it?

"Oh, Frank, how I love you! If only you knew."

But apparently he was not likely to know for some considerable time to come, for, besides the visiting-card and the bill, the entire contents of her purse consisted of two postage stamps and a threepenny bit. Her ticket cost nine shillings and ninepence. She remembered tendering half a sovereign to the booking-clerk and receiving threepence change; and now it seemed that that half sovereign had been all the money she had brought away with her. How was she to return; to purchase even a third-class ticket to take her back again; to send a telegram advising her husband of the plight she was in, with threepence for her all?

II. —THE WOMAN WHO MET HER

As she remained in a state of semi-stupefaction, mistily wondering what sort of nightmare Christmas this was going to be for her—for whom all the world had been full of the promise of good things only an hour or two ago!—the train rumbled into Liverpool Street. As she sat endeavouring to collect her thoughts, so as to decide upon some course of action, the carriage door was opened, and a woman looked in.

"From Chelmsford?"

Perceiving that the question was addressed to her, Mrs Bankes, still half-dazed, looked up, and answered,—

"No, from Colchester."

"That's right! Be quick, the train's late,—I've been waiting for you."

"For me?"

"Yes, for you. I've had instructions to meet you by this train."

Edith rose from her seat, instantly conscious that a sense of relief was being born within her.

"You've had—instructions? When?"

"Not half an hour ago. It wasn't certain that you were coming by this train, but in case you did I was to meet you and see you safe."

The sensation of relief was almost more than she could bear. How good he was! Frank had accurately gauged the extent of her folly, and had taken instant steps to guard her from the consequences of her own misconduct. How little was she deserving of such a husband? With a blinding mist before her eyes she got out on to the platform.

"Come," said the woman. "I've a cab waiting."

"A cab—shall we want a cab?"

"Of course we shall,—trust me for knowing what we want. You had better move yourself, there may be someone else here to meet you, and someone may see you whose recognition you had rather be without."

What did the woman mean? There was something in her tone which was not altogether agreeable. Could tidings of her escapade have already leaked out, and did she go in fear of the condemnatory glances of censorious friends? In a state of nervous doubt she pressed after the woman through the crowd. They reached a four-wheeler. Opening the door her companion let her enter first. When they had started she put a question on the subject which was preying on her mind, a little stammeringly.

"Does—anyone know of what I've done?"

Her companion's tone, as she replied, was dry—even grim.

"Just one or two. More than you perhaps imagine, or would quite care for if you knew. If you don't keep your eyes wide open this'll be the worst Christmas ever you spent in all your life."

Edith began to suspect that this might turn out to be only too true. Her heart sank lower. Amidst the noise made by the cab her voice was scarcely audible.

"Is he—so very—angry?"

"That's a pretty question to ask! You've made a mess of it—about as bad a mess as you could make, and then you wonder if folks are angry. I don't know much about it, I'm not told everything, and I don't want to be told, sometimes the less I know the better I'm pleased; but from what I have heard, I should say anger wasn't the word for it; and that you're in for about as bad a time as ever you had in all your days!"

Edith did not like her companion's manner,—she liked it less and less. Her voice was not that of an educated woman; her bearing, from one in her station, was unpleasantly familiar—at times, almost threatening. Mrs Bankes wondered why her husband had chosen such an agent, and how he had chanced on her.

"Where are you taking me?" she asked.

"Never mind where I'm taking you. Do as I do, and don't want to know more than you can help. As I've said, sometimes the less you know the more comfortable you feel."

"But I insist on knowing where you are taking me. I don't want to go too far away from the station; I wish to go back by the nine o'clock train."

"The devil you do!" The woman actually swore. Edith shuddered. What a dreadful creature she seemed. How could Frank have selected such a being to be her companion even for a fleeting hour. "Then you can take my word for it that you'll go back by no nine o'clock train—not much."

"Then by what train shall I return?"

"How should I know? Return! I shouldn't have thought that you'd have been anxious to return after what you've done. I should have thought that it would have been a little bit too warm for you down there."

What was the woman insinuating? Why did she use such exaggerated language? It could hardly have been warranted by any instructions which she had received from Frank.

"I think that you hardly understand the situation?"

The stranger cut her short.

"You're right there—I don't, and I don't want to. If you take my advice, so far as I'm concerned, you'll keep your mouth shut tight. Say what you've got to say to someone else, you'll soon have plenty to say it to, who'll want to hear all, and perhaps a bit besides. All I've to do is to see you safe; after I've done that, I don't want to see no more of you."

Edith was silent. She was beginning to be conscious of a feeling of vague distrust; to wonder if, in entering a cab with this woman, she had not made the biggest of all her mistakes. As she began to think, she perceived the improbability, to say the least, of Frank's having communicated with anyone in town. Proposing to take a holiday till after Christmas, he had intended remaining at the office that evening unusually late. It was extremely unlikely that he would have returned home until after seven; before then she had reached her journey's end. In any case he would hardly have had time to telegraph instructions for her to be met, even if he had suspected her destination. In any case, who was this woman? What were the instructions which she claimed to have received, that she should refuse to vouchsafe any information as to where she was taking her?

The more Mrs Bankes thought it over the more she was convinced that she had been the victim of some extraordinary misunderstanding, and the more desirous she became of opening the cab door, and jumping straightway out into the street. With some hazy idea of resorting to such an extremely desperate measure she leaned over towards the window. Immediately her companion gripped her by the shoulder.

"Stop that! What are you up to?"

"I think there's been some mistake."

Mrs Bankes spoke faintly. Her companion's voice was anything but faint as she replied.

"Don't you try any of your tricks with me. I shouldn't be surprised if there has been a mistake, and it's just to give you a chance of explaining how it came about that you're going where you are. My instructions are to see you safe, and I'm going to see you safe. I carry out my instructions whatever other folks may do; I've got something to see you safe with, and if you make any fuss you shall have a taste of what's inside—see?"

To Mrs Bankes' petrifaction, a revolver gleamed in the speaker's hand, the muzzle of which was pointed towards her head. It was a form of argument with which, at the moment, she felt wholly powerless to cope. Before she again found courage enough to enable her to speak, the cab drove up before a house. Her companion favoured her with a further hint or two.

"Here we are; and don't you make a sound or try to speak a word to anyone before we get inside, or—"

The sentence was not concluded; but the speaker moved the weapon, which she still held in her hand, in a fashion which, so far as Mrs Bankes was concerned, rounded it off with more than sufficient point.

III.   —A HOUSE OF THIEVES

The house in front of which they had stopped seemed empty. At least, the hurried, agitated glance which Mrs Bankes cast up and down failed to discover any sign of a light at either of the windows. She had not, however, much time allowed her for inspection. Her companion, gripping her arm with uncomfortable firmness, drew her towards the door, which she opened with a key held in her other hand. So soon as it was opened she drew Mrs Bankes inside with a force and suddenness which almost precipitated that lady headforemost on to the floor. Instantly the door was slammed, and Mrs Bankes found herself standing with the stranger in pitchy blackness. Nor did the sound of the other's voice add to her sense of comfort.

"Now I've done what I was told to do,—I've brought you safe. You'd better be on your best behaviour, or you'll quickly find yourself in worse trouble than you are already. Come this way." The woman dragged her along what seemed to be a passage. "Here's the stairs—up you go."

And up Mrs Bankes went, pushed and pulled up the unseen staircase in a way which was more than a little disconcerting. They reached what was apparently a landing. The stranger, throwing open a door, disclosed a room, immediately in front of them.

"In you go."

And in Mrs Bankes did go, propelled by a well-directed push from the rear. When she was in, the door was pulled to behind her. She heard the key turned in the lock outside. Retreating footsteps were distinctly audible. In a state of bewilderment, which was unlike anything she had ever been conscious of before, she glanced about her. She found herself in a small room, whose entire furniture consisted of a solitary wooden chair—and the back of that was broken. There was neither carpet nor table. The dirty, tawdry paper was peeling off the walls. The sole illumination proceeded from a candle stuck in a broken, battered tin candlestick, which stood upon the greasy mantelshelf.

She seated herself on the solitary chair. Her life was ordinarily placid and uneventful. So much of the unexpected had been crowded into the last few hours that her mental faculties were in a state of seemingly inexplicable confusion. This was running away with a vengeance! This was indeed playing with dignity the part of outraged and indignant wife! This was a pleasant prelude to the Christmas season! Where was she? Of what extraordinary misunderstanding was she the subject? For whom had she been mistaken? What had the other person done? What was the fate which was awaiting her? Or was it not possible that there had been no misunderstanding at all; but that her credulity had been played upon; that she had been tricked into entering a den of criminals, where she was destined to be the victim of some horrible outrage?

As she asked herself these and similar questions, to which she sought in vain for answers, she became conscious, all at once, of the sound of voices. She looked about her, and perceived for the first time that the apartment had two doors—the one through which she had entered and another immediately facing it. This second door had been covered with paper of the same pattern as that which was on the walls; and it was this peculiarity, probably, which had caused its existence to hitherto escape Mrs Bankes' notice. A moment's attention made plain the fact that it was through this door that the sound of voices came. Edith hesitated. Eavesdropping was not to her taste; but in circumstances such as hers she was surely entitled to take advantage of anything which might tend to elucidate the position she was in, or which would prepare her for whatever danger threatened. She stood close up to the door.

Apparently there was a room beyond. There seemed to be several speakers. They were engaged in an animated discussion. She could distinguish the tones of at least three voices. Presently distinct words and phrases began to reach her ears.

"If I had my way I'd cut the heart clean out of her."

She shuddered. Could the reference be to her? The expression of opinion seemingly met with the approbation of its hearers. Another voice became audible—coarse, rough, threatening, and yet, unless Mrs Bankes erred, its proprietor was feminine. Indeed to her it appeared that all the speakers were women.

"That's what I say. Let's make short work of her. No cackle, and no beating about the bush. She's done us, we'll do her—and waste no time about it either!" A third voice followed. "That's right; then let's have her in and get through with it as soon as possible."

The proposition seemed to be approved. Steps were heard approaching the door against which the listener stood. A key was turned. The door was flung open.

"Now then!—in here! and look sharp about it too!"

The words were addressed to Mrs Bankes as if she had been a dog. She shrank back. The command was repeated.

"Do you hear? Out you come! Or have I to fetch you? No nonsense, or it'll be the worse for you!"

As best she could, Mrs Bankes drew herself together.

"You are making some mistake," she said, and went into the other room.

She was conscious that her entry created some emotion which was akin to surprise. There were four women. They all looked at her with something very like astonishment; as if this pretty, graceful girl, every inch of her unmistakably a lady, dressed in such perfect taste, forming altogether such a pleasant picture for the eye to rest upon, was hardly the sort of person they had expected to see. And yet she was conscious that their amazement was not by any means of an agreeable nature; that it did not tend to make their feeling towards her one whit more cordial. On the contrary, in the rapid glances which they exchanged one with the other there was a rancorous gleam which suggested that a fresh element of personal dislike had been generated in their bosoms by the mere sight of her.

Her entrance was followed by an interval of silence, which was broken by Edith repeating her former assertions with such show of courage as she was capable of.

"There has been some mistake. If you will allow me, I think I can explain quite easily how it has happened. It is all owing to my foolish hastiness. I am quite willing to admit that the fault has been in great part mine."

Her offer to elucidate the situation, or, at any rate, the part which she had played in it, made with all humility, was not greeted with any show of heartiness. Rather the faces in front of her hardened, as if her words added fuel to the fire of their resentment.

"You're a pretty piece, upon my word! You look a fine lady, and no error! Anyone would think you were one, to hear you talk. You impudent cat, to try to carry it off with us. You shut your mouth, and don't you speak unless you're spoken to, or we'll soon shut it for you, and don't you make any mistake, my beauty. You forget where you are, and what you're here for."

"I assure you—"

"Catch her a clap over the jaw."

In obedience to the request, the woman who had bade her enter the room struck her in the mouth, with her clenched fist, with such violence that she reeled back, and all but fell to the floor. Her brain seemed to reel in harmony with her body. Never before in the whole course of her life had she been struck a blow. No action could have revealed to her more clearly the sort of company she was in.

Three of the women into whose presence she had been so unceremoniously introduced, were seated round a table whose jagged and time-stained surface was covered with a cloth. The one who had been the instigating cause of what seemed to Edith such an entirely unprovoked assault, was a short, thick-set woman of between forty and fifty years of age. She was dressed with a cheap flashiness which served to emphasise her natural vulgarity. Her cheeks were red; her eyes were small though bold; on her upper lip was more than the suggestion of a moustache. She looked like the not too respectable wife of some disreputable small publican; a likeness which was rendered the more obvious by the accident of her having in her hand a glass which was half filled with the drink of which, plainly enough, her soul was over-fond. On her left was a tall, scraggy woman, of about the same age, clad in rusty widow's weeds. She, like her companion, wore a bonnet, but hers was an emblem of the deepest woe. Even her hands were cased in black. Anyone seeing her casually would have taken her for the widow of some struggling tradesman, who, now that she was left alone in the world, had taken, as a last resource, to letting lodgings. The expression of her face was not an agreeable one; and no judge of character, who had once had a good look at it, would willingly have accepted her as a landlady. She had high cheek-bones; hollow, sallow cheeks, as though her side teeth had departed from their places; a long, pointed nose; wide, shapeless mouth, and she kept her thin lips tightly closed. She was not the sort of woman into whose sympathetic ears one would have been disposed to pour a tale of woe. And it was surprising, when she spoke, how disagreeable her voice sounded,—as if her small, mean, rasping nature had even got the better of her vocal organs.

But it was on the third person seated at the table that Edith's attention was, half unconsciously, chiefly centred. This she instinctively felt was the leading spirit present in the room, the one in whose hands her fate principally rested. The woman was of so distinct and even curious a personality that one wondered by what chance she found herself in such a gallery. She was so small as to be almost diminutive; but she was both young and pretty. One might wonder how much her fair hair, and the bloom on her cheeks, owed to artifice; but there could be no doubt as to the well-shaped mouth, the pouting lips, the dainty aquiline nose, the big bright eyes, shaded by unusually long lashes, and piquant, arched eyebrows. Yet it was in her eyes, charming though they were, that one read most clearly the storm warnings of her character. There was in them something daring, wild, relentless, suggestive of the masculine adventurer, to whom the world is an oyster, to be opened by the sharp blade of his keen wits.

She was oddly dressed, with a profusion of chiffons which became her small form peculiarly well. So far, Edith had not heard her voice, but, as Mrs Bankes reeled before the force of her assailant's blow, she broke into a peal of hearty laughter, which, under the circumstances, seemed out of place as proceeding from those pretty lips.

"Poor thing! She doesn't seem to like it! Give her another; teach her how to swallow a tooth or two."

But even the creature who had struck her seemed to shrink from a display of such gratuitous brutality.

"There's plenty more where that came from, and I expect she'll have 'em before I've done with her. But for the present I daresay she'll find that that's enough—it'll give her a taste of what's to follow."

Edith, regarding the speaker, realised what a typical virago she was, almost masculine in build, big and broad, slovenly in her attire; her draggled bonnet was a little on one side of her head, and her black serge dress covered with stains. To Mrs Bankes' frightened eyes, the lust of combat was written largely over her.

"I've got no time to waste. Let's put the slut through her paces, and have done with her. The sooner we're shut of her the better I'll be pleased."

It was the woman who resembled a publican's wife who spoke. No one said her nay. She spoke to Edith.

"First of all, hand over what you've got."

Edith stared at her bewildered. "Hand over what I've got? I don't understand. I've got nothing."

The woman brought down the palm of her hand with a bang upon the table.

"No blarney, hand over what you've got, before we take it from you."

"All I have is in there."

The young wife held out her purse with a trembling hand. The virago, snatching it from her, subjected its contents to a rude examination.

"Here's a card, a bill, two stamps, and a threepenny bit,—and that's all."

"That's all I have—every penny. I give you my word it is."

The four women stared at her, as if the surprise caused by her statement had deprived them of their power of speech. It was the publican's wife who was the first to find her tongue.

"Of all the beauties I ever heard of!—if you haven't got the cheek of fifty! Why, you yourself sent word that you'd got about four hundred pounds' worth!"

"I sent word? Four hundred pounds' worth of what?"

The lady became, on a sudden, very angry. "If you try that on with me, you two-faced cat, I'll smash your face in with my own hands!"

The little woman poured oil on the troubled waters—in a fashion of her own.

"Let's begin calmly, at any rate. Let me deal with this person, we may arrive at an understanding quicker that way—she seems to require understanding." She addressed herself to Edith, in a manner which that lady found sufficiently startling. "We will begin at the beginning. That will prevent our leaving anything in obscurity. There seems to be a good deal of obscurity about just now. You will remember that when you came out of Wandsworth jail—"

Mrs Bankes stared, and well she might.

"When I came out of Wandsworth jail!"

"Yes, when you came out of Wandsworth jail. You seem prepared to deny a good many things, but I take it that you can hardly be disposed to deny that you did come out of Wandsworth jail."

At that moment Mrs Bankes was prepared to deny nothing. Her tongue was parched and dry. It seemed to her that she must be suffering from nightmare, and that these things were taking place in some horrible dream. The speaker went on, as calmly and quietly as if she were treating of the most ordinary subjects in the most commonplace manner; yet there was a glitter in her eyes which did not promise well for the person she was addressing.

"I say that you will remember that when you came out of Wandsworth jail, as you have come out of other jails in the course of your not uneventful career, you were introduced, by a certain individual, to our society. Our rules and regulations were explained to you; you expressed yourself as being satisfied; you subscribed to them; you became a member. Not one of us who is here present has had the pleasure of meeting you personally before, or I am sure that we should have congratulated ourselves on securing so promising a recruit to our little circle. I do not flatter you when I assure you that you look a really ideal thief, capable of practising your profession to the utmost advantage in the best of good society."

Mrs Bankes shivered.

The speaker smiled.

The others only glared.

"When it was proposed to annex the Denyer jewels—"

"The Denyer jewels?"

Mrs Bankes gasped. A sudden gleam of light began to glimmer through the mist—a dreadful gleam.

"You seem fond of echoing my words! I say that when it was proposed to annex the Denyer jewels, you immediately volunteered to carry the business through. Your offer was accepted. You were provided with every necessary, and, if one may judge from your appearance, with a few luxuries as well; you were sent down to Colchester—all at our expense—and a place was found for you in Lady Denyer's household. Certain persons were associated with you in the enterprise, and among them, Mary Griffiths."

"Mary Griffiths?"

Fresh light was gaining access to the lady's bewildered brain, light which was growing more and more lurid.

"You may well start, and look uncomfortable at the mention of Mary Griffiths' name, especially when you reflect on the position she is now in, owing to your—shall we call it, discreet behaviour? You informed us that all was going on well, and yet, on the night on which you, yourself, had arranged that the *coup* should be brought off, almost immediately Mary Griffiths gained access to the house she was arrested. When we asked you to explain, you were so good as to tell us that it was absolutely necessary to allow her to be arrested in order to draw suspicion off yourself, and, by way of solace, you added the information that you had, at any rate, got hold of four hundred pounds' worth of her ladyship's jewels. From all we learnt we could not but suppose that you had made a slight mistake, and that by four hundred you meant four thousand. Jewels to the value of more than four thousand pounds appear to have gone; if you have not got them, then who has? The question is rather a nice one, don't you think?"

The speaker paused as if for a reply. None came. Mrs Bankes was trembling in every limb. She perceived, even more clearly than those in front of her, how close she was standing to the brink of a chasm.

"When we perceived your reluctance to communicate with us, our doubts as to your perfect trustworthiness began to amount to something stronger than suspicion—particularly when we learnt that, not content with betraying Mary Griffiths, you proposed to betray us too; to slip away to a quiet little shelter of your own, and there have a good time on the proceeds of the property which, whosesoever it was, had been procured, so far as you were concerned, very much at our expense. So, since it had clearly become a question of diamond cut diamond, we contrived a little scheme by means of which we hoped to lure you up to town. Our little scheme has succeeded even beyond our expectations. You came to town; you came here; and now that we have got you here, you may take my word for it that we don't mean to let you go till we have had an opportunity of crying quits. First of all, hand over those jewels. Not, you understand, four hundred, but four thousand pounds' worth."

"But I haven't got them. I assure you—"

"Silence! We don't want any of your assurances, we don't want words from you of any sort or kind. I fancy that at talk we should find you more than a match for us. I'll tell you what we're going to do. We're going to ask you to hand over those jewels, and if you don't hand them over at once, to our satisfaction, we're going to strip you. If we don't find them concealed in your clothing, as, for my part, I think we probably shall do, we're going to find out where they are concealed, if we have to kill you to do it. I tell you, frankly, that I should have as little compunction in killing you as I should have in killing a snake which had tried to bite me. For such as you, plain killing is too good. Hand over those jewels."

"I have no jewels! For God's sake, listen to me! There is some dreadful mistake."

"That's enough of that. Penfold, strip her. I daresay you can manage her single-handed; but if you want assistance, I shall be happy to give you mine."

The virago, addressed as Penfold, grinned, not agreeably.

"I sha'n't want assistance, not with the likes of her. I can handle her as easy as if she was a baby."

IV.   —OUT OF THE FRYING-PAN

Penfold proceeded to put her words to the proof. Without any sort of warning, she took Edith by the throat, and, advancing her foot, tripped her over on to the floor with an ease which was positively ludicrous. And, having got her down, choking her with one huge hand, while with the other she began to tear her clothes from off her with as scant formality as she might have plucked the feathers from a fowl, Edith made not the slightest attempt at resistance. Not only was there no fight left in her, but she was being throttled. If that iron grasp about her slender throat was not soon relaxed, she would, ere long, become a runaway wife indeed, and for ever. Before, however, that consummation had been achieved, and she was actually and finally throttled, a diversion was caused by the unceremonious entrance of still another woman, who was holding a paper in her hand. Without any sort of prelude she addressed herself to all and sundry.

"Clara Harvey's been too much for us. She's declined to swallow the bait we offered her, she saw the hook behind it, as I expected she would. She's given us the slip, and apparently got clean away, because she's had the impudence to send me this telegram."

The new-comer read aloud from the piece of paper she was holding, which was now seen to be a telegraph form.

"So sorry cannot accept kind invitation to come to town. Have business engagement, which I am now starting to fill. Good-bye, dearest, in case I should not see you again for very long time, which fear I sha'n't. Say good-bye for me to the other dears. Hope dear Mary won't suffer much, but we have all of us to be in trouble in our turn. Best love.—CLARA."

The reading of this curiously and extravagantly-worded telegram, was followed by a chorus of exclamations.

"What nonsense are you talking?" "What are you reading from?" "Who's been kidding you?" "Clara's here!"

It was the new-comer's turn to exclaim. "Clara's here? Where?"

"Here!"

Her attention was directed to the figure of Mrs Bankes, who was still recumbent on the floor, though fortunately Penfold had somewhat softened the vigour of her attentions. The new-comer stared at the prostrate lady.

"Clara! That's not Clara!"

"Not Clara? Don't talk rubbish! It's her, right enough!"

"I don't know who that is, and I don't know what you're playing off on me, but I do know that's not Clara Harvey. I've known her pretty well all my life; if I don't know her, I don't know who does, and I tell you that's no more Clara Harvey than I am."

On the faces of the four women were looks of stupefied amazement. Penfold shook the recipient of her tender mercies.

"Now then, wake up there, you ain't quite dead. Ain't you, Clara?"

"No!" Mrs Bankes just managed to gasp.

On the table lay her purse, with its contents displayed to the public gaze. The new-comer took up the visiting card.

"What's this? Mrs Frank Bankes, The Chestnuts, Tuesdays, 4 to 6."

"I'm Mrs Frank Bankes," murmured the owner of that name.

The new-comer darted forward.

"Not Mrs Frank Bankes, of Colchester? Not the wife of Frank Bankes, the solicitor, who's undertaken the prosecution of Mary Griffiths?"

"I'm his wife."

The new-comer evinced all the symptoms of mental disturbance. She stared at Edith as if she were a ghost. Then looked at the others with eyes in which were both anger and amazement.

"What—what's the meaning of this? What tomfoolery have you been up to? How came she here?"

The little woman advanced to the front.

"It is for her to explain, not us. She came here with Ricketts as Clara Harvey; she allowed us to believe she was Clara Harvey. You know neither of us four has ever seen Clara Harvey; we never supposed, therefore, that she could be anyone else!" She spoke to Edith. "Why did you pass yourself off as someone else?"

"I didn't. I told you there was a mistake. I wanted to explain but you wouldn't let me."

"But you came here with Ricketts?"

"Not of my own free will. I didn't want to come, but she made me. She threatened to shoot me if I tried to get out of the cab."

"But how came you to be with Ricketts at all? Do you know her?"

"If you mean by Ricketts the person who brought me here, I never saw her before in my life. When she came to me in the railway carriage, I thought my husband had sent her to meet me. I was in great distress, or I should have been more cautious."

"Look here, Mrs Bankes, what has happened has been your fault, not ours. We certainly were not desirous of your presence, so perhaps you will just explain by what curious accident you are here."

Mrs Bankes did explain, lamely enough, and with plentiful lack of dignity.

Her audience listened with all their ears.

"I am Mrs Bankes, of Colchester. This afternoon I quarrelled with my husband—I see now that I was altogether in the wrong." If only Frank could have heard! "I was beside myself with passion. I said that I would run away, and—I ran away. When I got to London someone came to me in the train. I thought my husband had sent her to take me back again, so—I went with her, but—she brought me here instead—you wouldn't listen to me, so—"

She stopped short, something seemed to be choking her. But she had said enough to make her meaning pretty plain.

"Ricketts is a fool." They were the first words the lady in widow's weeds had uttered. They seemed to meet with general approval.

"Rickett's is not the only fool." The addition was the little woman's. This expression of opinion was also adopted. "For all I know, Mrs Bankes, you may, on ordinary occasions, be a person remarkable for common-sense; but you must forgive my saying that, on this occasion, it is not that quality in your conduct which strikes one most. You are the wife of a man who is no friend of ours; you have forced yourself into our confidence; you have tricked us into treating you with alarming frankness; you have engineered yourself into a position in which you will be able to do us serious mischief. For us it now becomes a question of self-preservation. What are we to do with her?"

"Don't let her go back to her husband."

This suggestion also came from the lady in weeds. An irrepressible shudder went all over Mrs Bankes. She would have protested, however feebly, against so terrible a proposition, had not her tongue refused its office. Never had she supposed it possible that she would have been treated with contempt by anyone—and by a gang of thieves!

The five women drew together at one side of the room. They entered into agitated discussion, conducted, however, in whispers, so as to be inaudible to the anxious lady close at hand. The consultation could not have been carried far before the room door was again thrown open, and the woman, Ricketts, who had been primarily the cause of all the mischief, came rushing in.

"Quick!—the coppers! they're at the door!—the other way."

The woman was a picture of excitement and alarm. As soon as she had spoken she turned and fled as rapidly as she had come. Her words fell like a bombshell amidst the little group of women. Without an attempt at comment they rushed after her, bustling each other in their panic flight. Almost before she learned what had happened, and certainly before she could guess what was about to happen, Mrs Bankes found herself alone. Suddenly there was the sound of violent knocking at the street door; a loud crash; heavy footsteps were heard ascending the stairs. Three or four men came into the room. One of them, advancing, laid his hand upon her shoulder. He turned to a man behind him.

"They've had the office and done a bolt. I daresay they are trying the roof; go up and see. Take somebody with you." The man addressed walked quickly from the room, two others going with him.

"You are my prisoner."

V.   —INTO THE FIRE

Mrs Bankes looked up at the speaker with ashen cheeks.

"Your prisoner? What do you mean? Who are you?"

"You know very well who I am, though, since you ask, I don't mind telling you that I'm a detective officer of police, named Macarthy, which, no doubt, is all quite news to you. How comes it that you weren't so nimble on your pins as those friends of yours?"

"Friends of mine?"

"They are friends of yours, I take it. You're a regular happy family, aren't you? And a nice little lot you seem to be. You, at anyrate, will be separated from them for a time. Hold out your hands."

He did not wait for her to hold out her hands, he held them out for her. In an instant handcuffs were girdling her dainty wrists. This did seem to be the most terrible catastrophe of all, that she, Edith Bankes, should be arrested at Christmas-time, as a common thief, and handcuffed!

"You are making a horrible mistake, I am not the person you take me for."

"I don't see how you can make that out, since I haven't said who I do take you for as yet. Of course you can cheek it out if you like, but don't you think it would seem too thin? Do you expect us to believe that only ladies of first-class character are to be found in a house like this—the foulest den in London?"

"I assure you, officer, that it is only owing to the most extraordinary misapprehension."

"Of course—not a doubt of it; it always is like that. Take my advice and keep a still tongue—anything you say 'll be used against you. Sorry to have to use the bracelets, we don't generally, with a lady, but, in a place like this, we take no chances. Jones, take her off, and let Wright go with you. I'm going over this place, and then I'll come straight on."

"But I implore you to listen to me. I am Mrs Bankes—"

"Very pleased to meet you, Mrs Bankes; hope to see you again a little later on. Now off you go; don't be silly. You don't want us to carry you, I suppose —it might spoil your pretty clothes!"

He gave her what was meant as a good-natured push; but to her, unaccustomed to come into physical contact with policemen, it was as if the heavens were falling. A younger man took her by the arm.

"Now then. Downstairs!"

She went downstairs, the officer gripping her firmly. The house seemed full of men. In the street were half a dozen more. Her companion called one of them to her. Presently she found herself walking between two constables, each having hold of an arm, handcuffed, to the station house. And even then she was unable to adequately realise the situation. It did seem incredible that she, a woman of position, the wife of a man of reputation, could be hauled off to jail without even knowing with what crime she was charged. She made still another effort to induce her captors to hear reason.

"I do assure you that you are making a dreadful mistake. I am Mrs Bankes —"

Sergeant Jones interrupted her.

"All right, you've said that before. We've been ordered to take you to the station, and if you're a duchess it makes no difference to us, we're going to take you. You can explain all about it when you're there."

What was the use of attempting to argue with such impossible creatures? Fate was hard on her. Her heart was sinking down into her shoes. Was she actually to spend a night in a police cell, after undergoing goodness only knew what indignities? What an inauguration of the Christmas season? What would be her husband's feelings? What would her relations think? What would her acquaintances say? What a tale to be told against her throughout the whole remainder of her life! The horror of it all!

As they passed out of the narrow street in which stood that house of ill omen, just as they had turned the corner, six or seven figures appeared out of the darkness, and without uttering a sound, or word of warning, precipitated themselves upon the advancing trio. Before Mrs Bankes had an inkling of their purpose she found herself being torn from the clutches of her captors, each of whom, with what seemed to be a cloth thrown over his head, was being dragged backward on to the ground. In what appeared little more than an instant she was freed at the expense of her arms being torn nearly out of their sockets, and was being hurried along the pavement under the guidance of a tall individual in a long dark overcoat, who continually urged her, by word and action, to use her utmost speed.

"Who are you? Where are you taking me?" she managed to articulate. Her conductor's reply was not entirely satisfactory.

"Move yourself. It's all right, coast's clear, only don't stop talking. I've got a cab round the corner, this way."

He whirled her round into an alley which she would hardly have noticed if it had not been for him. In the dim light a hansom stood waiting. He lifted her in without a with-your-leave or by-your-leave, sprang in after her, and in a moment the horse, urged by its driver, tore off at the top of its speed. So soon as they had started the man at her side broke into a peal of laughter, which, despite its heartiness, had about it a peculiar quality of silence, beginning at the same time to talk with surprising volubility.

"Neat, wasn't it? Did you ever see anything neater? I fancy I scored off those infernal coppers that time, what do you think? I heard you were going to be raided, in fact I saw them starting, so I whipped up a few trusty pals, boys who wouldn't stick at a trifle, and I've got you away from them at any rate; it'll be your own fault, my dear, if, after this, you're buckled again. I should like to see Macarthy's face when he hears what's happened to those chaps of his. Aren't you very much obliged to me?"

Edith was not by any means certain. She ventured on an inquiry.

"Who are you?"

"I'm Captain Jim."

"Captain Jim?"

"Yes, you must be a raw hand if you've never heard of Captain Jim. Why, it's only a week or two since I came out from doing my last five years, and I've made things move since I've been out, I tell you. A word to the wise—I've got the biggest thing in my eye ever you heard of. Some of that lot in your gang have got grit, that I do know, and if you're the sort of girl I take you for, you're just the one I want—we'll bring it off between us, just me and you together. What do you say to that?"

"Thank you, but I—I'm afraid you've made a mistake—"

"Oh, blow your mistakes, I don't believe it! You wouldn't have been where you were if you hadn't got the right stuff in you. Let me take those darbies off, they can't feel comfortable on those nice little wrists of yours; darn their eyes for putting them on you."

The handcuffs did gall her. She offered no objection to his removing them with the aid of a key which he took from his pocket. When they were off he tossed them up into the air, catching them as they came down.

"You beauties! you've buckled many a good man; wouldn't I like to buckle a copper with you for a change? I'd make him look funny!"

The cab had been dashing along without any diminution of speed. It turned round still another corner. Captain Jim looked out. "Keep your eyes skinned. My place is along here. Bill—that's the cabman, he's a pal of mine—don't want to stop any longer than he can help, for fear of being spotted,—you never know who's looking; so when I give the word jump out like lightning."

"But I want to explain to you—"

"Stow your explanations till we get inside. Then you and me'll have a good old palaver. Now then."

The cab drew up. Somehow, she herself scarcely knew how, Edith found herself standing on the pavement with Captain Jim. Almost before she felt the ground beneath her feet the cab was off.

"Pretty smart that. Bill can move when he wants to, trust him to get the right sort of cattle. Now then, here we are at home." He turned towards the house behind them. She made a further attempt at expostulation—but she was too far gone to do so with effect.

"It's all a mistake, I want to tell you it's all a mistake."

"Tell me all about it when we get inside. You're not up to the mark, I can see. A pick-me-up will put you to rights."

He had been opening the door with a latchkey while he had been speaking. He hustled her through it, in spite of her feeble effort at resistance, leading the way into an apartment which appeared to be used as a sitting-room. The man looked round with an air of pride.

"Not a bad kind of crib, is it? And I have got a bedroom what is better than this,—you trust me to get the proper sort of place. There's some as would give a hundred pounds, and more, to find me in here—but they've got to find someone who'll give them the office. I don't think you will, what do you think? By George, you're a ripper! You look like glass, you do, I'd no idea you were such a beauty. Why, you'd look well in any company, I know what I'm talking about, I do. You mark my words! I'm going in for a clean hundred thousand pounds, and I'm going to touch it too, and you're the very sort I want to come in with me. We'll go shares, fifty thousand pounds a-piece! What do you say to that? You wait a minute, and I'll tell you all about it, I want to say a word to my old landlady."

He left the room. She was afraid that he would lock the door behind him, but he was evidently too wholly unsuspicious of the true state of the case to think of doing anything of the kind. In a moment her resolution was formed, with such strength as was left to her. She waited till she heard that his footsteps had receded along the passage. Then she too stole from the room. She crept along the passage with as little noise as possible. She reached the front door. The hall was in darkness; she fumbled with the latch, the sound reaching the keen ears of Captain Jim.

"What's that? Who's there?"

She found the handle; the door was open. Captain Jim came running along the passage. But with all his haste, he was too late. She was through the door, half a dozen paces away. The street was a mean one, dark and deserted. But, some hundred yards off, there was the gleam of lights, the roar of traffic, and evidently close at hand was some big thoroughfare. If she could only reach it she might be safe. Despair—the consciousness that it was now or never—lent her wings. She ran as she had never run before. Yet the man behind her ran faster still. She knew he gained. Another effort—still she might be at the corner first. As she reached it, he caught her by the shoulder. His voice was hoarse with rage.

"What the devil does this mean? What little game do you think you're up to?"

"Help! Help!" she screamed.

Just as the man was beginning to draw her back into the side street someone came hurrying towards her across the pavement. Someone, who, without the slightest hesitation, struck Captain Jim full in the face, with such force and such science, that that gentleman went down like a ninepin.

"You villain!" exclaimed a voice—which sounded to the girl like a voice from heaven. "What are you doing to this lady?"

"Frank!" she cried.

"Edith? Great heavens! is it you?"

In another moment the wife was crying in her husband's arms.

"Oh, Frank, take me away, before they kill me."

Captain Jim had regained his feet. He seemed disposed to bluster—though evidently not completely at his ease.

"What did you hit me for? Who do you think you're knocking about? What do you mean by interfering between my wife and me?"

"Your wife—you hound? Think yourself lucky if I let you go. Say another word and I'll call that constable, and give you into custody."

As it chanced, at that moment a policeman was seen approaching. At sight of him, Captain Jim, apparently completely at a loss to understand the situation, slunk off, muttering curses beneath his breath. Mr Bankes hailed a passing hansom. When he got into it he found that his wife had fainted.

VI—AFTERWARDS

They returned by the nine o'clock train. The strange happenings herein set forth took place in a very much shorter time than it has taken to tell of them. She told her tale of wonder as they travelled homewards, he listening with open-mouthed amazement, interpolating occasional suggestions as to what he would like to do to some of the characters treated of in the lady's narrative.

When the Christmas guests arrived upon the morrow they little guessed what was the real inspiration of the exceeding warmth with which their hostess greeted them. Never was there a happier Christmas gathering, "a more united family." Everything went off without a hitch.

Mary Griffiths was tried for her share in the robbery of the Denyer jewels, and Frank Bankes was solicitor for the prosecution. She was found guilty. Previous convictions having been proved against her, she was sentenced to a term of penal servitude.

Mr and Mrs Bankes have heard nothing of that gang of dreadful women who got the lady in their clutches owing to such a very singular misunderstanding. Nor of Captain Jim. Truth to tell they have made no enquiries with a view of hearing, being desirous that no one but themselves should know that Mrs Bankes was ever—even for so short a space of time—a runaway wife.

She has never felt disposed to run away since, and come what may, she is absolutely convinced that she never will.

THE END